STITCHED

**#1: "The First Day of
the Rest of her Life"**

STITCHED

#1: "The First Day of the Rest of her Life"

Story by Mariah McCourt
Art by Aaron Alexovich

NEW YORK

STITCHED

STITCHED #1
"The First Day of the Rest of Her Life"

MARIAH McCOURT – Story
AARON ALEXOVICH – Art, Lettering and Cover
DREW RAUSCH – Color
SASHA KIMIATEK – Production Coordinator
MARIAH McCOURT – Editor
JEFF WHITMAN – Assistant Managing Editor
JIM SALICRUP
Editor-in-Chief

Charmz is an imprint of Papercutz.

ISBN HC: 978-1-62991-775-7
ISBN PB: 978-1-62991-774-0

Printed in China
May 2017

Charmz books may be purchased for business or promotional use.
For information on bulk purchases please contact Macmillan
Corporate and Premium Sales Department at
(800) 221-7945 x5442

Distributed by Macmillan
First CHARMZ Printing

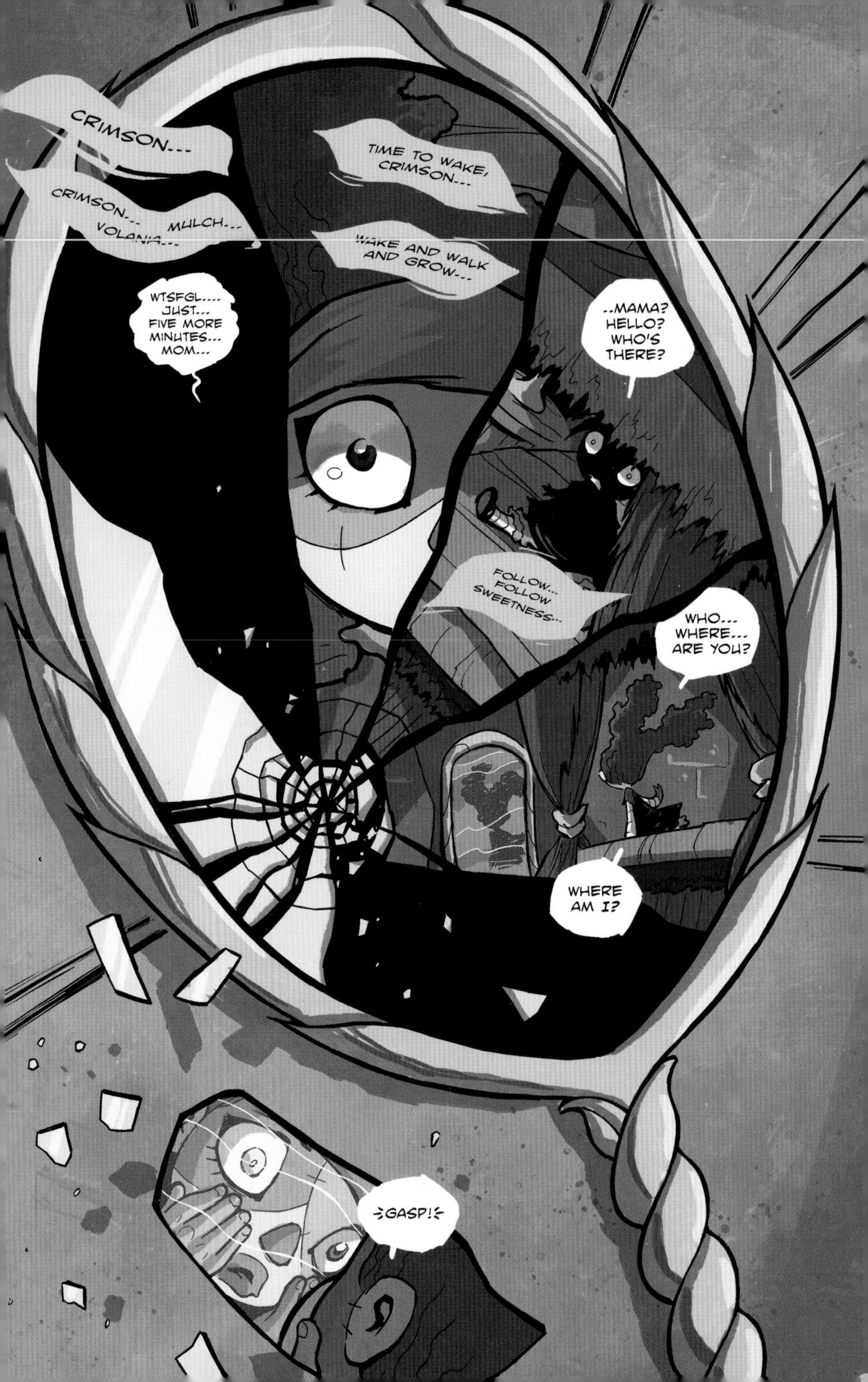
CRIMSON...
CRIMSON... VOLANIA... MULCH...
TIME TO WAKE, CRIMSON...
WAKE AND WALK AND GROW...
WTSFGL.... JUST... FIVE MORE MINUTES... MOM...
..MAMA? HELLO? WHO'S THERE?
FOLLOW... FOLLOW SWEETNESS...
WHO... WHERE... ARE YOU?
WHERE AM I?
GASP!

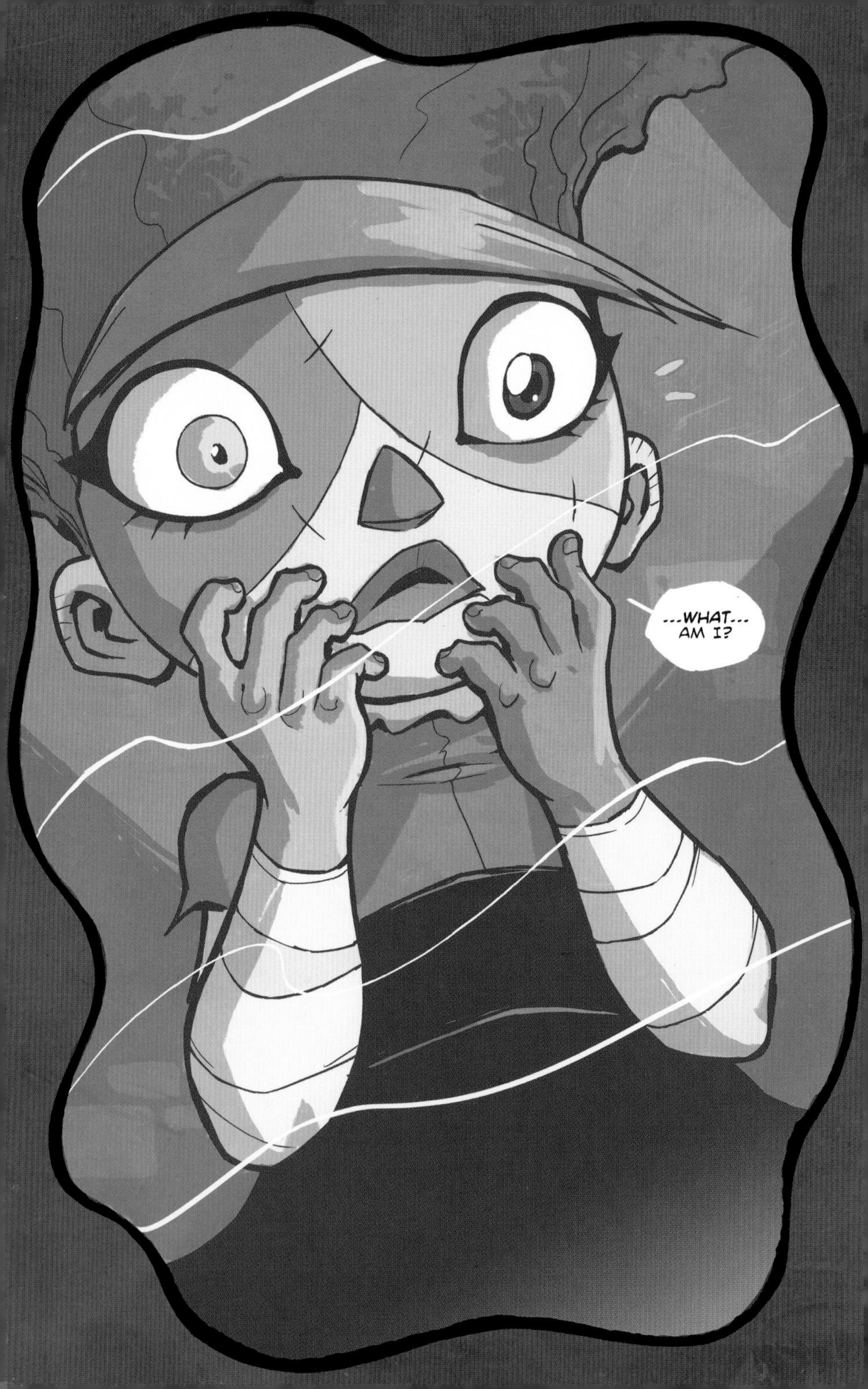
---WHAT--- AM I?

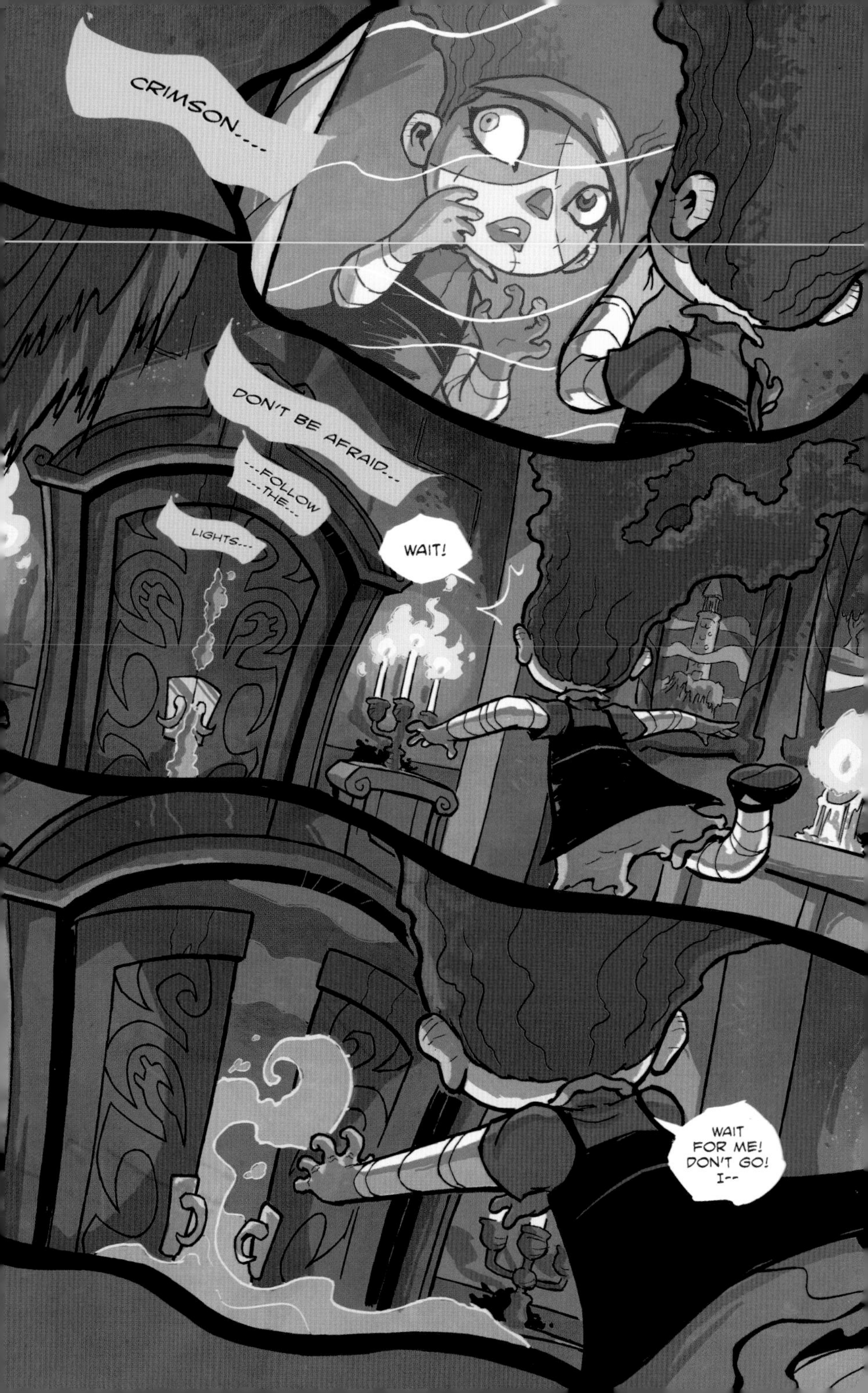
CRIMSON....
DON'T BE AFRAID...
--FOLLOW ---THE---
LIGHTS---
WAIT!
WAIT FOR ME! DON'T GO! I--

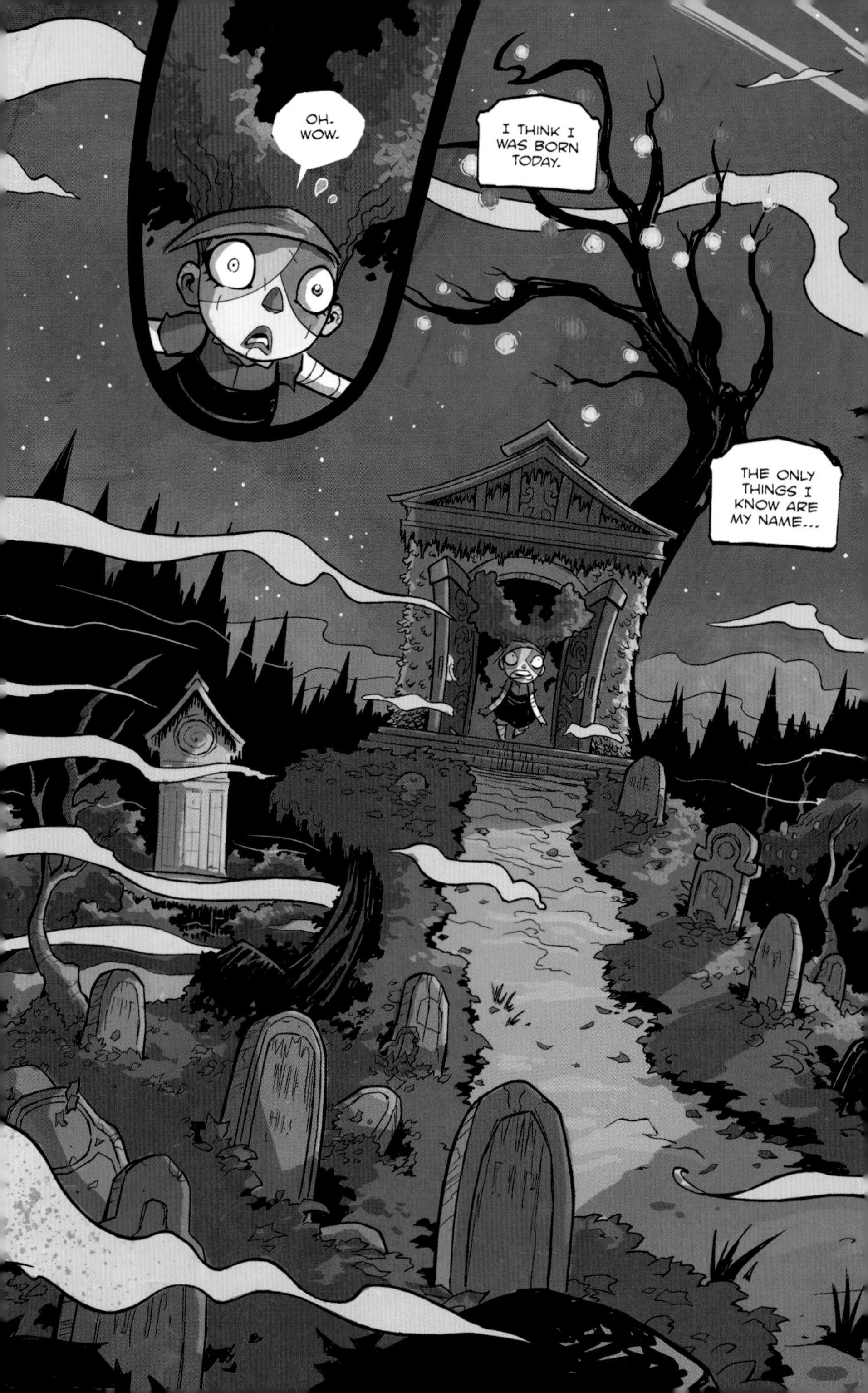
OH. WOW.
I THINK I WAS BORN TODAY.
THE ONLY THINGS I KNOW ARE MY NAME...

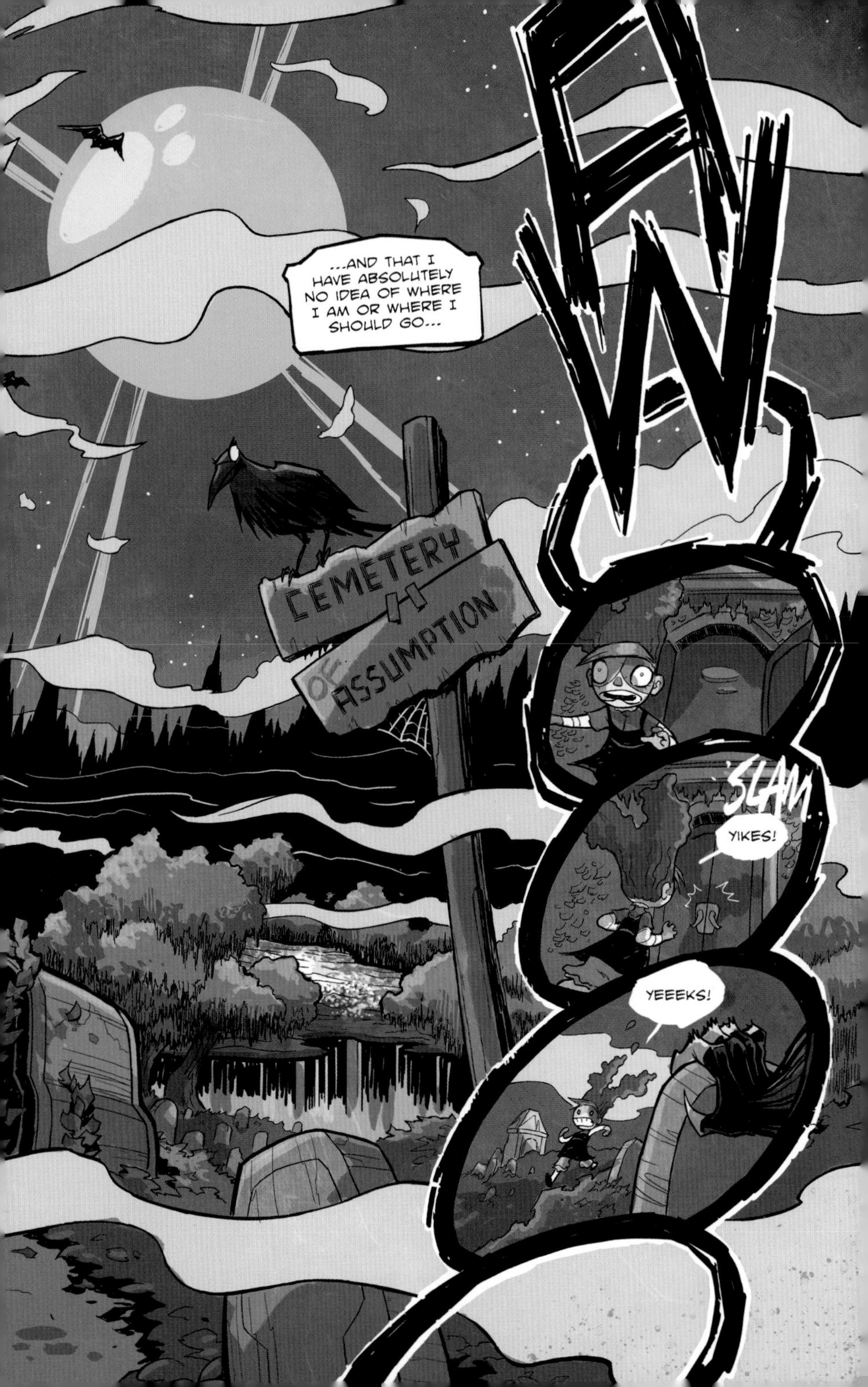
...AND THAT I HAVE ABSOLUTELY NO IDEA OF WHERE I AM OR WHERE I SHOULD GO...
CEMETERY OF ASSUMPTION
EW
SLAM
YIKES!
YEEEKS!

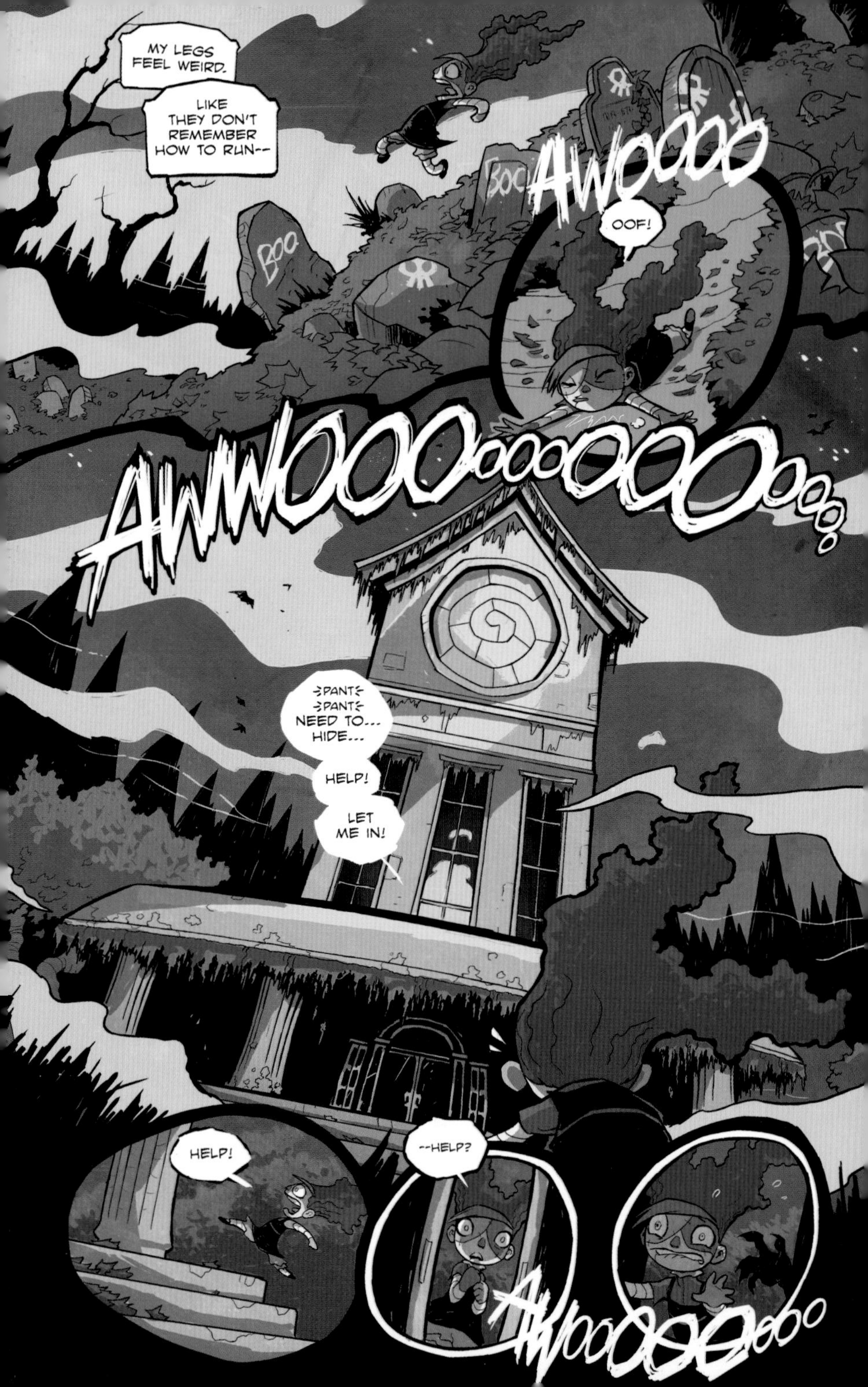
MY LEGS FEEL WEIRD.
LIKE THEY DON'T REMEMBER HOW TO RUN--
AWOOOO
OOF!
AWWOOOoooooOOOOooo
PANT PANT NEED TO... HIDE...
HELP!
LET ME IN!
HELP!
--HELP?
AWOOOOOOOooo

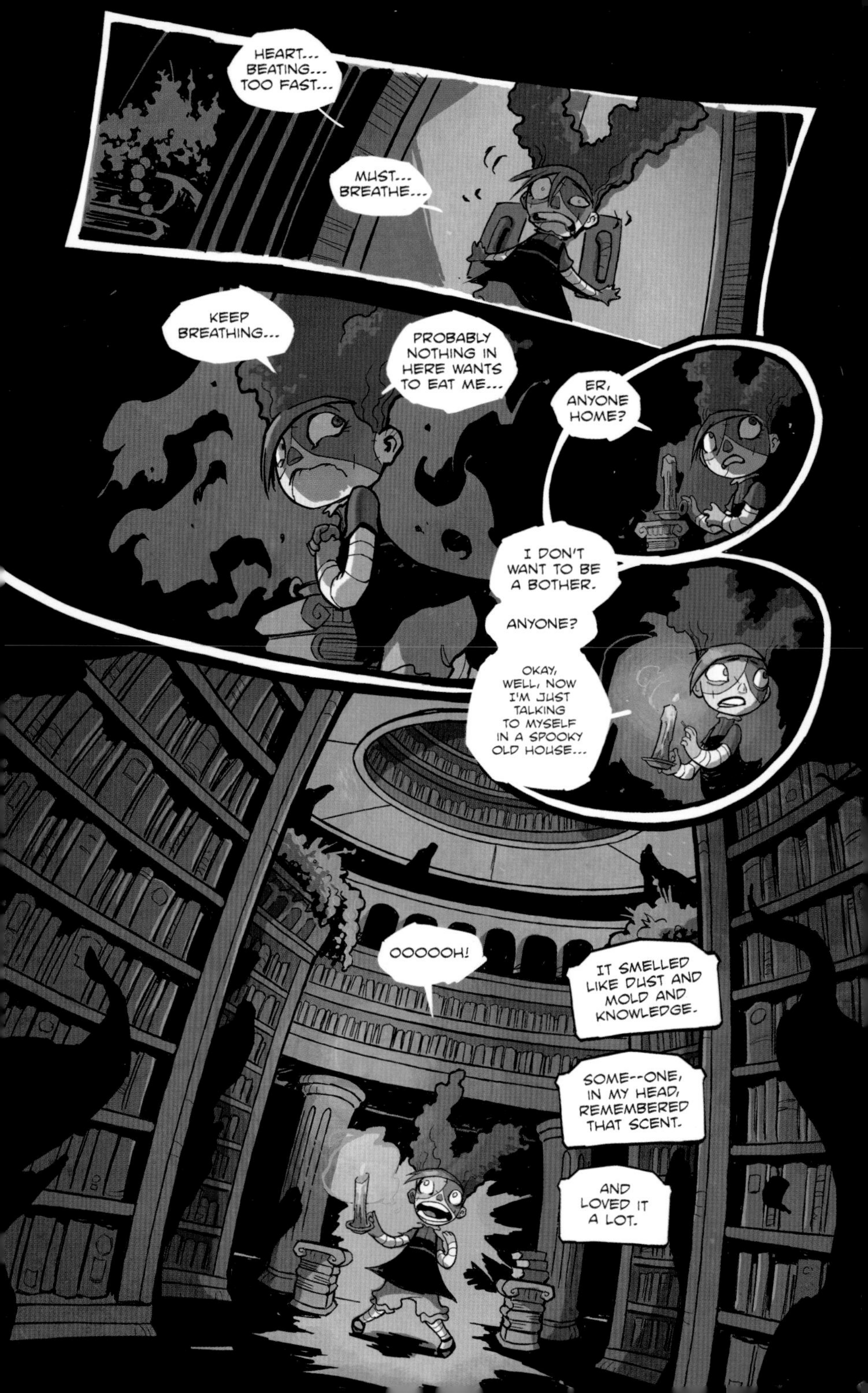
HEART... BEATING... TOO FAST...
MUST... BREATHE...
KEEP BREATHING...
PROBABLY NOTHING IN HERE WANTS TO EAT ME...
ER, ANYONE HOME?
I DON'T WANT TO BE A BOTHER.
ANYONE?
OKAY, WELL, NOW I'M JUST TALKING TO MYSELF IN A SPOOKY OLD HOUSE...
OOOOOH!
IT SMELLED LIKE DUST AND MOLD AND KNOWLEDGE.
SOME--ONE, IN MY HEAD, REMEMBERED THAT SCENT.
AND LOVED IT A LOT.

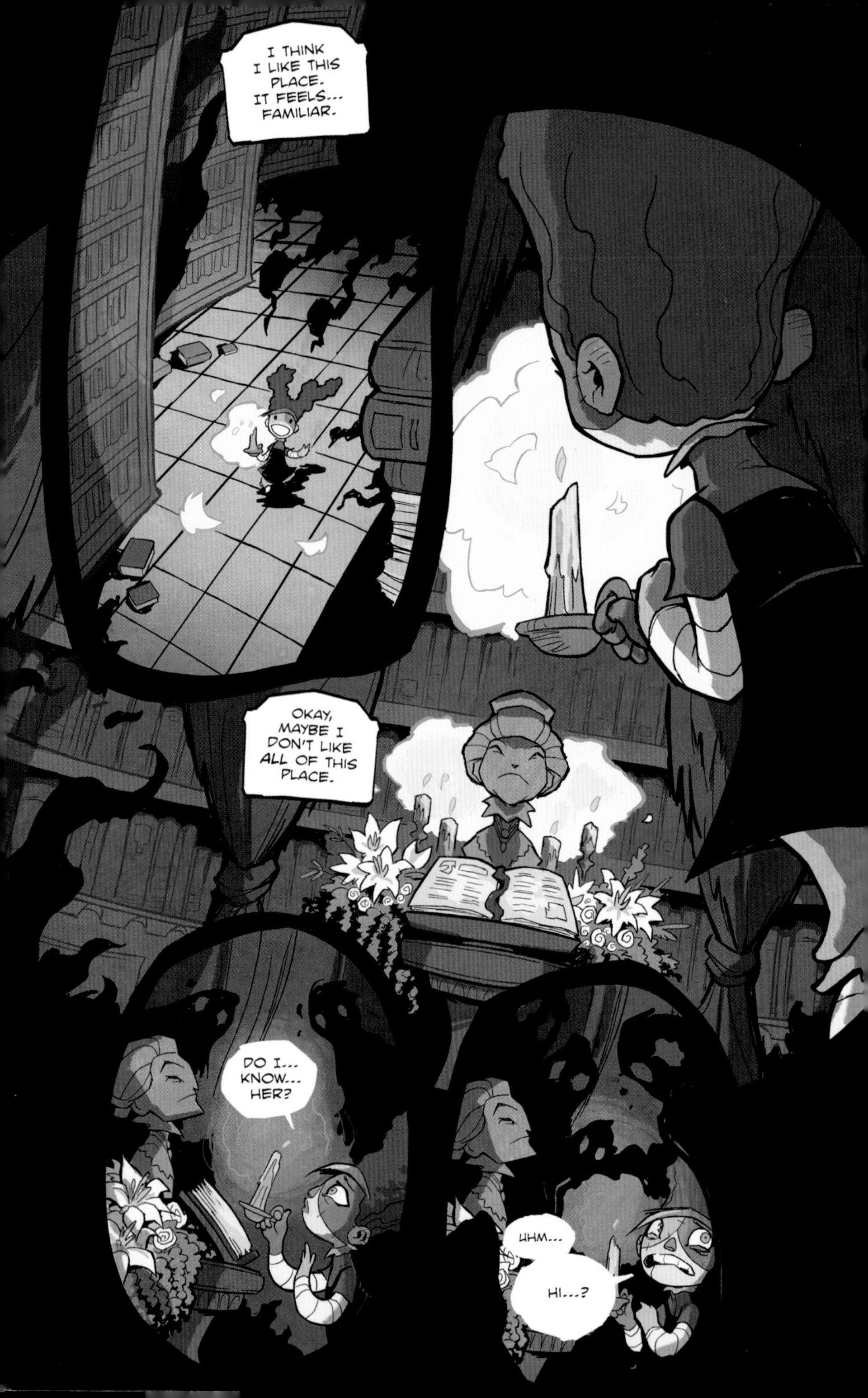
I THINK I LIKE THIS PLACE. IT FEELS... FAMILIAR.
OKAY, MAYBE I DON'T LIKE ALL OF THIS PLACE.
DO I... KNOW... HER?
UHM...
HI...?

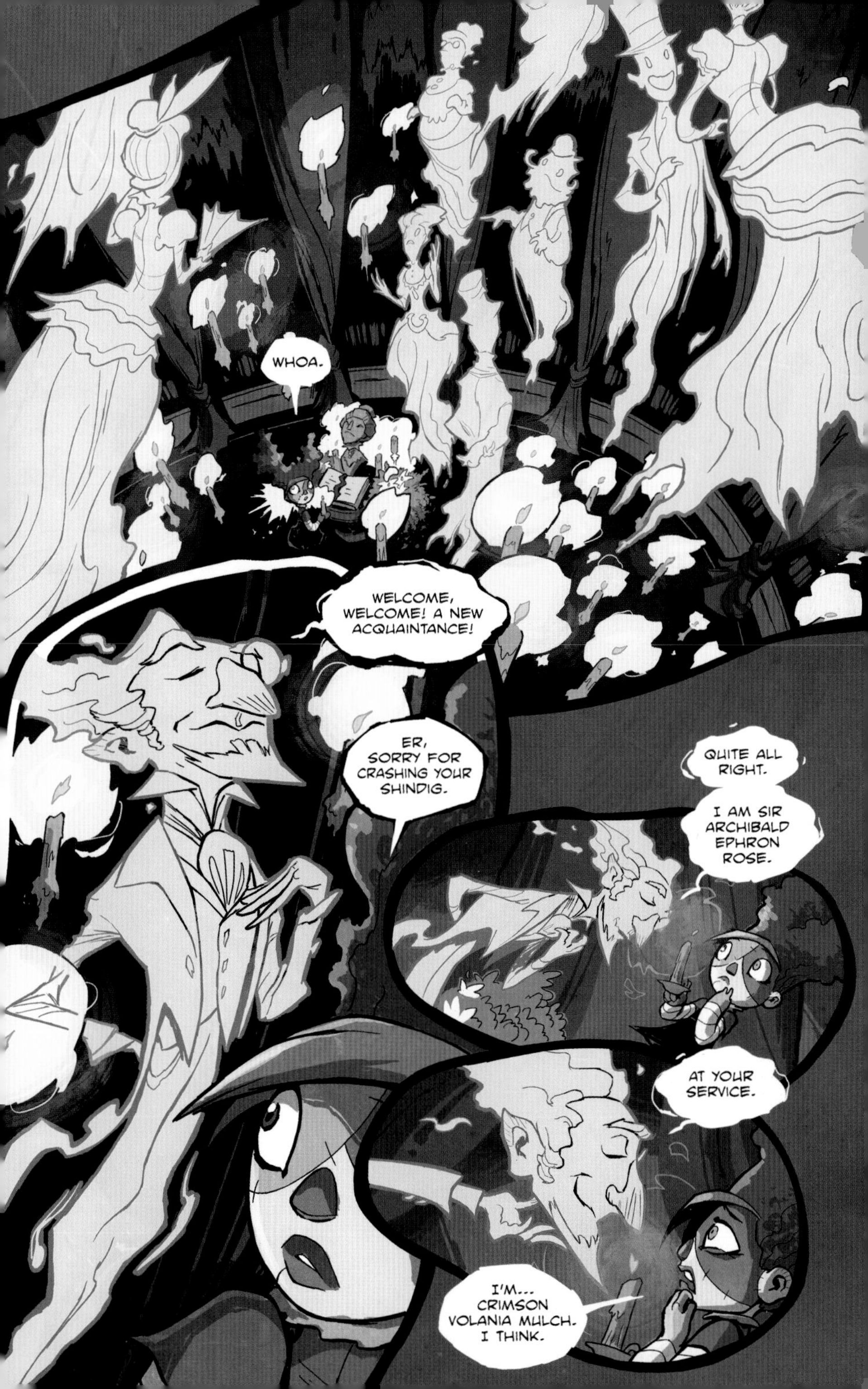
WHOA.
WELCOME, WELCOME! A NEW ACQUAINTANCE!
ER, SORRY FOR CRASHING YOUR SHINDIG.
QUITE ALL RIGHT.
I AM SIR ARCHIBALD EPHRON ROSE.
AT YOUR SERVICE.
I'M... CRIMSON VOLANIA MULCH. I THINK.

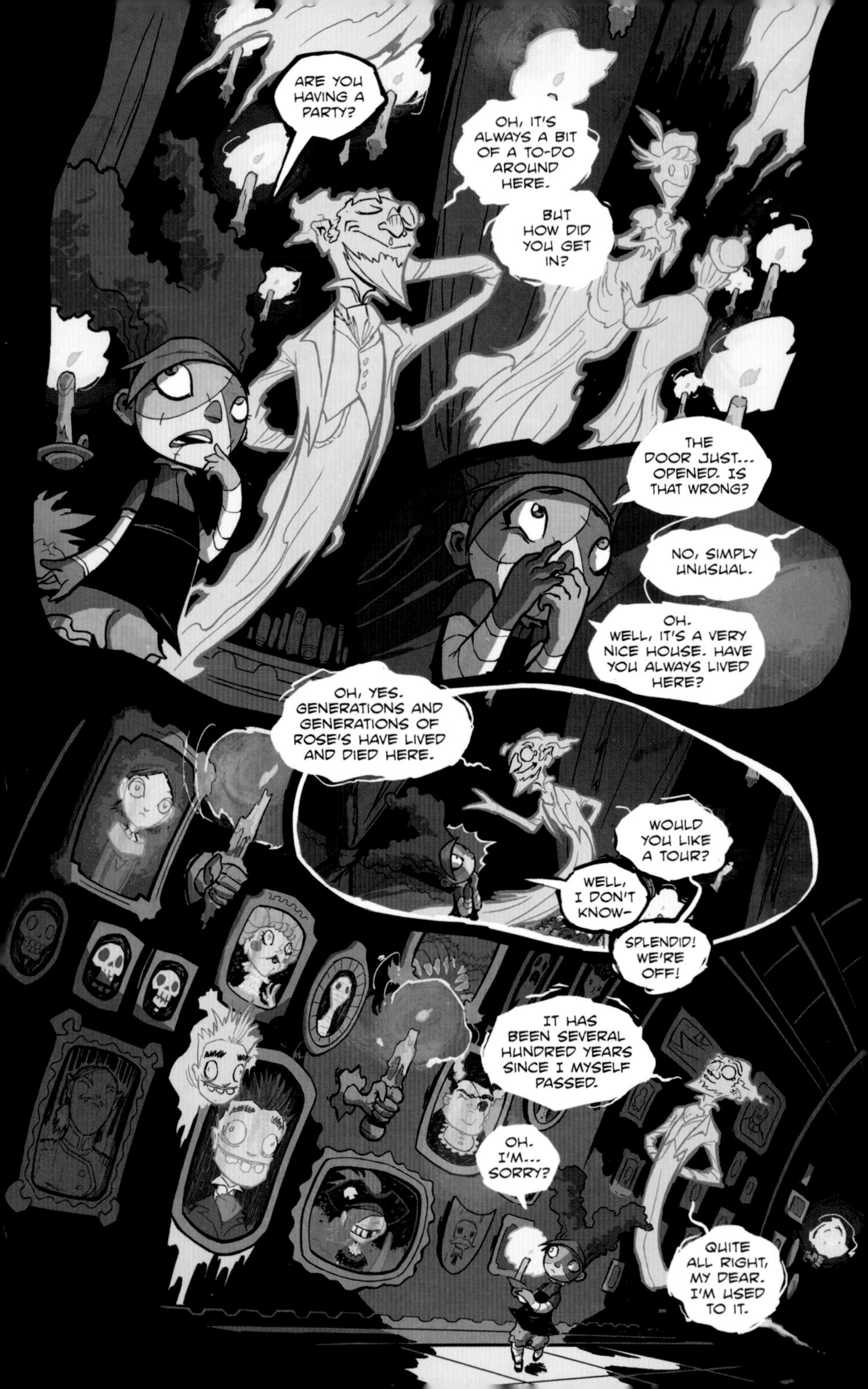
ARE YOU HAVING A PARTY?
OH, IT'S ALWAYS A BIT OF A TO-DO AROUND HERE.
BUT HOW DID YOU GET IN?
THE DOOR JUST... OPENED. IS THAT WRONG?
NO, SIMPLY UNUSUAL.
OH. WELL, IT'S A VERY NICE HOUSE. HAVE YOU ALWAYS LIVED HERE?
OH, YES. GENERATIONS AND GENERATIONS OF ROSE'S HAVE LIVED AND DIED HERE.
WOULD YOU LIKE A TOUR?
WELL, I DON'T KNOW-
SPLENDID! WE'RE OFF!
IT HAS BEEN SEVERAL HUNDRED YEARS SINCE I MYSELF PASSED.
OH. I'M... SORRY?
QUITE ALL RIGHT, MY DEAR. I'M USED TO IT.

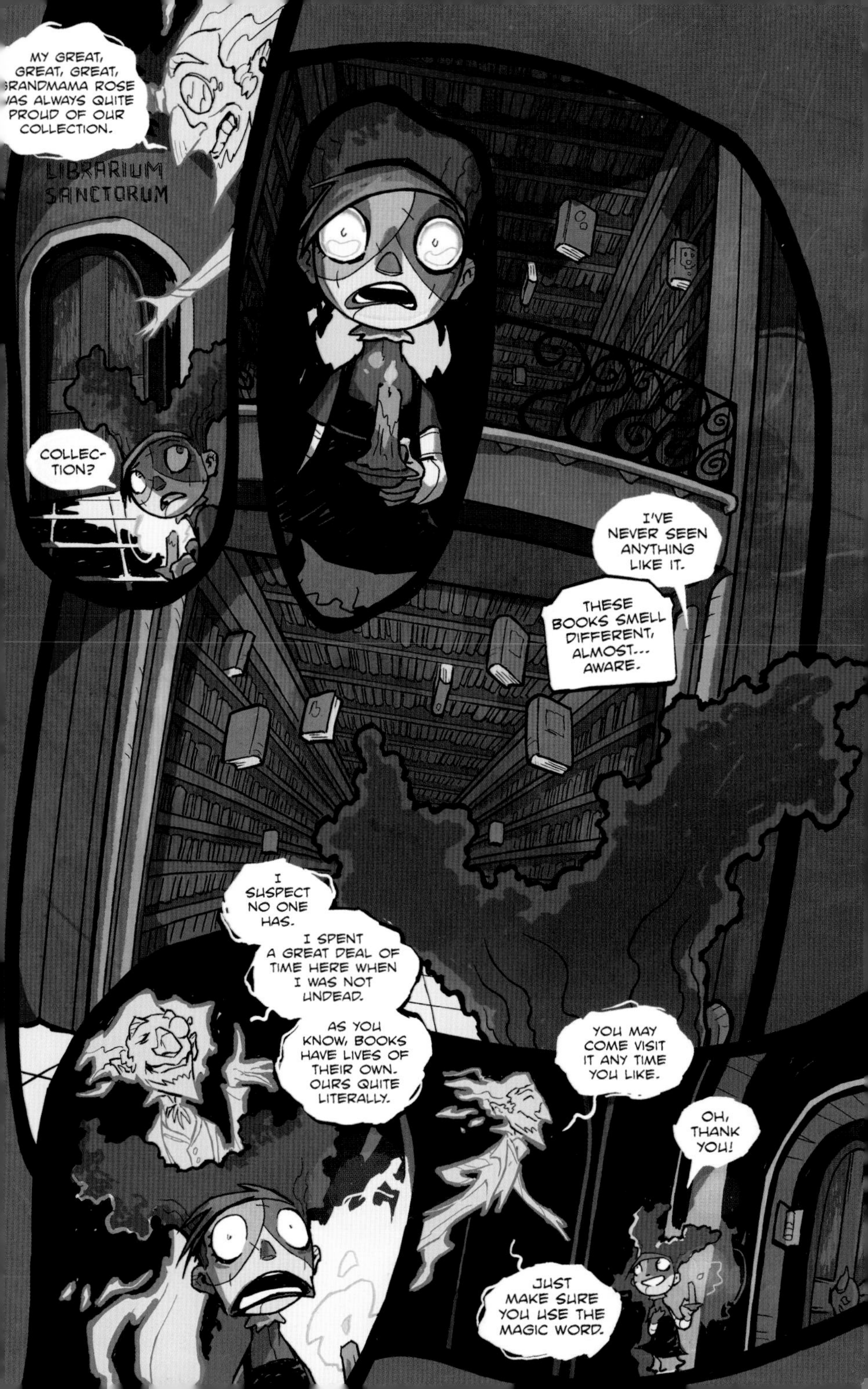
MY GREAT, GREAT, GREAT, GRANDMAMA ROSE WAS ALWAYS QUITE PROUD OF OUR COLLECTION.
LIBRARIUM SANCTORUM
COLLECTION?
I'VE NEVER SEEN ANYTHING LIKE IT.
THESE BOOKS SMELL DIFFERENT, ALMOST... AWARE.
I SUSPECT NO ONE HAS.
I SPENT A GREAT DEAL OF TIME HERE WHEN I WAS NOT UNDEAD.
AS YOU KNOW, BOOKS HAVE LIVES OF THEIR OWN. OURS QUITE LITERALLY.
YOU MAY COME VISIT IT ANY TIME YOU LIKE.
OH, THANK YOU!
JUST MAKE SURE YOU USE THE MAGIC WORD.

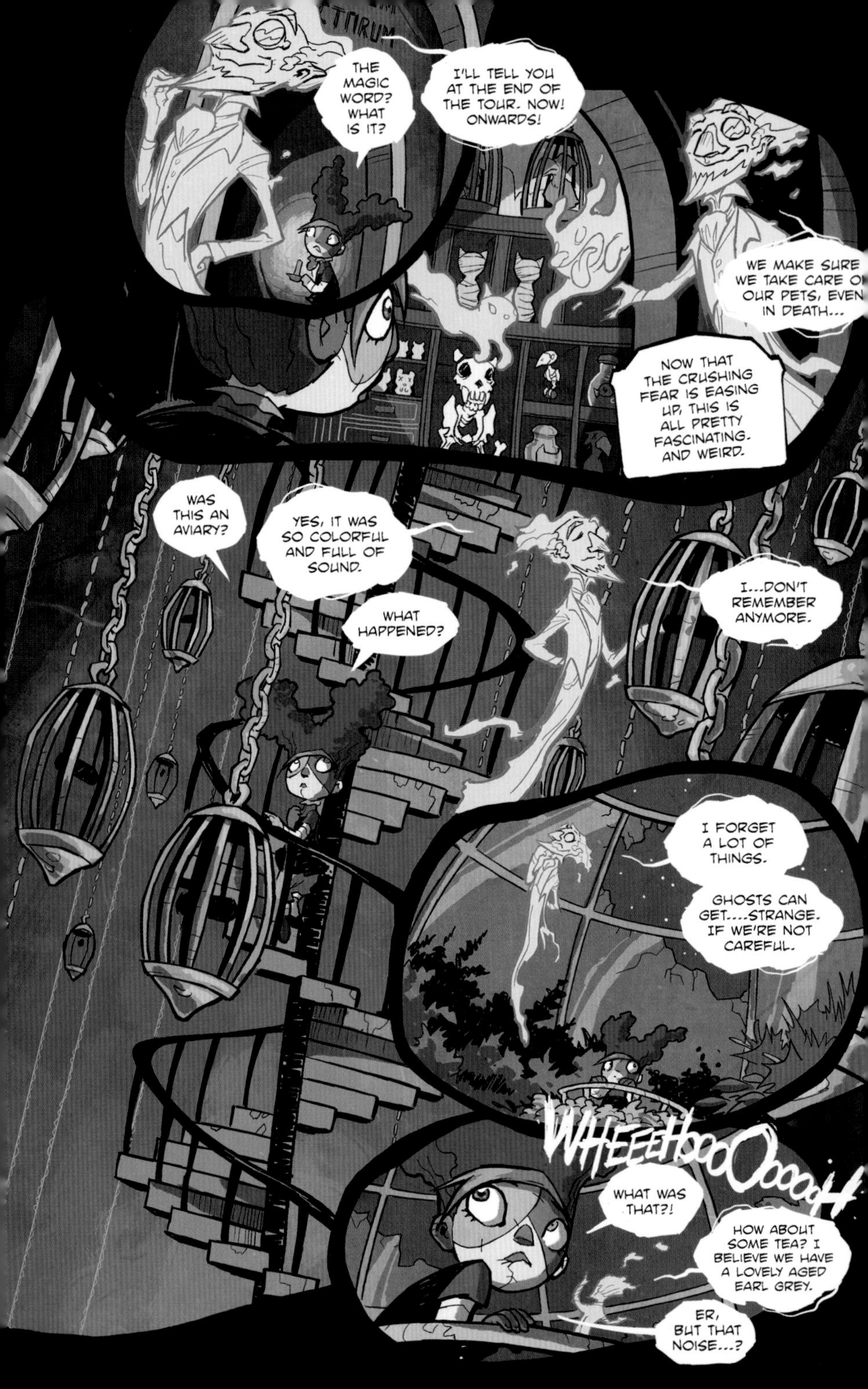
THE MAGIC WORD? WHAT IS IT?
I'LL TELL YOU AT THE END OF THE TOUR. NOW! ONWARDS!
WE MAKE SURE WE TAKE CARE OF OUR PETS, EVEN IN DEATH...
NOW THAT THE CRUSHING FEAR IS EASING UP, THIS IS ALL PRETTY FASCINATING. AND WEIRD.
WAS THIS AN AVIARY?
YES, IT WAS SO COLORFUL AND FULL OF SOUND.
WHAT HAPPENED?
I...DON'T REMEMBER ANYMORE.
I FORGET A LOT OF THINGS.
GHOSTS CAN GET....STRANGE. IF WE'RE NOT CAREFUL.
WHEEEHooOOoooH!
WHAT WAS THAT?!
HOW ABOUT SOME TEA? I BELIEVE WE HAVE A LOVELY AGED EARL GREY.
ER, BUT THAT NOISE...?

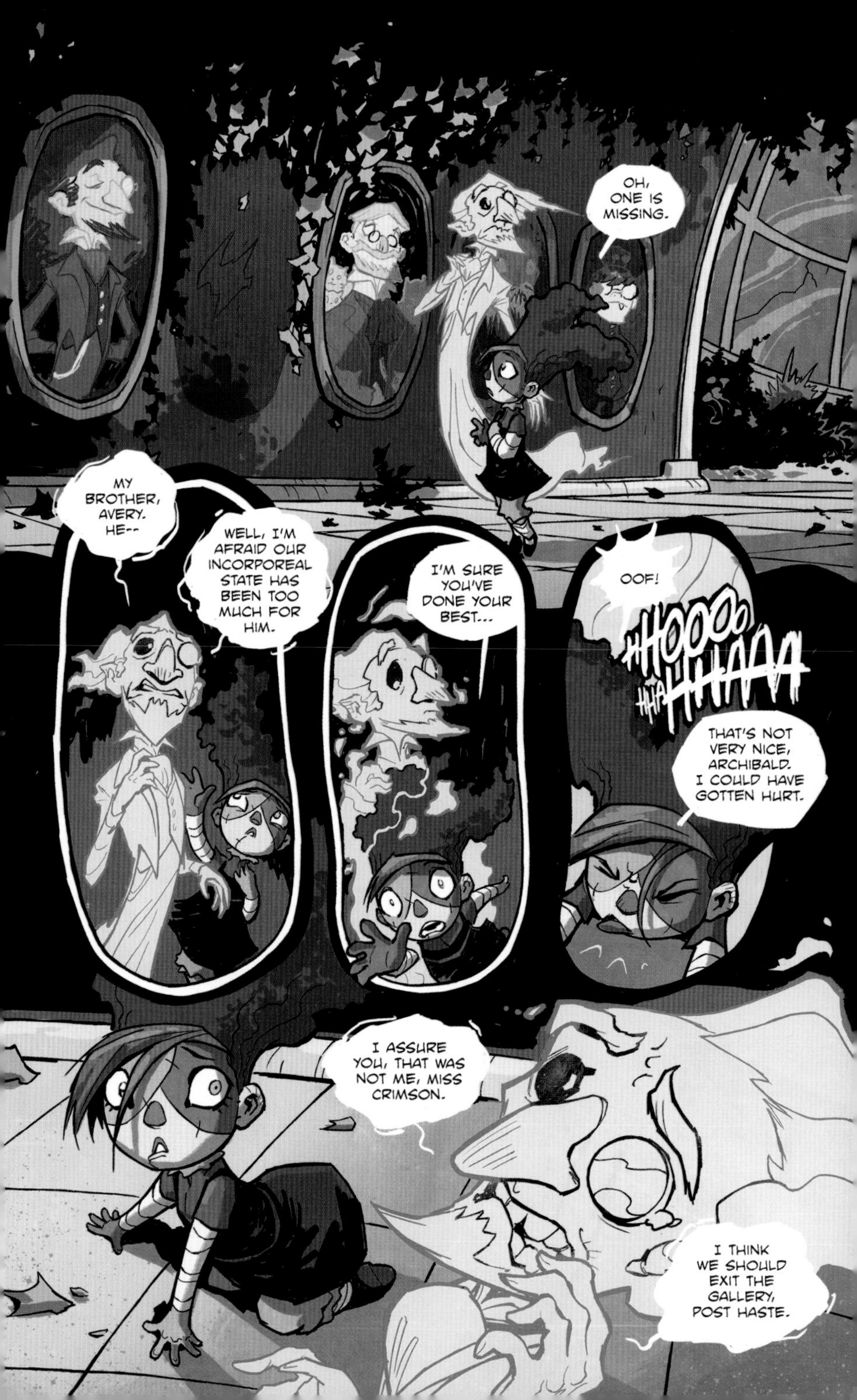
OH, ONE IS MISSING.
MY BROTHER, AVERY. HE--
WELL, I'M AFRAID OUR INCORPOREAL STATE HAS BEEN TOO MUCH FOR HIM.
I'M SURE YOU'VE DONE YOUR BEST...
OOF!
HHOOOo HHAHHAAA
THAT'S NOT VERY NICE, ARCHIBALD. I COULD HAVE GOTTEN HURT.
I ASSURE YOU, THAT WAS NOT ME, MISS CRIMSON.
I THINK WE SHOULD EXIT THE GALLERY, POST HASTE.

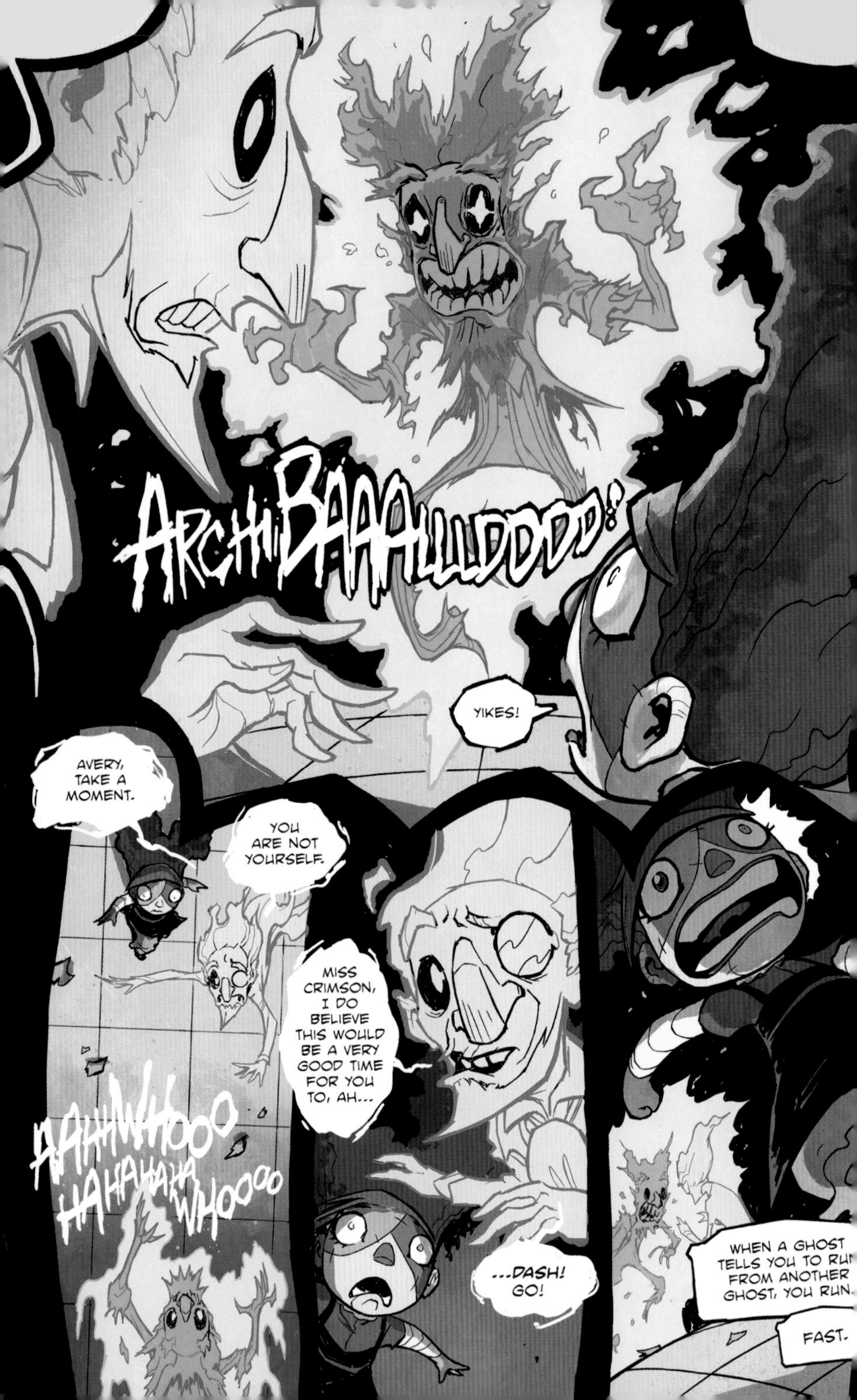
ARCHIBAAALLLDDDD!
YIKES!
AVERY, TAKE A MOMENT.
YOU ARE NOT YOURSELF.
MISS CRIMSON, I DO BELIEVE THIS WOULD BE A VERY GOOD TIME FOR YOU TO, AH...
AAHHWHOOO HAHAHAHA WHOOOO
...DASH! GO!
WHEN A GHOST TELLS YOU TO RUN FROM ANOTHER GHOST, YOU RUN.
FAST.

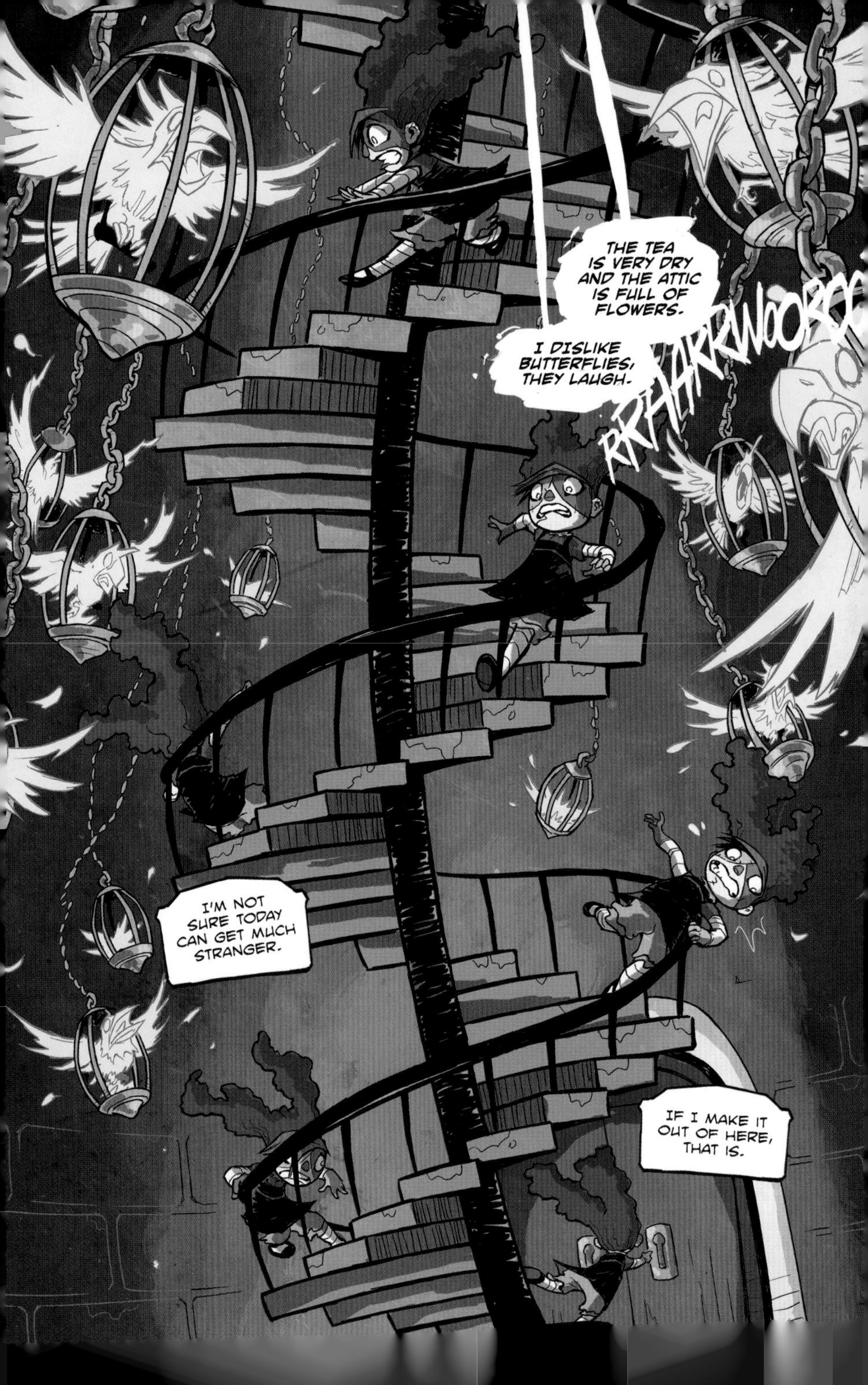
THE TEA IS VERY DRY AND THE ATTIC IS FULL OF FLOWERS.
I DISLIKE BUTTERFLIES, THEY LAUGH.
RRHARRWOOROO
I'M NOT SURE TODAY CAN GET MUCH STRANGER.
IF I MAKE IT OUT OF HERE, THAT IS.

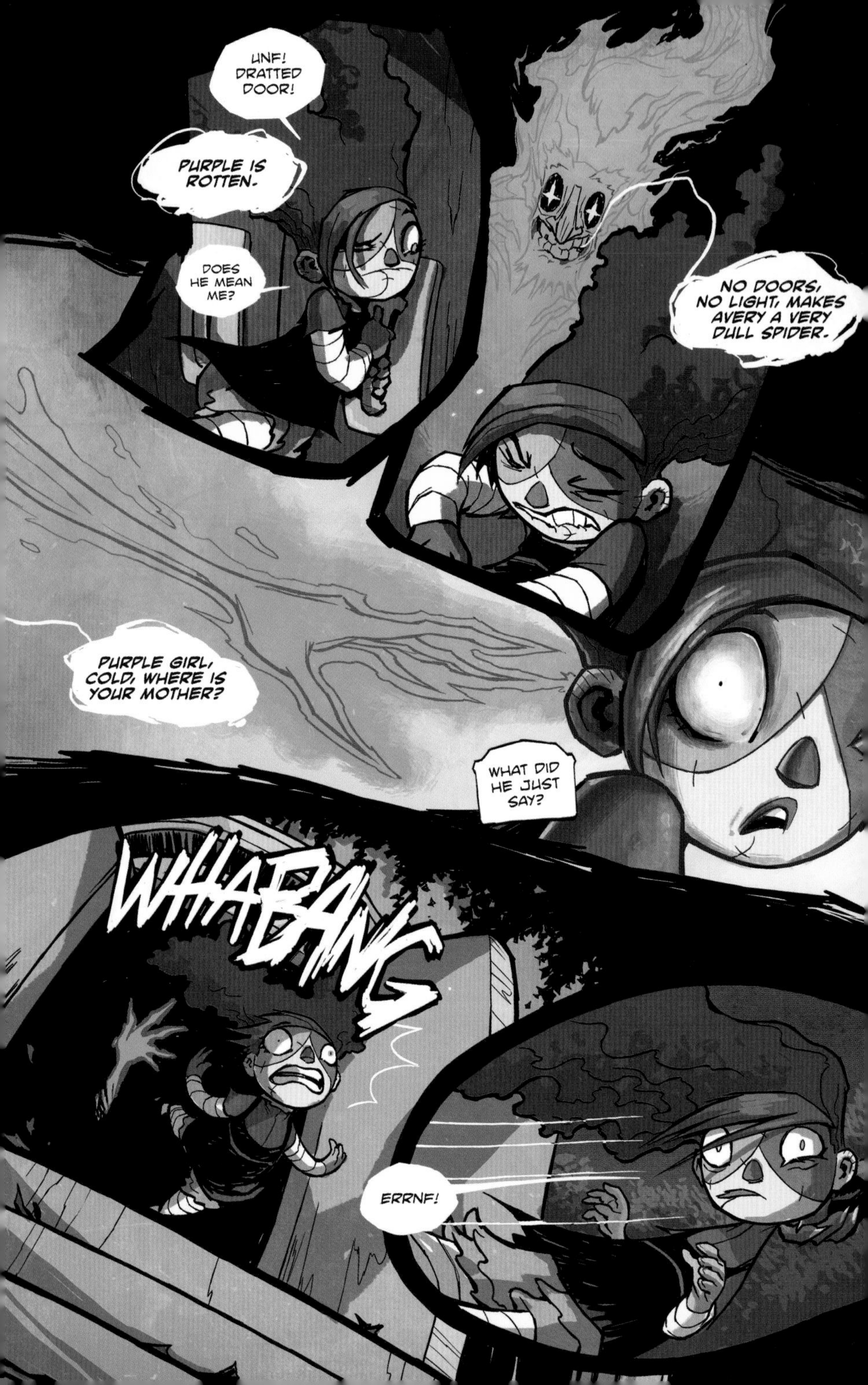
UNF! DRATTED DOOR!
PURPLE IS ROTTEN.
DOES HE MEAN ME?
NO DOORS, NO LIGHT, MAKES AVERY A VERY DULL SPIDER.
PURPLE GIRL, COLD, WHERE IS YOUR MOTHER?
WHAT DID HE JUST SAY?
WHABANG
ERRNF!

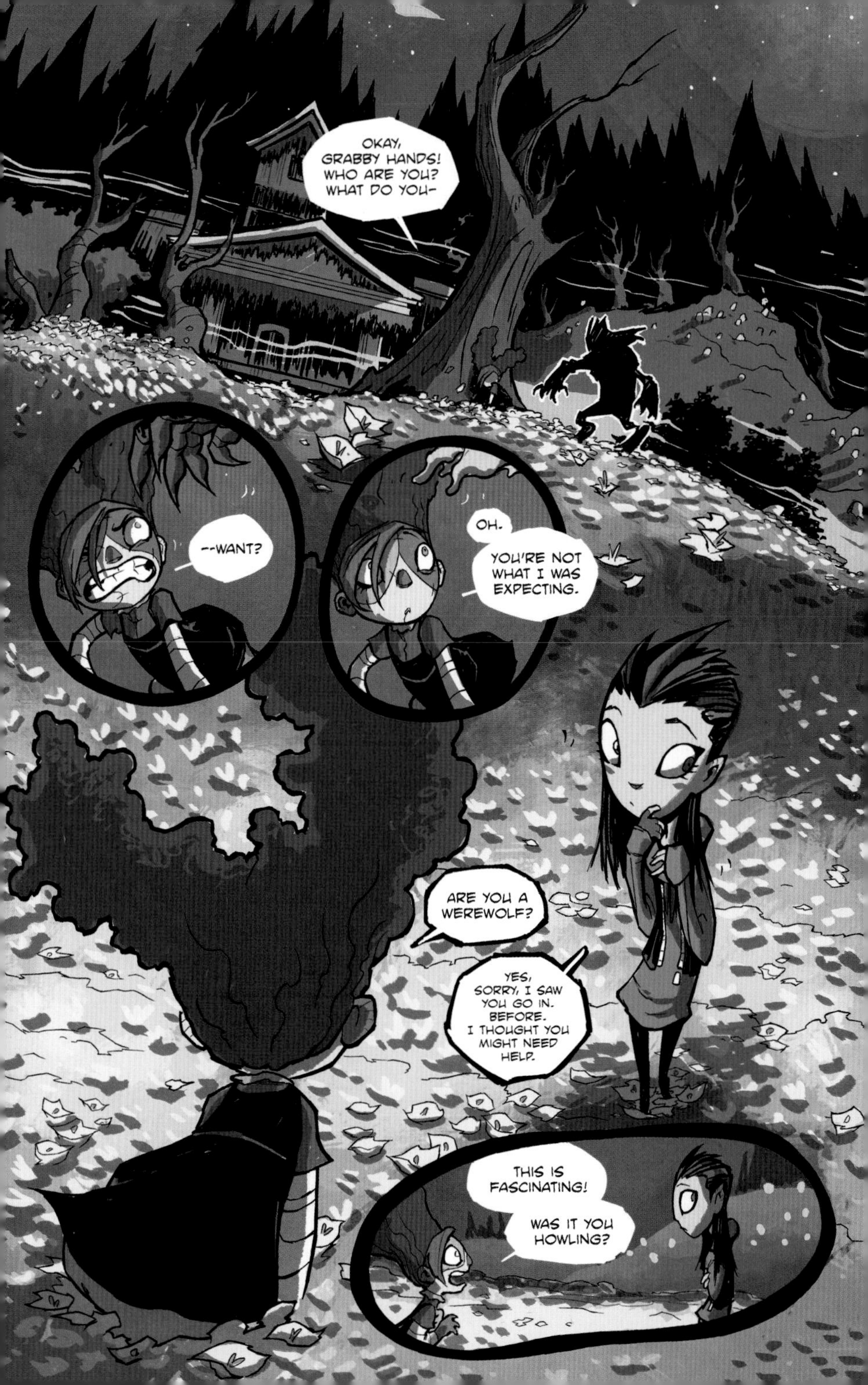
OKAY, GRABBY HANDS! WHO ARE YOU? WHAT DO YOU-
--WANT?
OH.
YOU'RE NOT WHAT I WAS EXPECTING.
ARE YOU A WEREWOLF?
YES, SORRY, I SAW YOU GO IN. BEFORE. I THOUGHT YOU MIGHT NEED HELP.
THIS IS FASCINATING!
WAS IT YOU HOWLING?

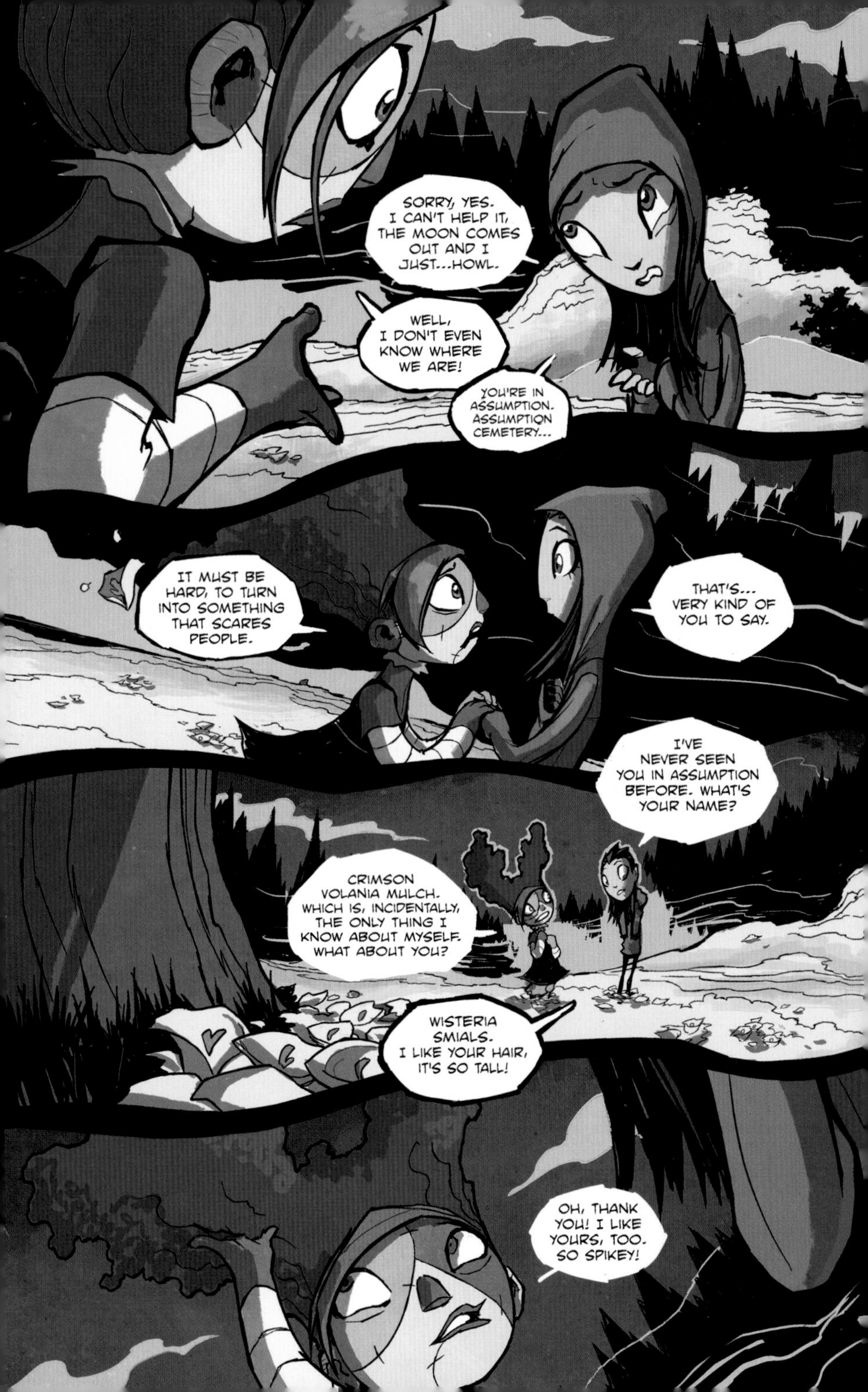
SORRY, YES. I CAN'T HELP IT, THE MOON COMES OUT AND I JUST...HOWL.
WELL, I DON'T EVEN KNOW WHERE WE ARE!
YOU'RE IN ASSUMPTION. ASSUMPTION CEMETERY...
IT MUST BE HARD, TO TURN INTO SOMETHING THAT SCARES PEOPLE.
THAT'S... VERY KIND OF YOU TO SAY.
I'VE NEVER SEEN YOU IN ASSUMPTION BEFORE. WHAT'S YOUR NAME?
CRIMSON VOLANIA MULCH. WHICH IS, INCIDENTALLY, THE ONLY THING I KNOW ABOUT MYSELF. WHAT ABOUT YOU?
WISTERIA SMIALS. I LIKE YOUR HAIR, IT'S SO TALL!
OH, THANK YOU! I LIKE YOURS, TOO. SO SPIKEY!

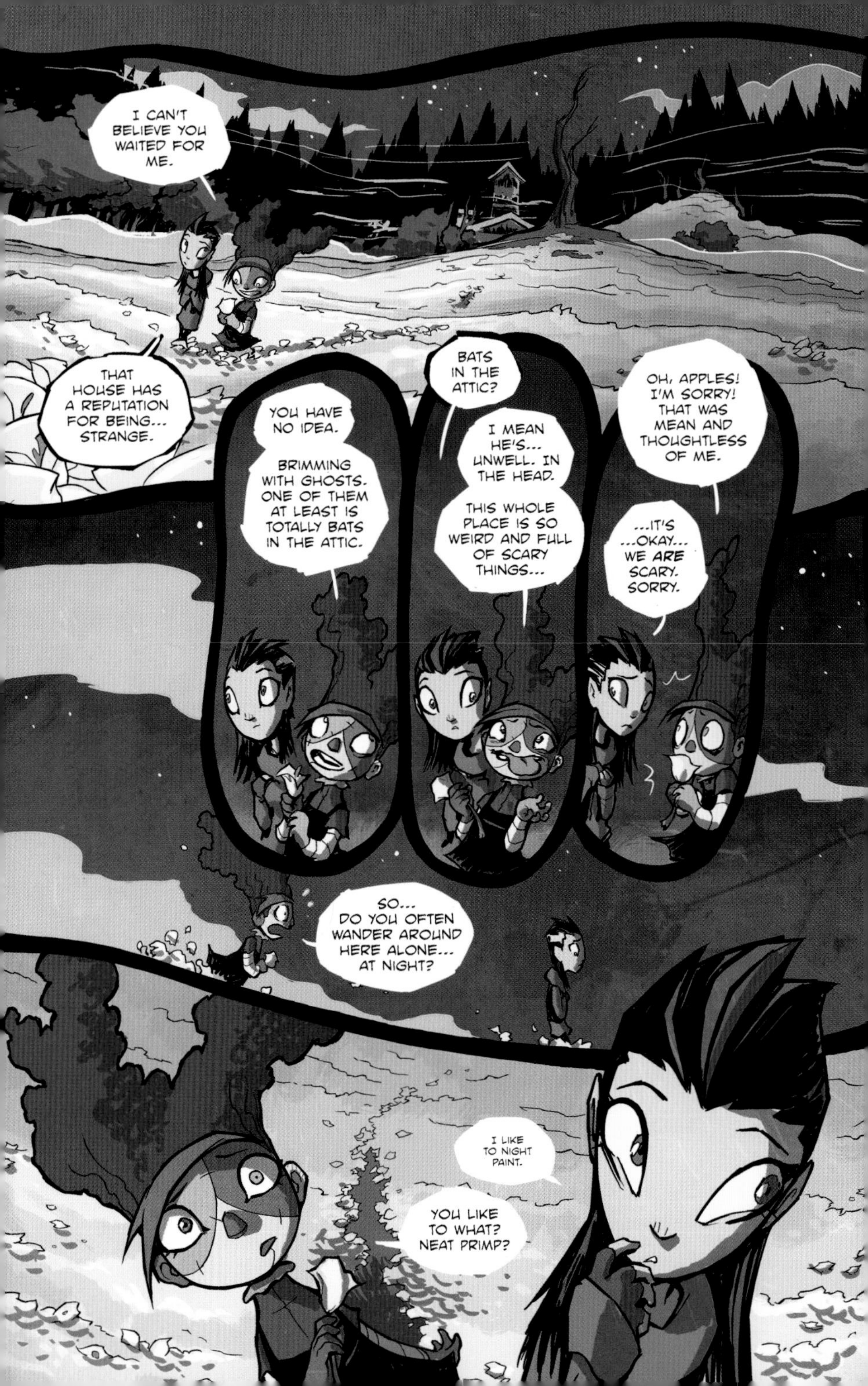
I CAN'T BELIEVE YOU WAITED FOR ME.
THAT HOUSE HAS A REPUTATION FOR BEING... STRANGE.
YOU HAVE NO IDEA.
BRIMMING WITH GHOSTS. ONE OF THEM AT LEAST IS TOTALLY BATS IN THE ATTIC.
BATS IN THE ATTIC?
I MEAN HE'S... UNWELL. IN THE HEAD.
THIS WHOLE PLACE IS SO WEIRD AND FULL OF SCARY THINGS...
OH, APPLES! I'M SORRY! THAT WAS MEAN AND THOUGHTLESS OF ME.
...IT'S ...OKAY... WE ARE SCARY. SORRY.
SO... DO YOU OFTEN WANDER AROUND HERE ALONE... AT NIGHT?
I LIKE TO NIGHT PAINT.
YOU LIKE TO WHAT? NEAT PRIMP?

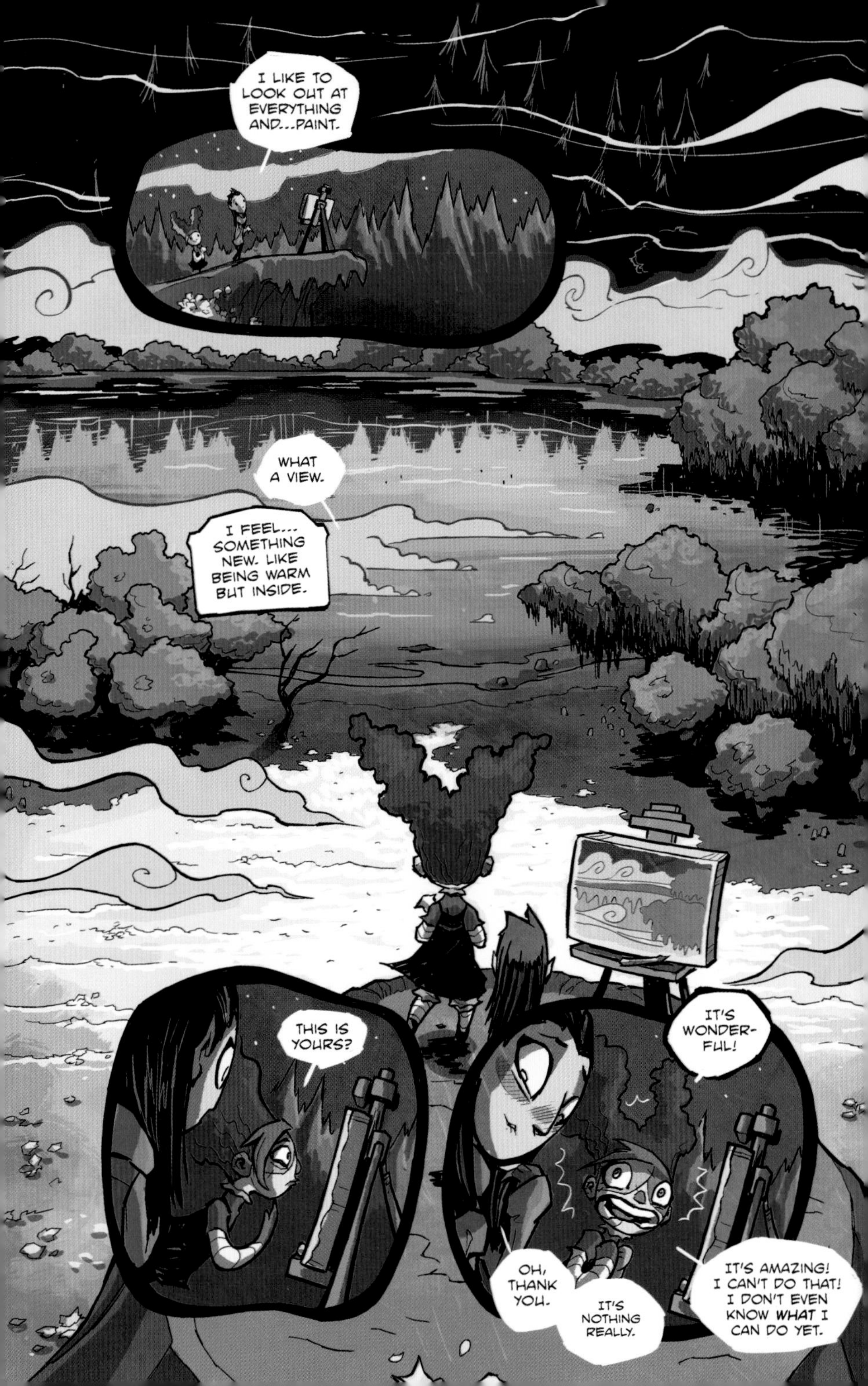
I LIKE TO LOOK OUT AT EVERYTHING AND...PAINT.
WHAT A VIEW.
I FEEL... SOMETHING NEW. LIKE BEING WARM BUT INSIDE.
THIS IS YOURS?
IT'S WONDER-FUL!
OH, THANK YOU.
IT'S NOTHING REALLY.
IT'S AMAZING! I CAN'T DO THAT! I DON'T EVEN KNOW **WHAT** I CAN DO YET.

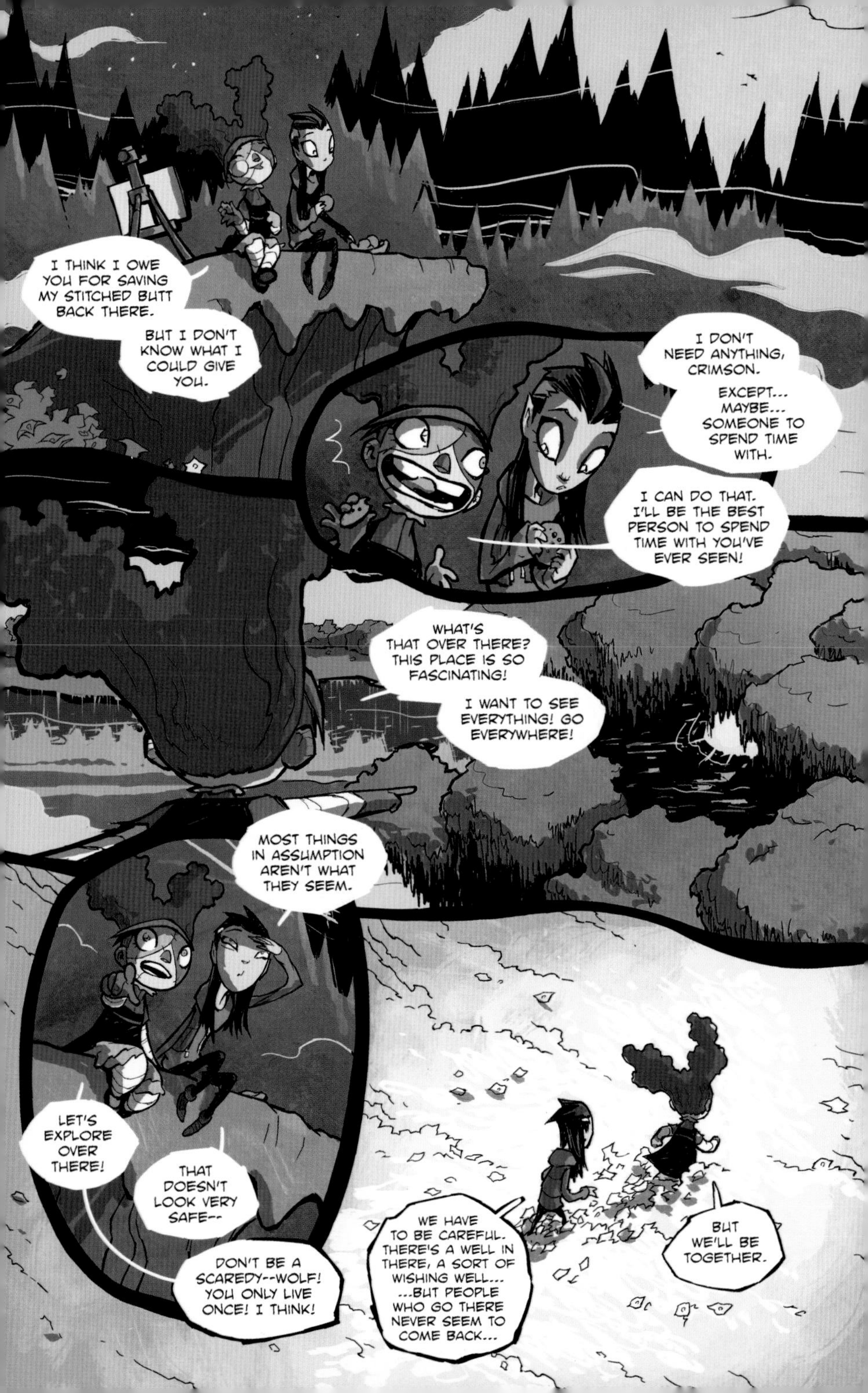
I THINK I OWE YOU FOR SAVING MY STITCHED BUTT BACK THERE.
BUT I DON'T KNOW WHAT I COULD GIVE YOU.
I DON'T NEED ANYTHING, CRIMSON.
EXCEPT... MAYBE... SOMEONE TO SPEND TIME WITH.
I CAN DO THAT. I'LL BE THE BEST PERSON TO SPEND TIME WITH YOU'VE EVER SEEN!
WHAT'S THAT OVER THERE? THIS PLACE IS SO FASCINATING!
I WANT TO SEE EVERYTHING! GO EVERYWHERE!
MOST THINGS IN ASSUMPTION AREN'T WHAT THEY SEEM.
LET'S EXPLORE OVER THERE!
THAT DOESN'T LOOK VERY SAFE--
DON'T BE A SCAREDY--WOLF! YOU ONLY LIVE ONCE! I THINK!
WE HAVE TO BE CAREFUL. THERE'S A WELL IN THERE, A SORT OF WISHING WELL... ...BUT PEOPLE WHO GO THERE NEVER SEEM TO COME BACK...
BUT WE'LL BE TOGETHER.

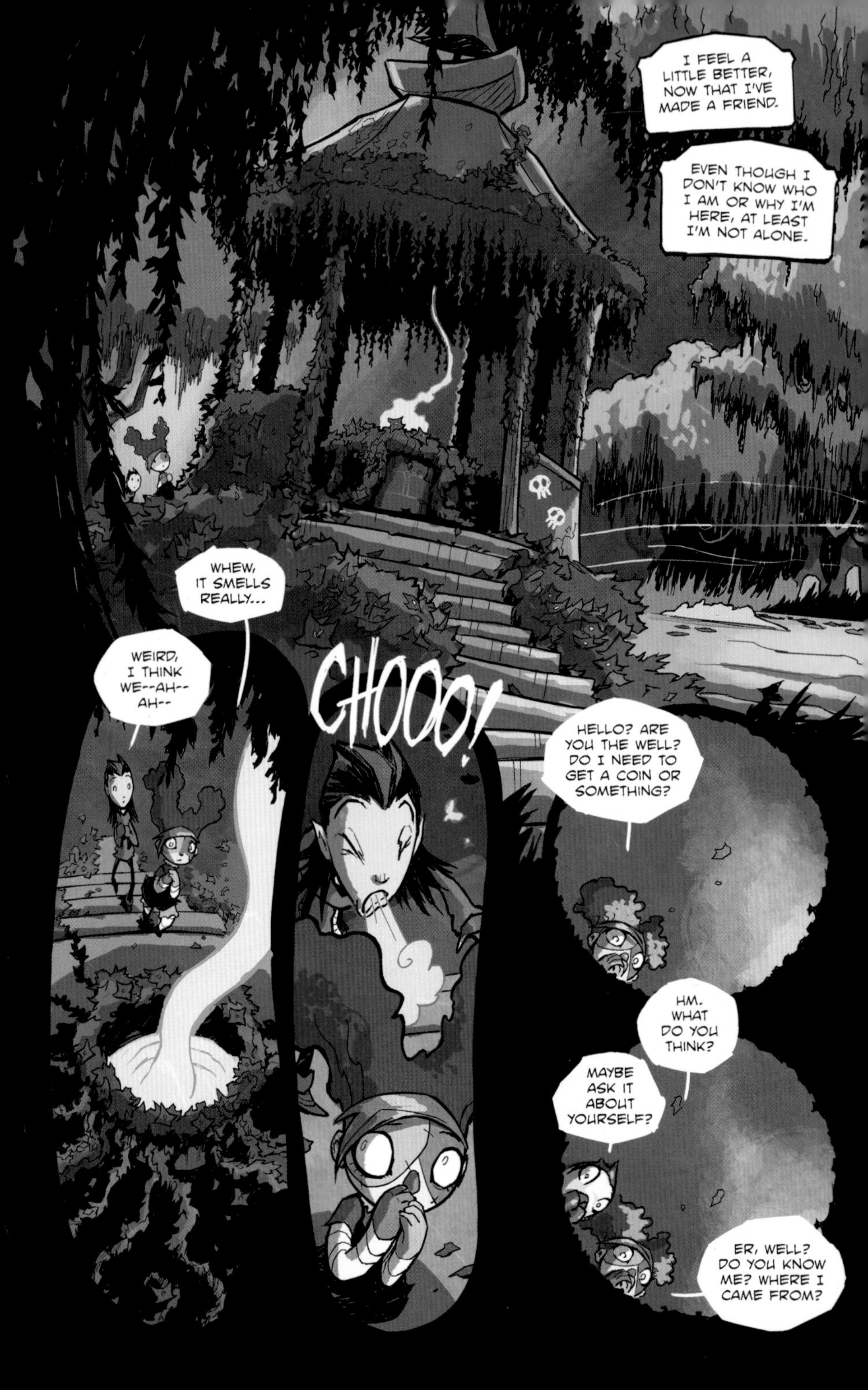
I FEEL A LITTLE BETTER, NOW THAT I'VE MADE A FRIEND.
EVEN THOUGH I DON'T KNOW WHO I AM OR WHY I'M HERE, AT LEAST I'M NOT ALONE.
WHEW, IT SMELLS REALLY...
WEIRD, I THINK WE--AH--AH--
CHOOO!
HELLO? ARE YOU THE WELL? DO I NEED TO GET A COIN OR SOMETHING?
HM. WHAT DO YOU THINK?
MAYBE ASK IT ABOUT YOURSELF?
ER, WELL? DO YOU KNOW ME? WHERE I CAME FROM?

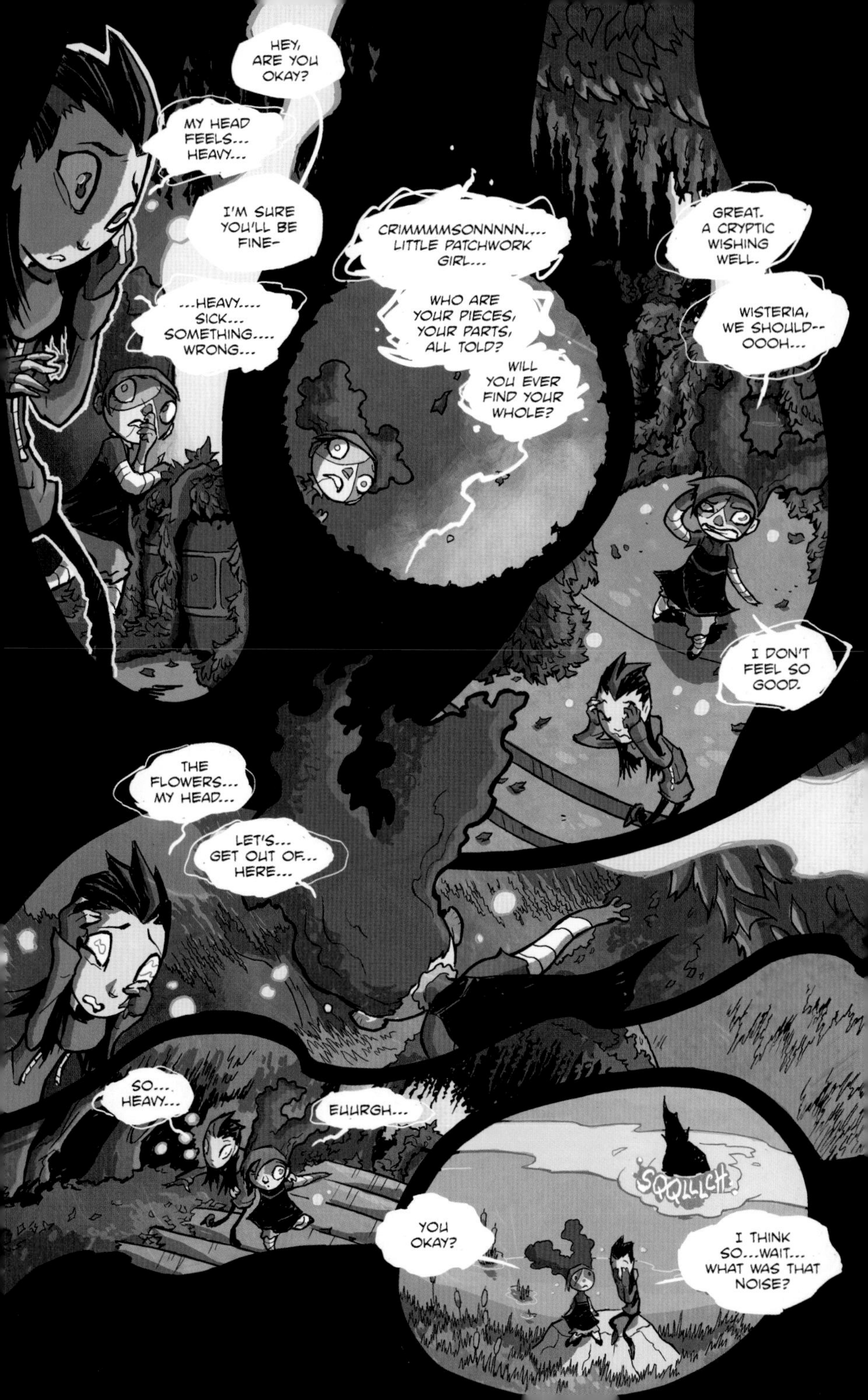
HEY, ARE YOU OKAY?
MY HEAD FEELS... HEAVY...
I'M SURE YOU'LL BE FINE-
...HEAVY.... SICK... SOMETHING.... WRONG...
CRIMMMMSONNNNN.... LITTLE PATCHWORK GIRL...
WHO ARE YOUR PIECES, YOUR PARTS, ALL TOLD?
WILL YOU EVER FIND YOUR WHOLE?
GREAT. A CRYPTIC WISHING WELL.
WISTERIA, WE SHOULD-- OOOH...
I DON'T FEEL SO GOOD.
THE FLOWERS... MY HEAD...
LET'S... GET OUT OF... HERE...
SO... HEAVY...
EUURGH...
SQQLLLCH
YOU OKAY?
I THINK SO...WAIT... WHAT WAS THAT NOISE?

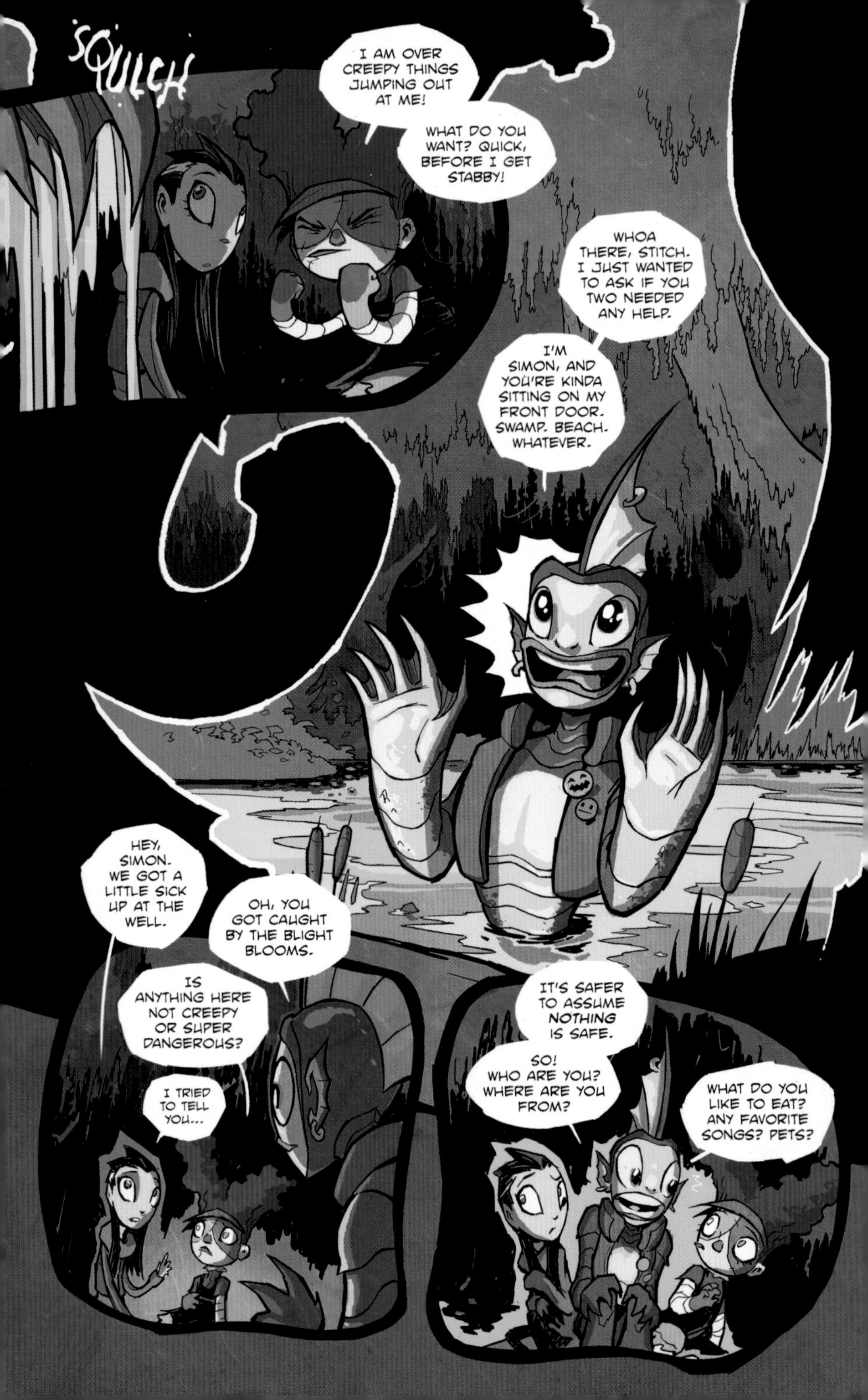
SQUILCH
I AM OVER CREEPY THINGS JUMPING OUT AT ME!
WHAT DO YOU WANT? QUICK, BEFORE I GET STABBY!
WHOA THERE, STITCH. I JUST WANTED TO ASK IF YOU TWO NEEDED ANY HELP.
I'M SIMON, AND YOU'RE KINDA SITTING ON MY FRONT DOOR. SWAMP. BEACH. WHATEVER.
HEY, SIMON. WE GOT A LITTLE SICK UP AT THE WELL.
OH, YOU GOT CAUGHT BY THE BLIGHT BLOOMS.
IS ANYTHING HERE NOT CREEPY OR SUPER DANGEROUS?
I TRIED TO TELL YOU...
IT'S SAFER TO ASSUME NOTHING IS SAFE.
SO! WHO ARE YOU? WHERE ARE YOU FROM?
WHAT DO YOU LIKE TO EAT? ANY FAVORITE SONGS? PETS?

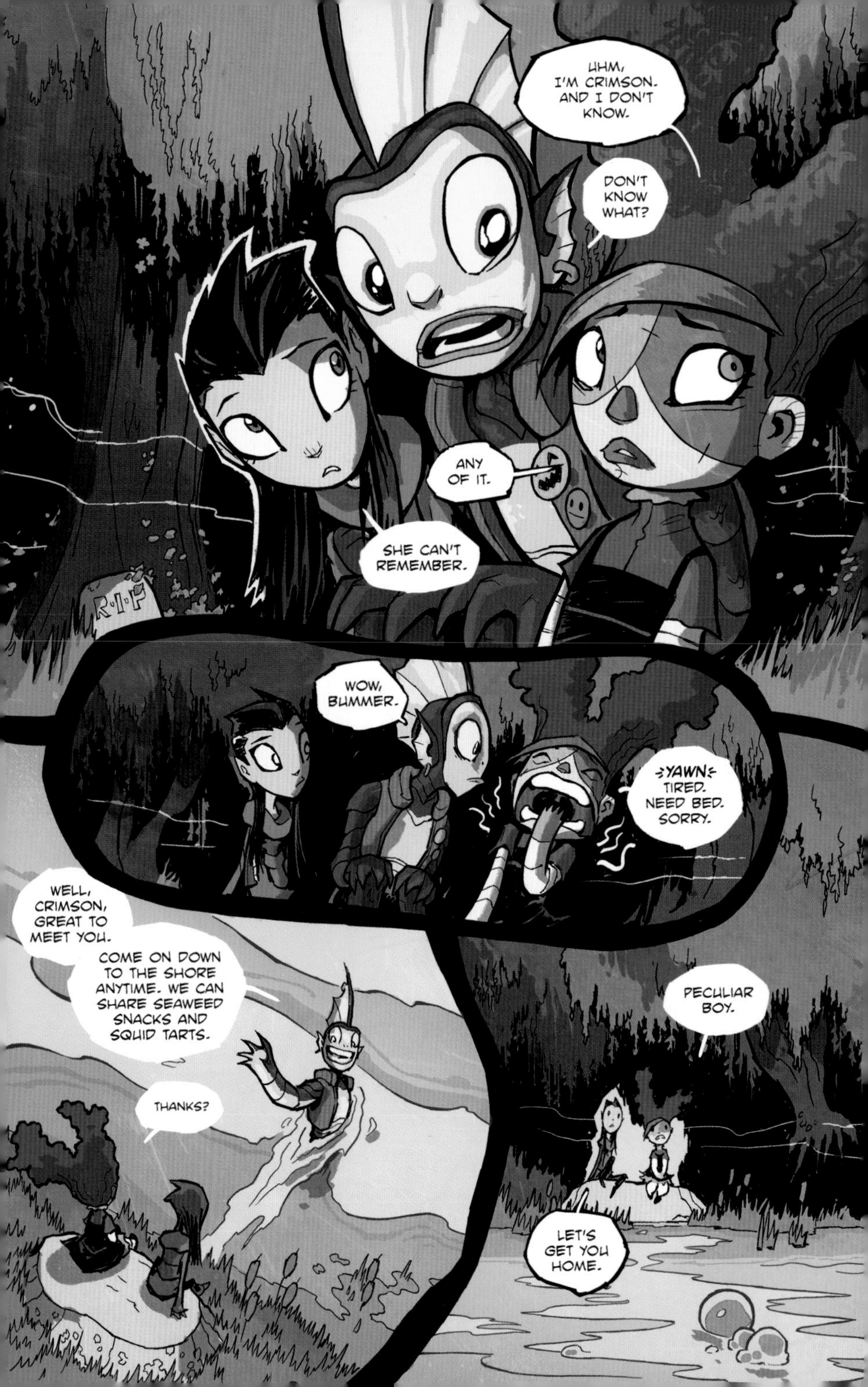
UHM, I'M CRIMSON. AND I DON'T KNOW.
DON'T KNOW WHAT?
ANY OF IT.
SHE CAN'T REMEMBER.
R.I.P.
WOW, BUMMER.
YAWN TIRED. NEED BED. SORRY.
WELL, CRIMSON, GREAT TO MEET YOU.
COME ON DOWN TO THE SHORE ANYTIME. WE CAN SHARE SEAWEED SNACKS AND SQUID TARTS.
THANKS?
PECULIAR BOY.
LET'S GET YOU HOME.

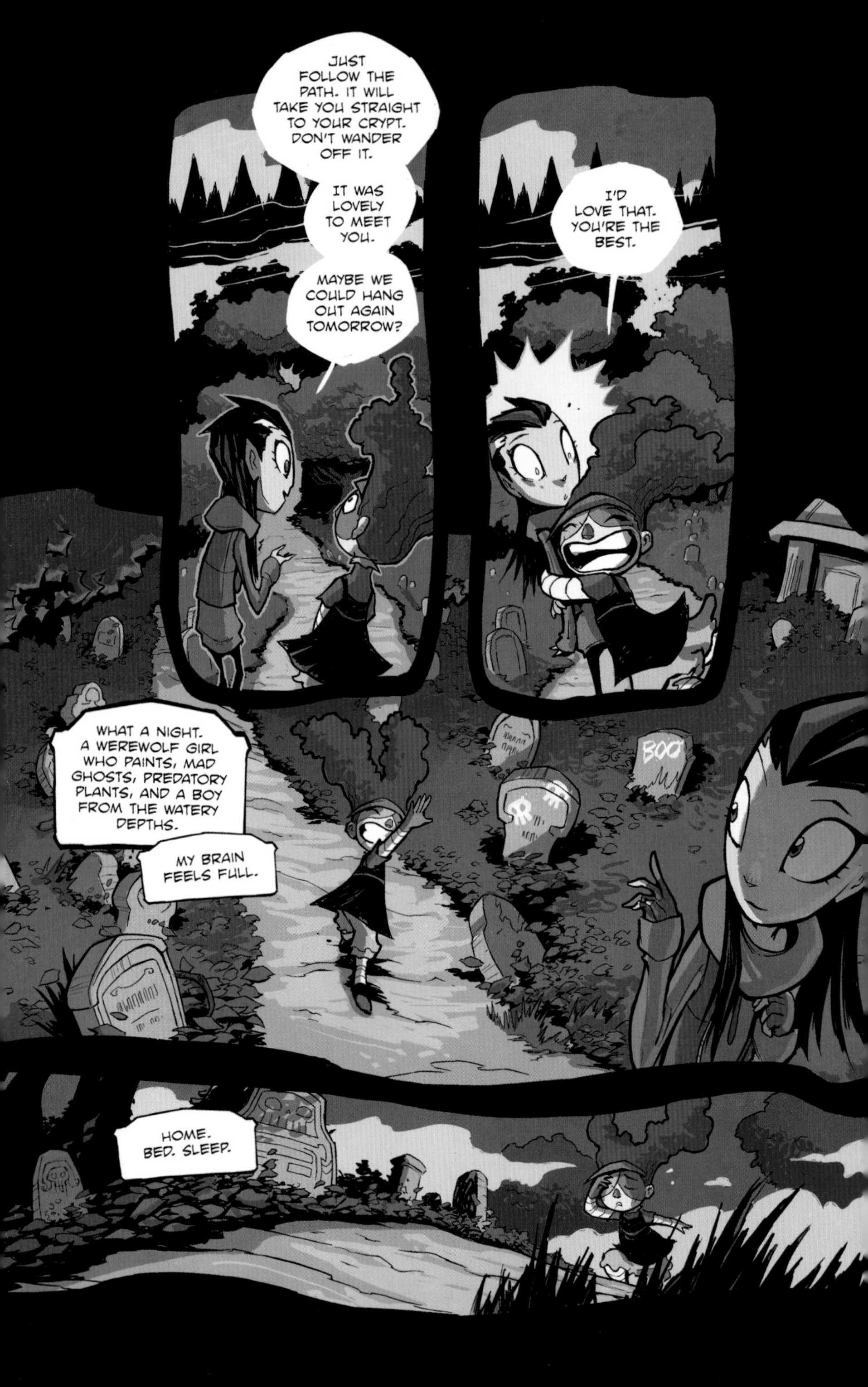
JUST FOLLOW THE PATH. IT WILL TAKE YOU STRAIGHT TO YOUR CRYPT. DON'T WANDER OFF IT.
IT WAS LOVELY TO MEET YOU.
MAYBE WE COULD HANG OUT AGAIN TOMORROW?
I'D LOVE THAT. YOU'RE THE BEST.
WHAT A NIGHT. A WEREWOLF GIRL WHO PAINTS, MAD GHOSTS, PREDATORY PLANTS, AND A BOY FROM THE WATERY DEPTHS.
MY BRAIN FEELS FULL.
BOO
HOME. BED. SLEEP.

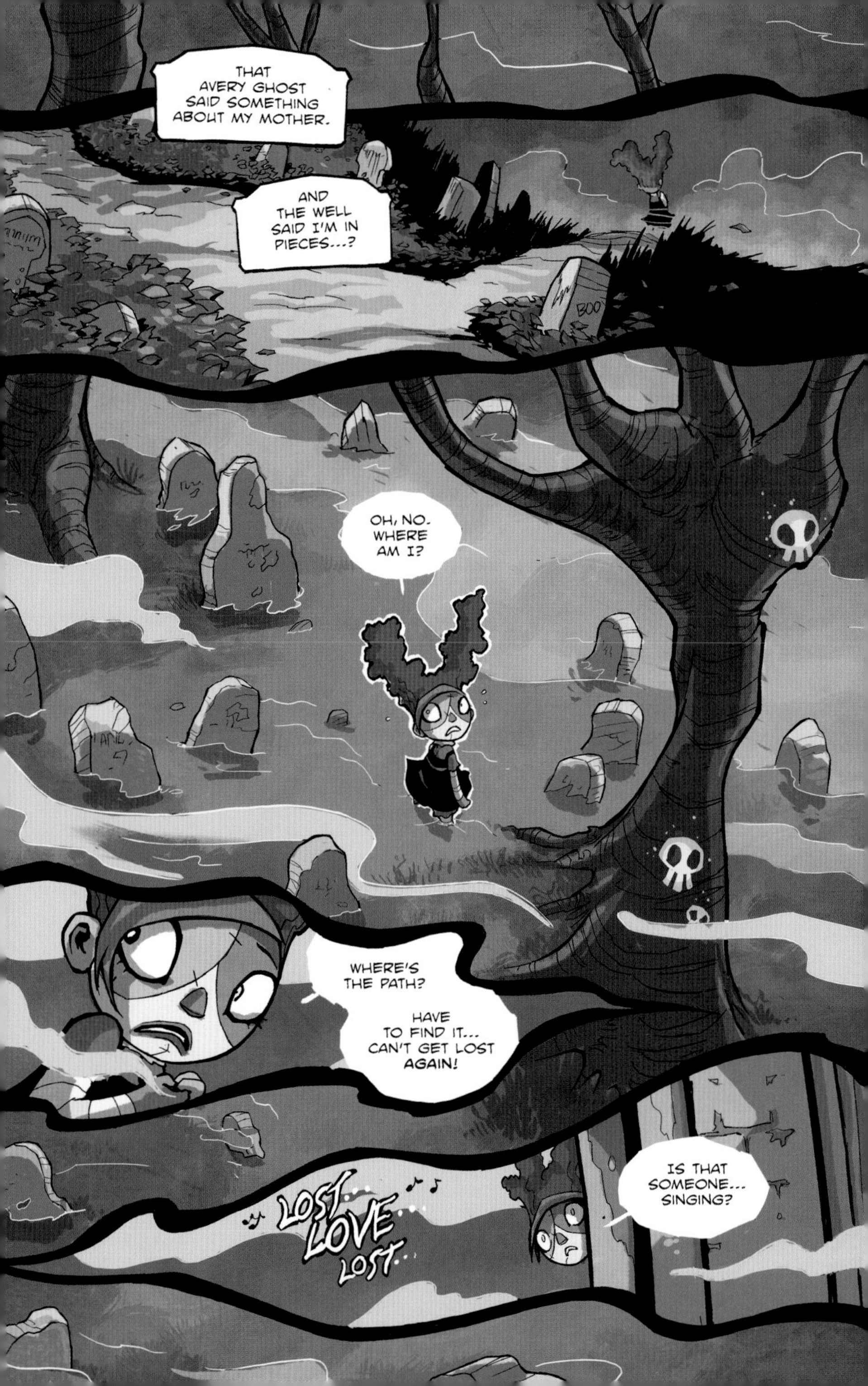
THAT AVERY GHOST SAID SOMETHING ABOUT MY MOTHER.
AND THE WELL SAID I'M IN PIECES...?
BOO
OH, NO. WHERE AM I?
WHERE'S THE PATH?
HAVE TO FIND IT... CAN'T GET LOST AGAIN!
LOST... LOVE... LOST...
IS THAT SOMEONE... SINGING?

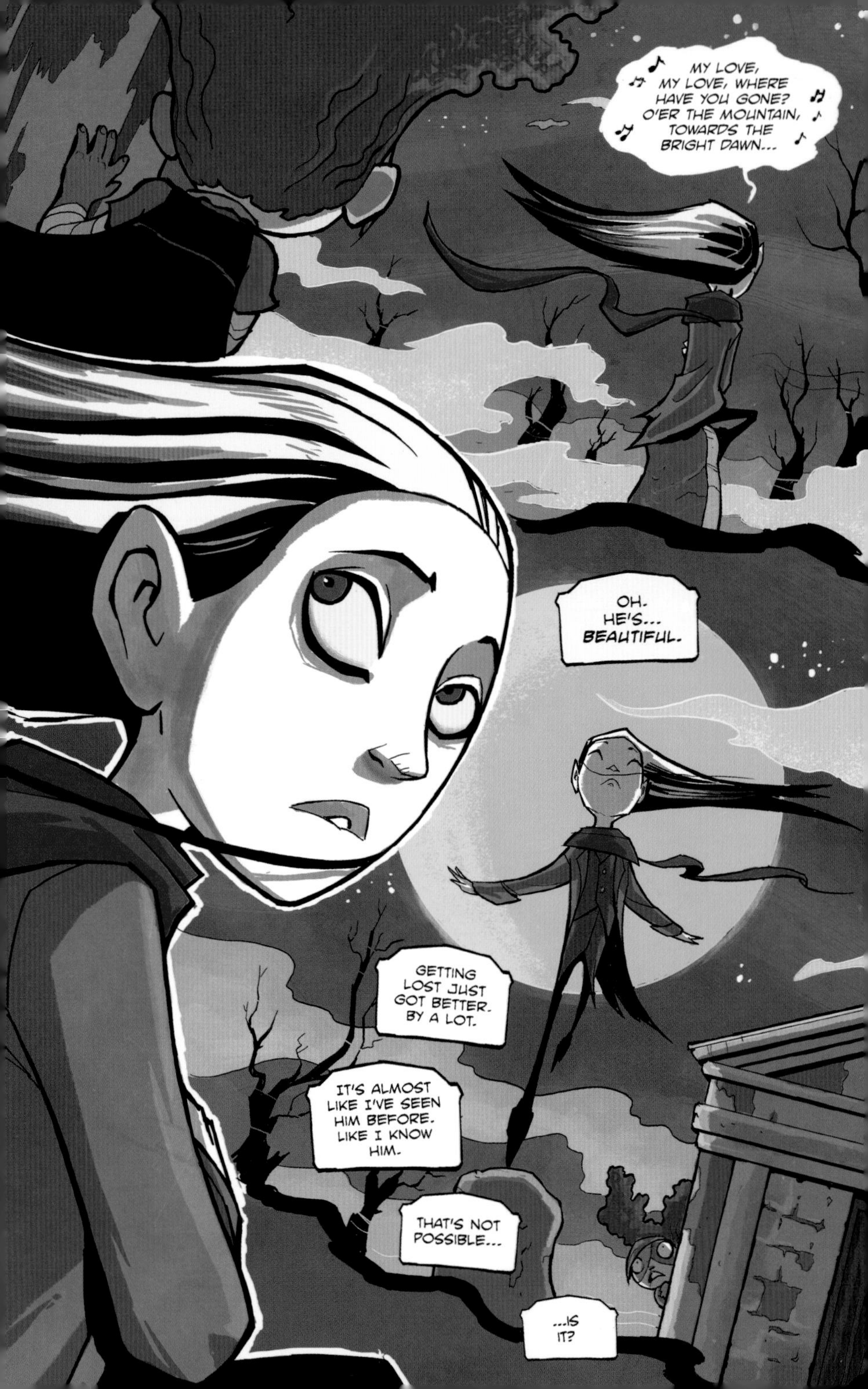
MY LOVE, MY LOVE, WHERE HAVE YOU GONE? O'ER THE MOUNTAIN, TOWARDS THE BRIGHT DAWN...
OH. HE'S... BEAUTIFUL.
GETTING LOST JUST GOT BETTER. BY A LOT.
IT'S ALMOST LIKE I'VE SEEN HIM BEFORE. LIKE I KNOW HIM.
THAT'S NOT POSSIBLE...
...IS IT?

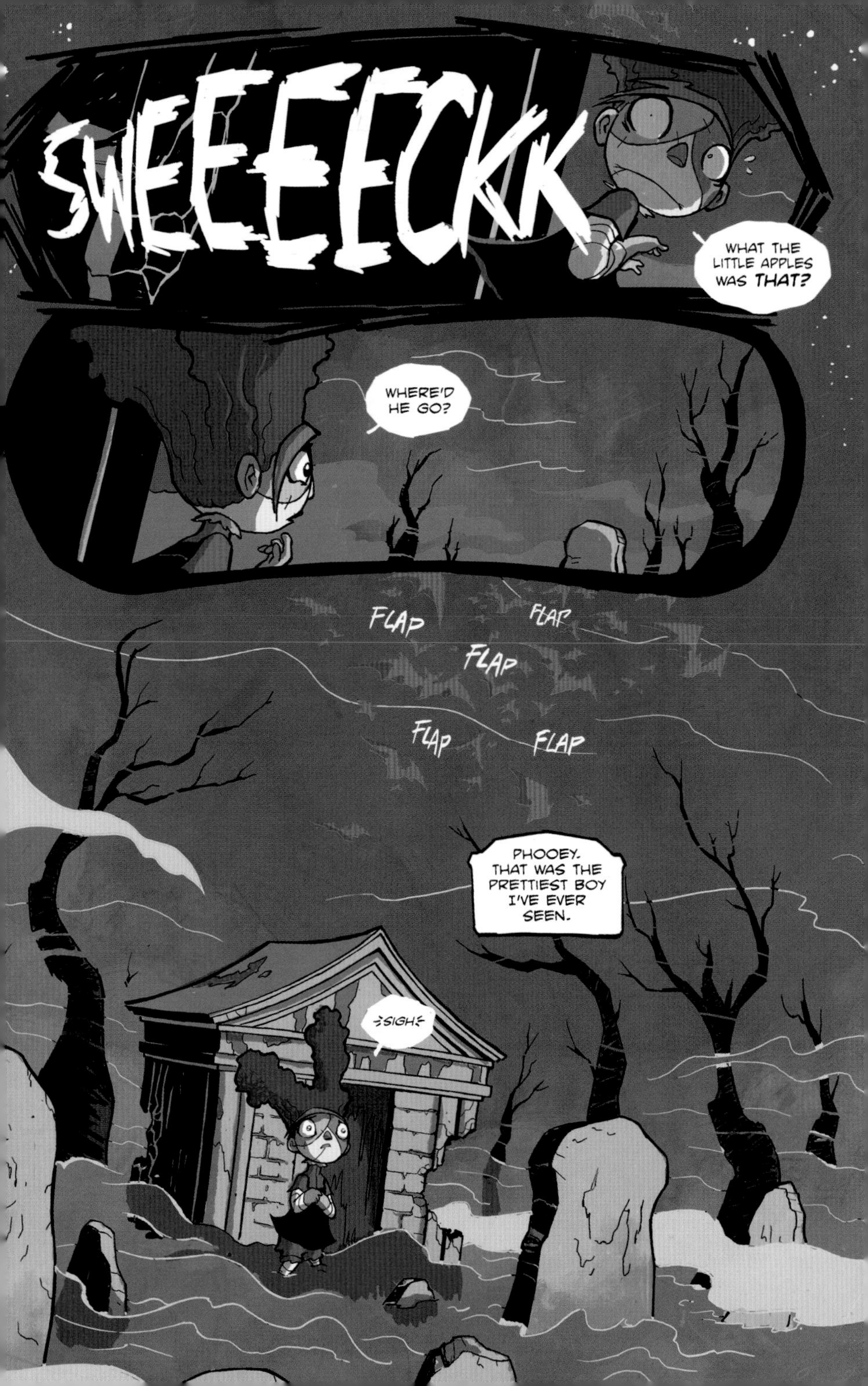
SWEEEECKK
WHAT THE LITTLE APPLES WAS THAT?
WHERE'D HE GO?
FLAP
FLAP
FLAP
FLAP
FLAP
PHOOEY. THAT WAS THE PRETTIEST BOY I'VE EVER SEEN.
SIGH

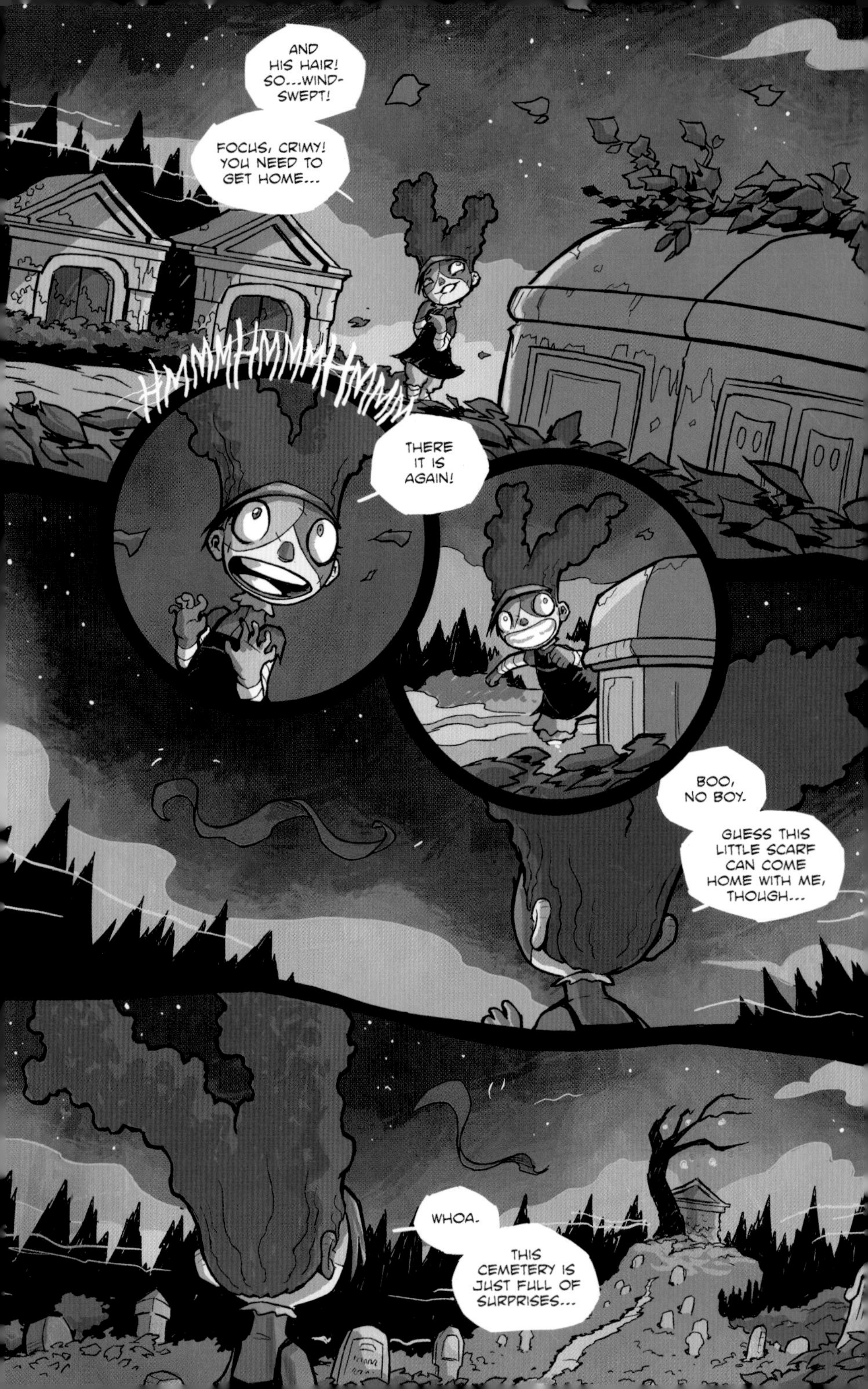
AND HIS HAIR! SO...WIND-SWEPT!
FOCUS, CRIMY! YOU NEED TO GET HOME...
HMMMHMMMHMMM
THERE IT IS AGAIN!
BOO, NO BOY.
GUESS THIS LITTLE SCARF CAN COME HOME WITH ME, THOUGH...
WHOA.
THIS CEMETERY IS JUST FULL OF SURPRISES...

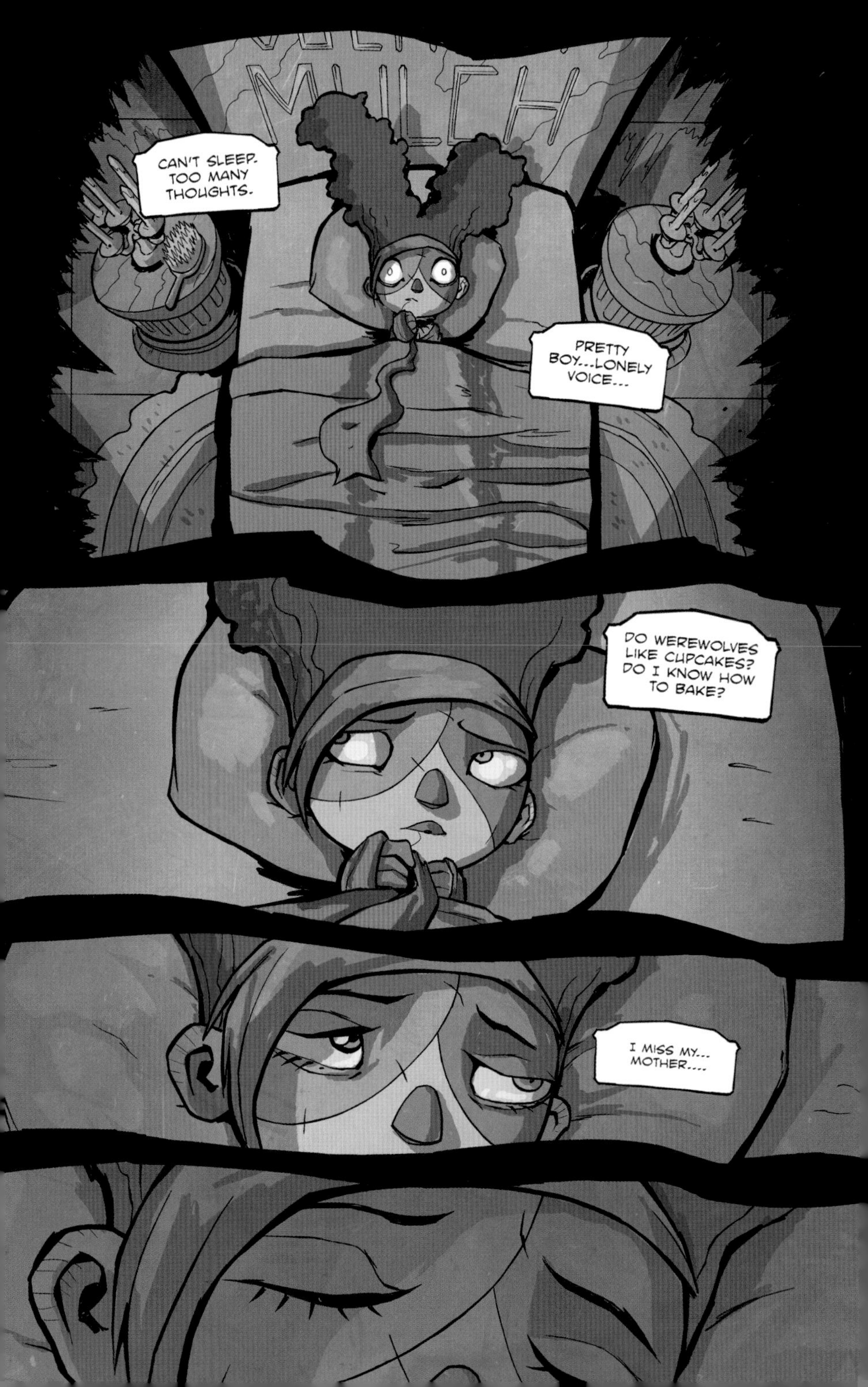

CAN'T SLEEP. TOO MANY THOUGHTS.
PRETTY BOY...LONELY VOICE...
DO WEREWOLVES LIKE CUPCAKES? DO I KNOW HOW TO BAKE?
I MISS MY... MOTHER....

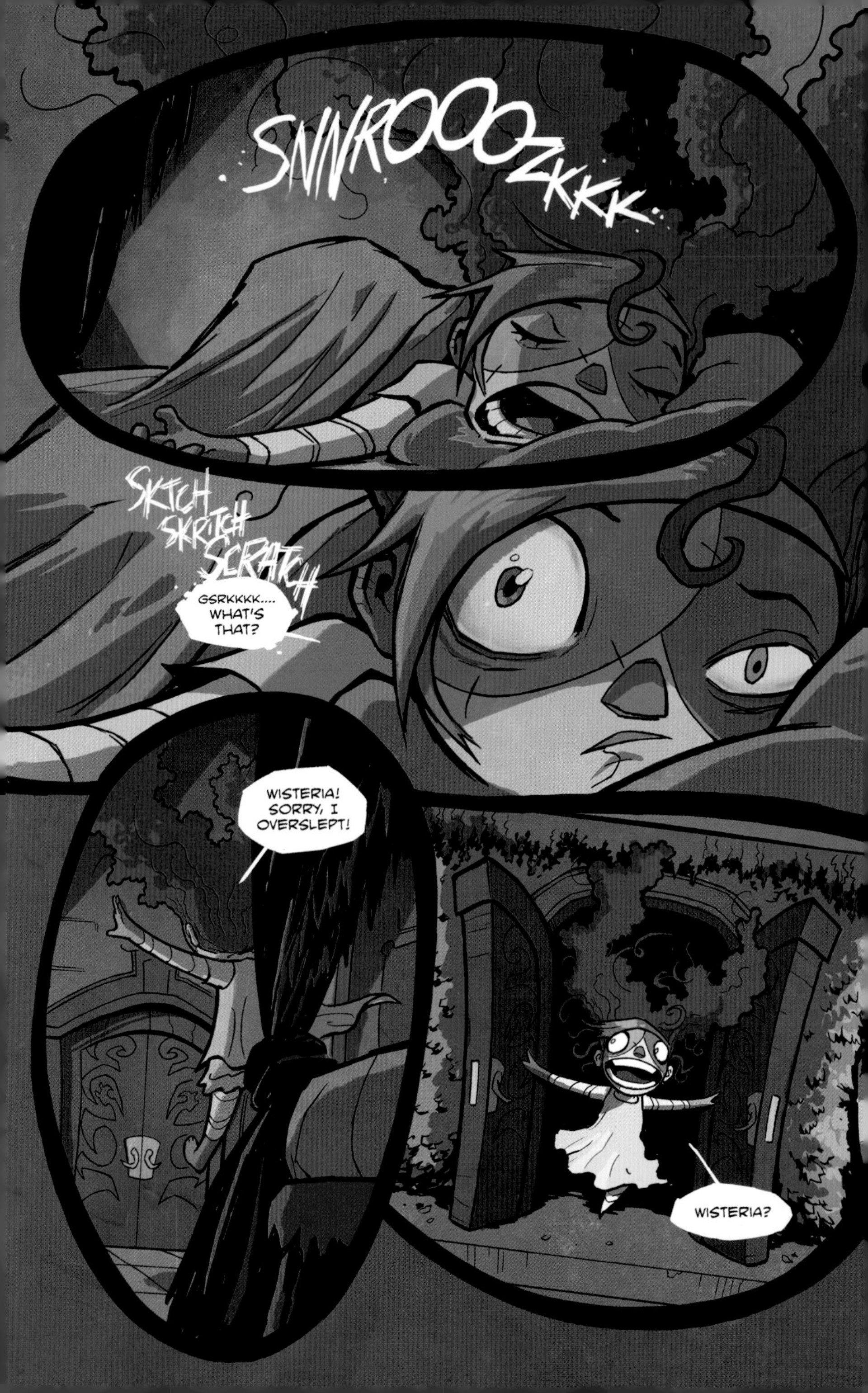
SNNROOOZKKK
SKTCH SKRITCH SCRATCH
GSRKKKK.... WHAT'S THAT?
WISTERIA! SORRY, I OVERSLEPT!
WISTERIA?

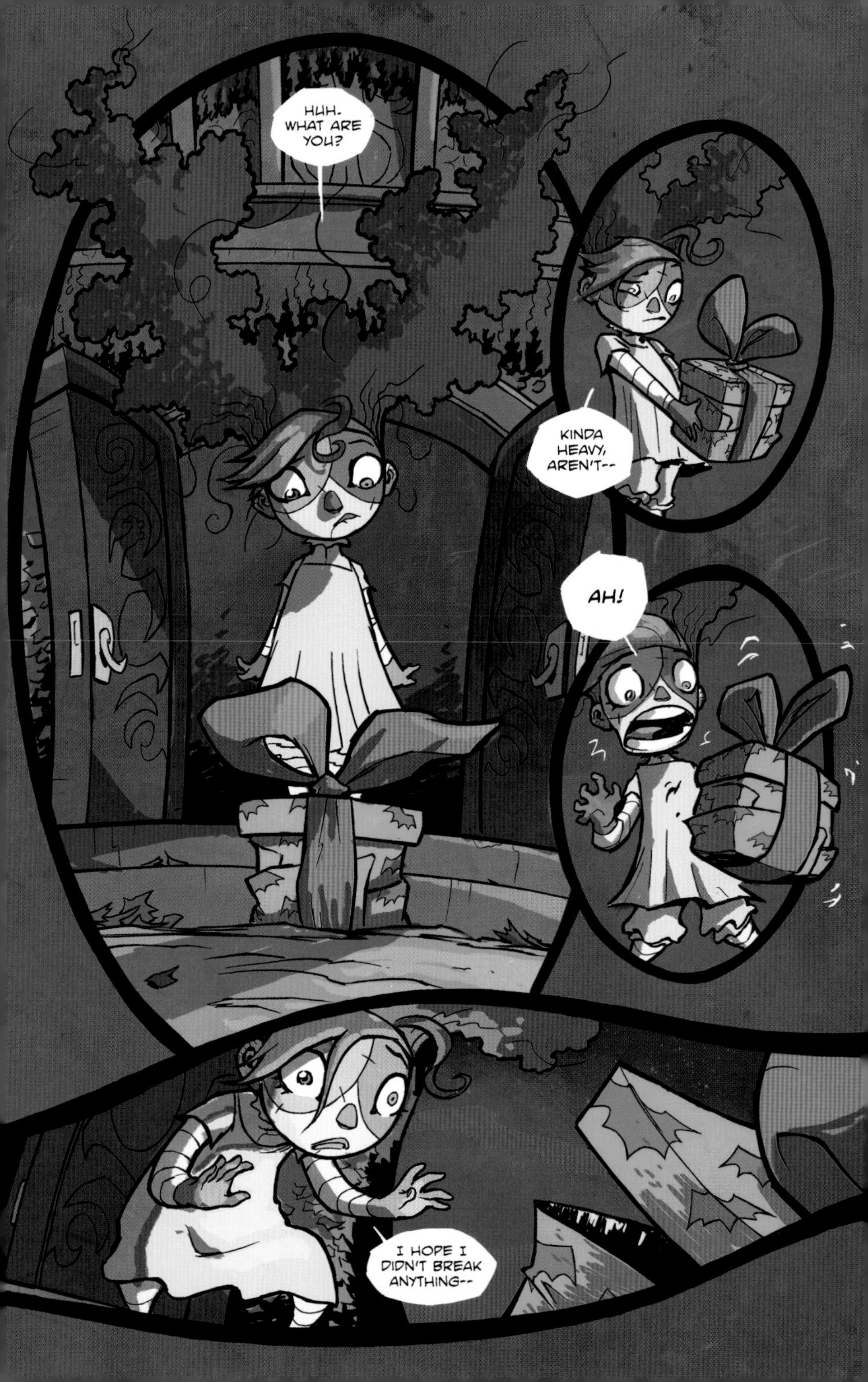
HUH. WHAT ARE YOU?
KINDA HEAVY, AREN'T--
AH!
I HOPE I DIDN'T BREAK ANYTHING--

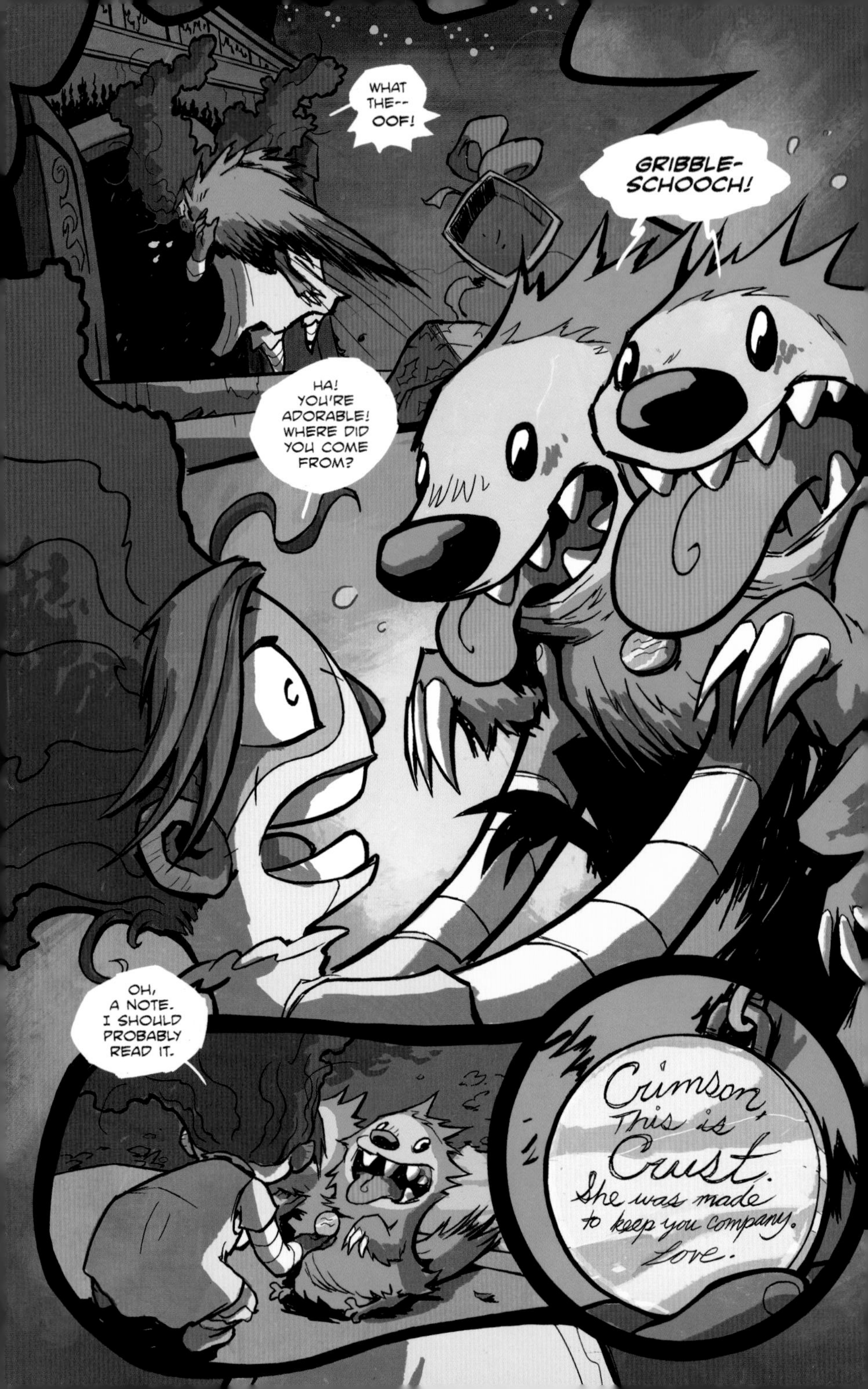
WHAT THE-- OOF!
GRIBBLE-SCHOOCH!
HA! YOU'RE ADORABLE! WHERE DID YOU COME FROM?
OH, A NOTE. I SHOULD PROBABLY READ IT.
Crimson, This is Crust. She was made to keep you company. Love.

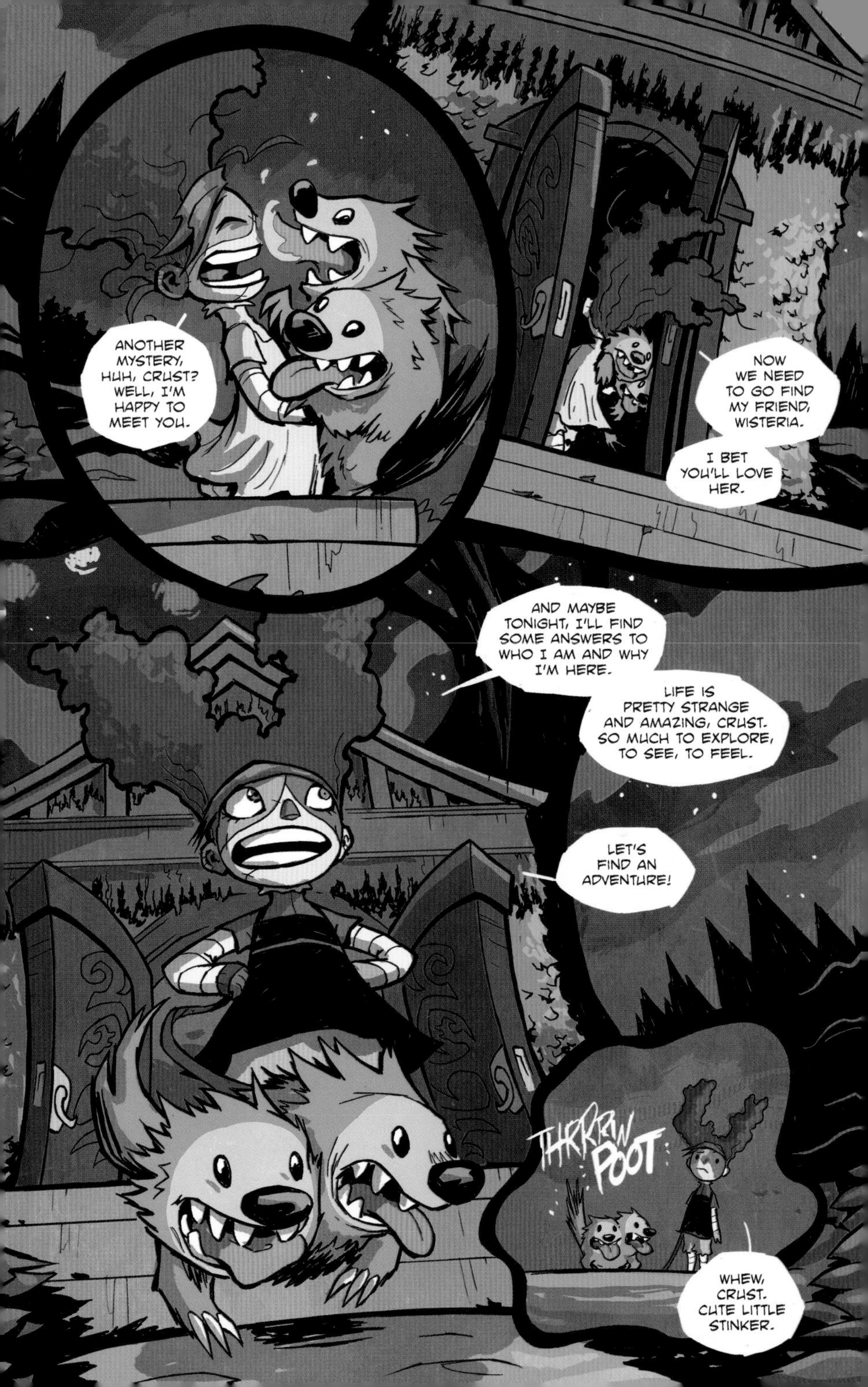
ANOTHER MYSTERY, HUH, CRUST? WELL, I'M HAPPY TO MEET YOU.
NOW WE NEED TO GO FIND MY FRIEND, WISTERIA.
I BET YOU'LL LOVE HER.
AND MAYBE TONIGHT, I'LL FIND SOME ANSWERS TO WHO I AM AND WHY I'M HERE.
LIFE IS PRETTY STRANGE AND AMAZING, CRUST. SO MUCH TO EXPLORE, TO SEE, TO FEEL.
LET'S FIND AN ADVENTURE!
THRRRW POOT
WHEW, CRUST. CUTE LITTLE STINKER.

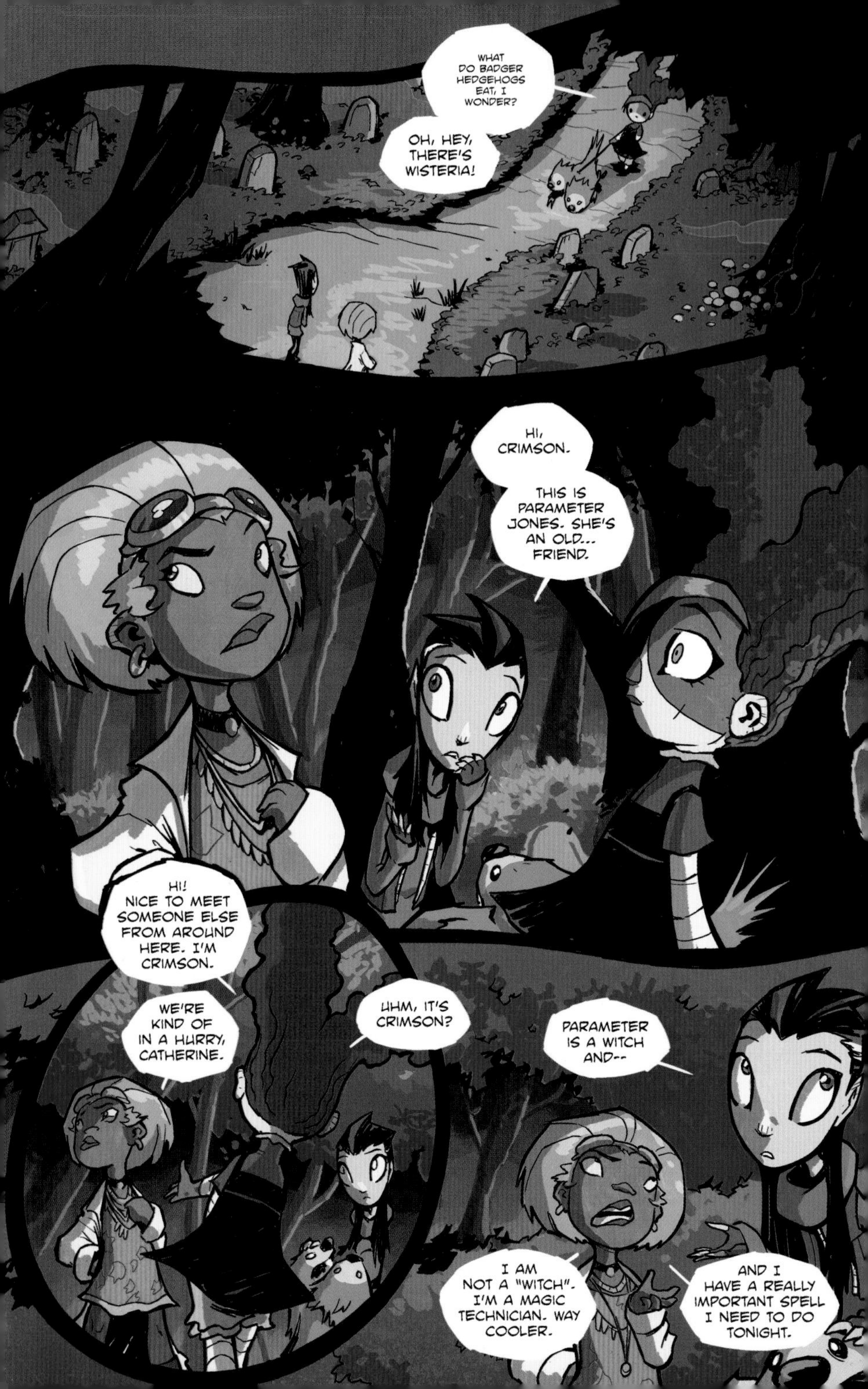
WHAT DO BADGER HEDGEHOGS EAT, I WONDER?
OH, HEY, THERE'S WISTERIA!
HI, CRIMSON.
THIS IS PARAMETER JONES. SHE'S AN OLD... FRIEND.
HI! NICE TO MEET SOMEONE ELSE FROM AROUND HERE. I'M CRIMSON.
WE'RE KIND OF IN A HURRY, CATHERINE.
UHM, IT'S CRIMSON?
PARAMETER IS A WITCH AND--
I AM NOT A "WITCH". I'M A MAGIC TECHNICIAN. WAY COOLER.
AND I HAVE A REALLY IMPORTANT SPELL I NEED TO DO TONIGHT.

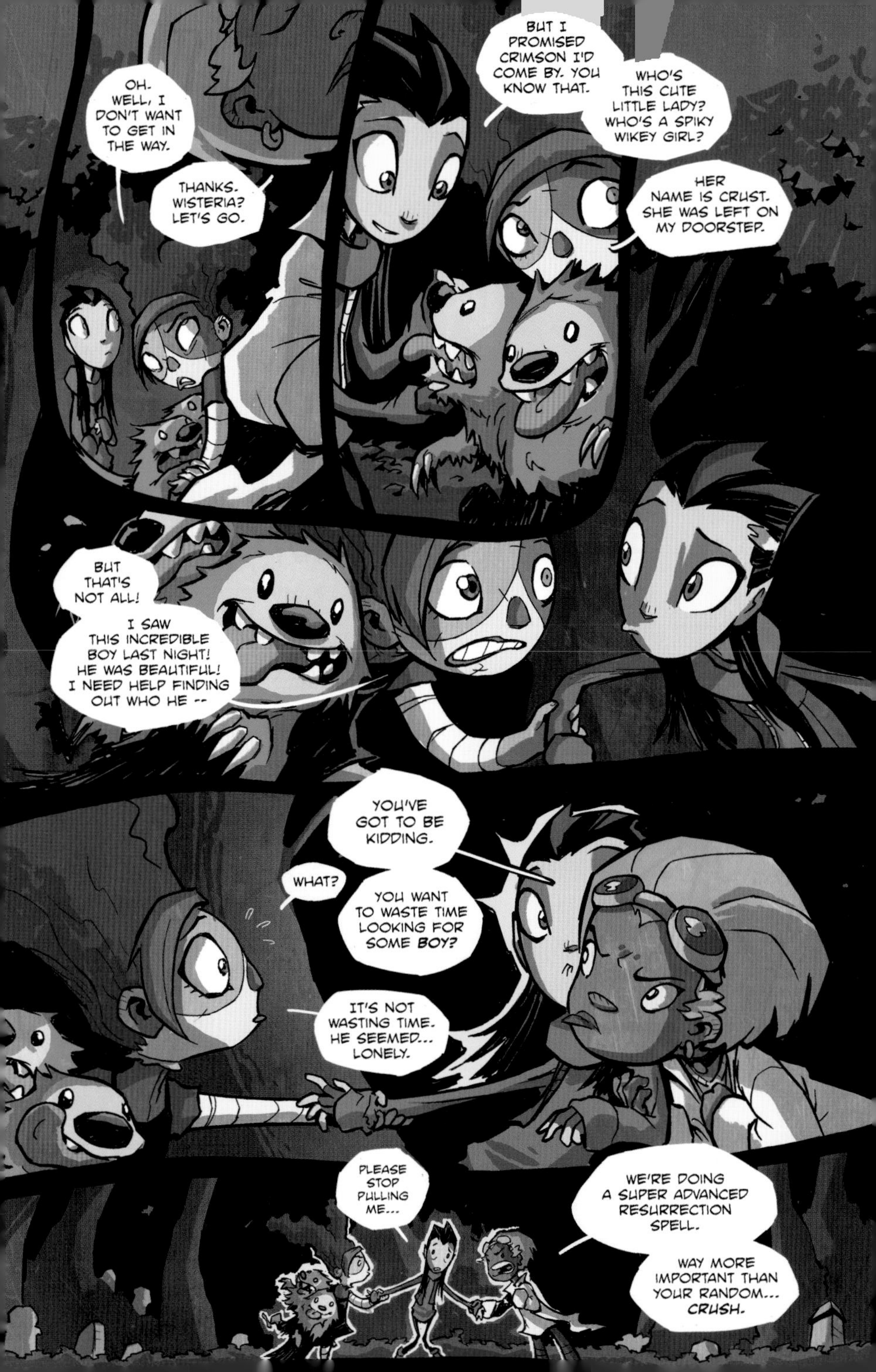
OH. WELL, I DON'T WANT TO GET IN THE WAY.
THANKS. WISTERIA? LET'S GO.
BUT I PROMISED CRIMSON I'D COME BY. YOU KNOW THAT.
WHO'S THIS CUTE LITTLE LADY? WHO'S A SPIKY WIKEY GIRL?
HER NAME IS CRUST. SHE WAS LEFT ON MY DOORSTEP.
BUT THAT'S NOT ALL!
I SAW THIS INCREDIBLE BOY LAST NIGHT! HE WAS BEAUTIFUL! I NEED HELP FINDING OUT WHO HE --
YOU'VE GOT TO BE KIDDING.
WHAT?
YOU WANT TO WASTE TIME LOOKING FOR SOME BOY?
IT'S NOT WASTING TIME. HE SEEMED... LONELY.
PLEASE STOP PULLING ME...
WE'RE DOING A SUPER ADVANCED RESURRECTION SPELL.
WAY MORE IMPORTANT THAN YOUR RANDOM... CRUSH.

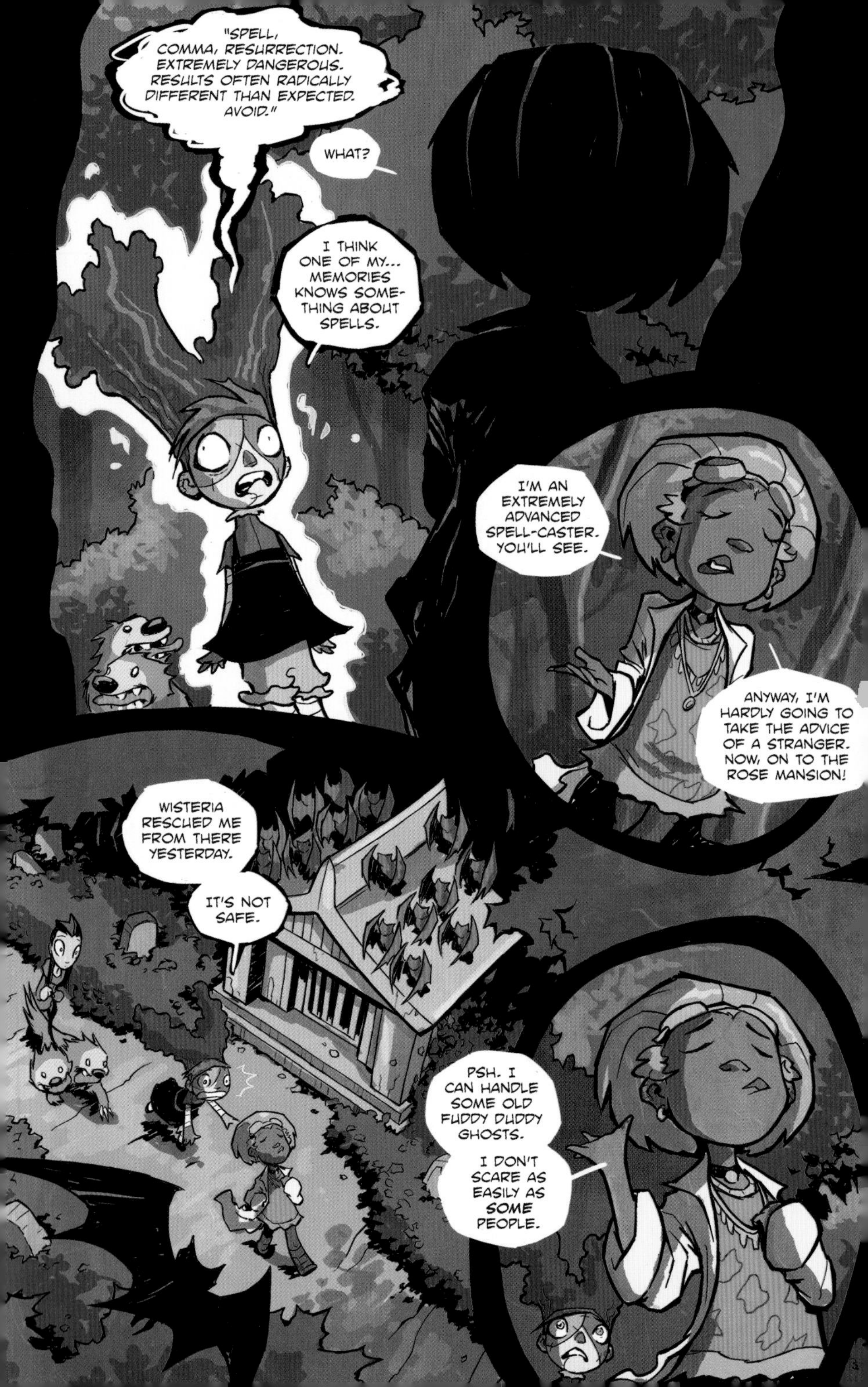
"SPELL, COMMA, RESURRECTION. EXTREMELY DANGEROUS. RESULTS OFTEN RADICALLY DIFFERENT THAN EXPECTED. AVOID."
WHAT?
I THINK ONE OF MY... MEMORIES KNOWS SOMETHING ABOUT SPELLS.
I'M AN EXTREMELY ADVANCED SPELL-CASTER. YOU'LL SEE.
ANYWAY, I'M HARDLY GOING TO TAKE THE ADVICE OF A STRANGER. NOW, ON TO THE ROSE MANSION!
WISTERIA RESCUED ME FROM THERE YESTERDAY.
IT'S NOT SAFE.
PSH. I CAN HANDLE SOME OLD FUDDY DUDDY GHOSTS.
I DON'T SCARE AS EASILY AS **SOME** PEOPLE.

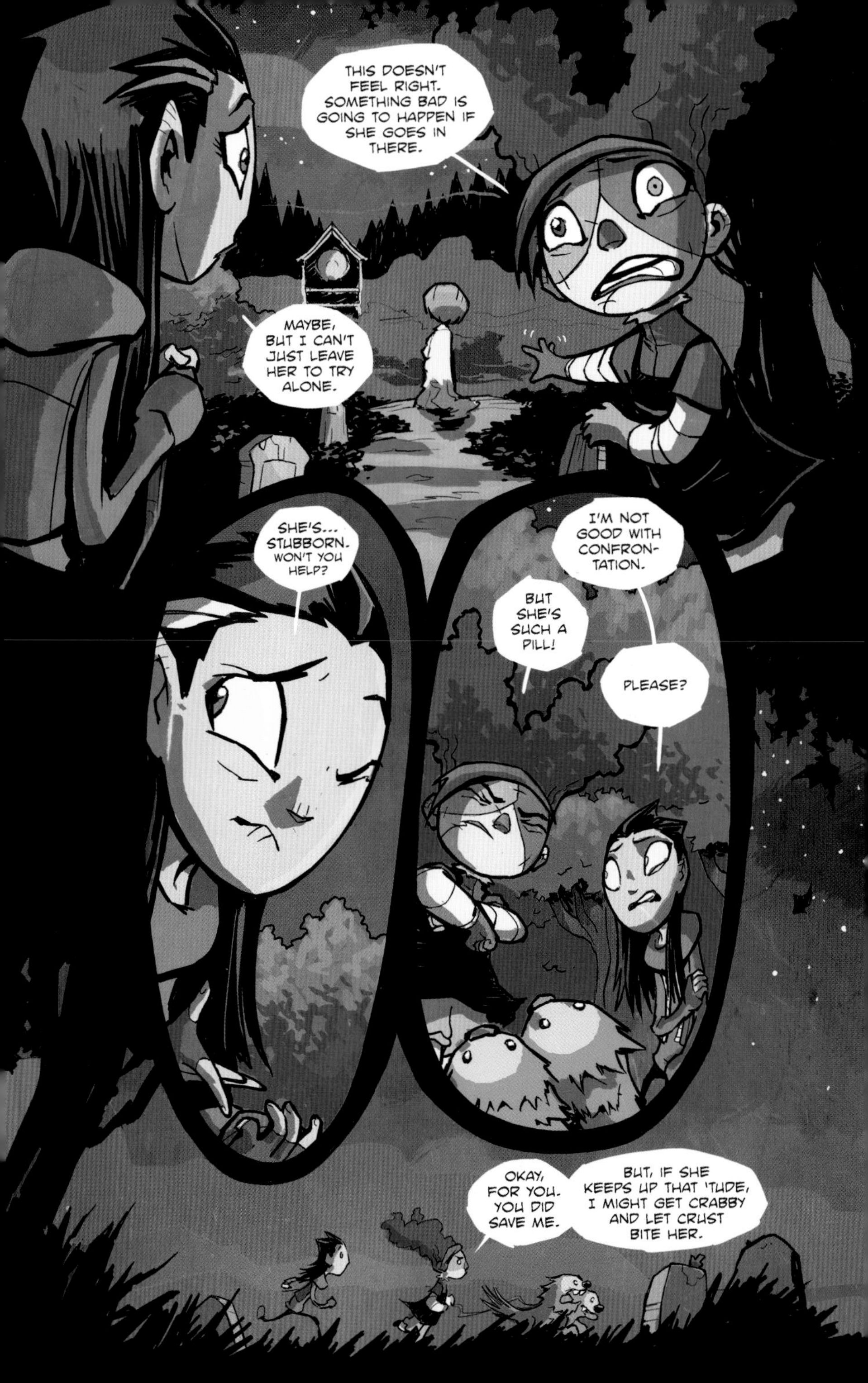
THIS DOESN'T FEEL RIGHT. SOMETHING BAD IS GOING TO HAPPEN IF SHE GOES IN THERE.
MAYBE, BUT I CAN'T JUST LEAVE HER TO TRY ALONE.
SHE'S... STUBBORN. WON'T YOU HELP?
I'M NOT GOOD WITH CONFRON-TATION.
BUT SHE'S SUCH A PILL!
PLEASE?
OKAY, FOR YOU. YOU DID SAVE ME.
BUT, IF SHE KEEPS UP THAT 'TUDE, I MIGHT GET CRABBY AND LET CRUST BITE HER.

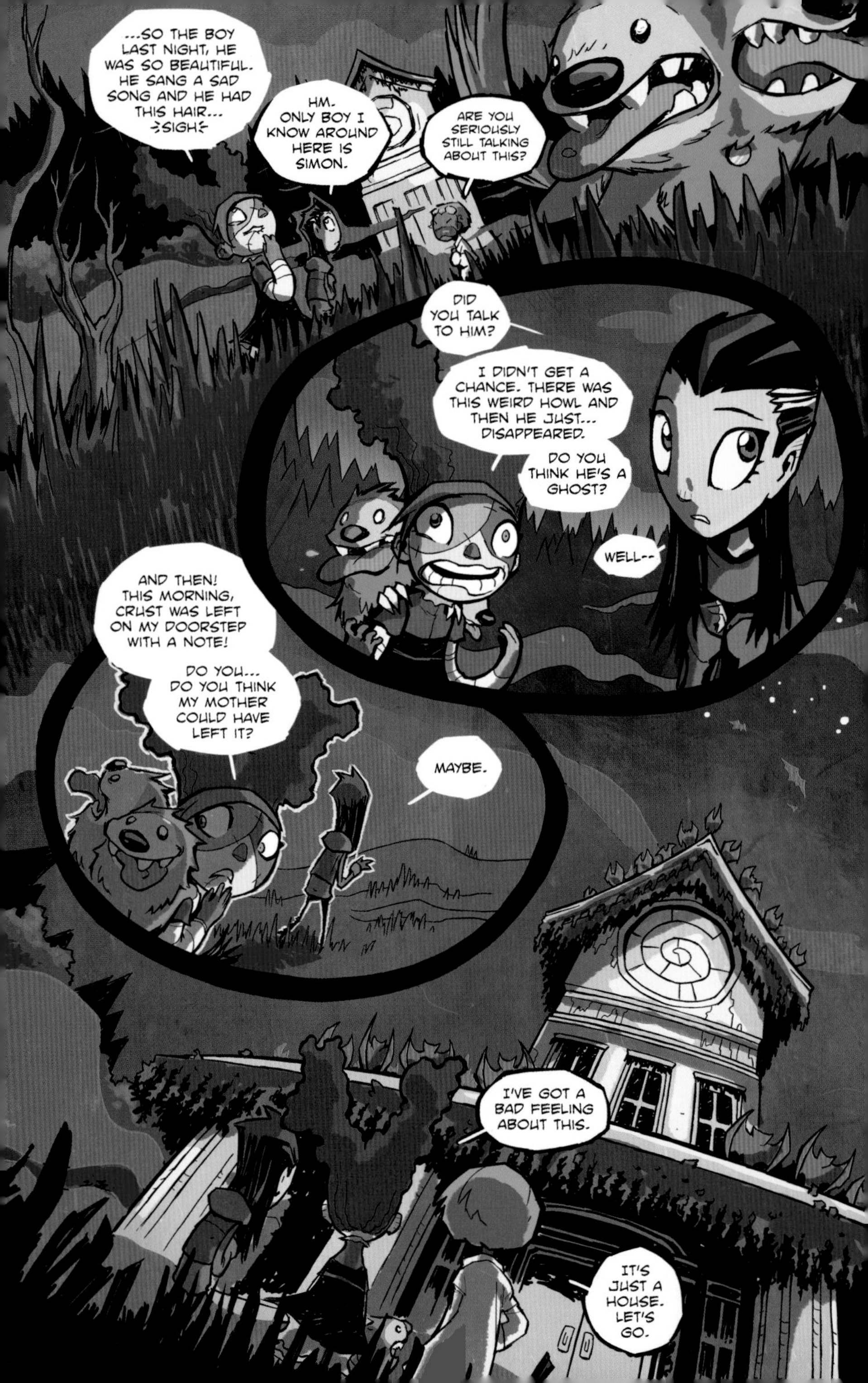
...SO THE BOY LAST NIGHT, HE WAS SO BEAUTIFUL. HE SANG A SAD SONG AND HE HAD THIS HAIR... ⋟SIGH⋞
HM. ONLY BOY I KNOW AROUND HERE IS SIMON.
ARE YOU SERIOUSLY STILL TALKING ABOUT THIS?
DID YOU TALK TO HIM?
I DIDN'T GET A CHANCE. THERE WAS THIS WEIRD HOWL AND THEN HE JUST... DISAPPEARED.
DO YOU THINK HE'S A GHOST?
WELL--
AND THEN! THIS MORNING, CRUST WAS LEFT ON MY DOORSTEP WITH A NOTE!
DO YOU... DO YOU THINK MY MOTHER COULD HAVE LEFT IT?
MAYBE.
I'VE GOT A BAD FEELING ABOUT THIS.
IT'S JUST A HOUSE. LET'S GO.

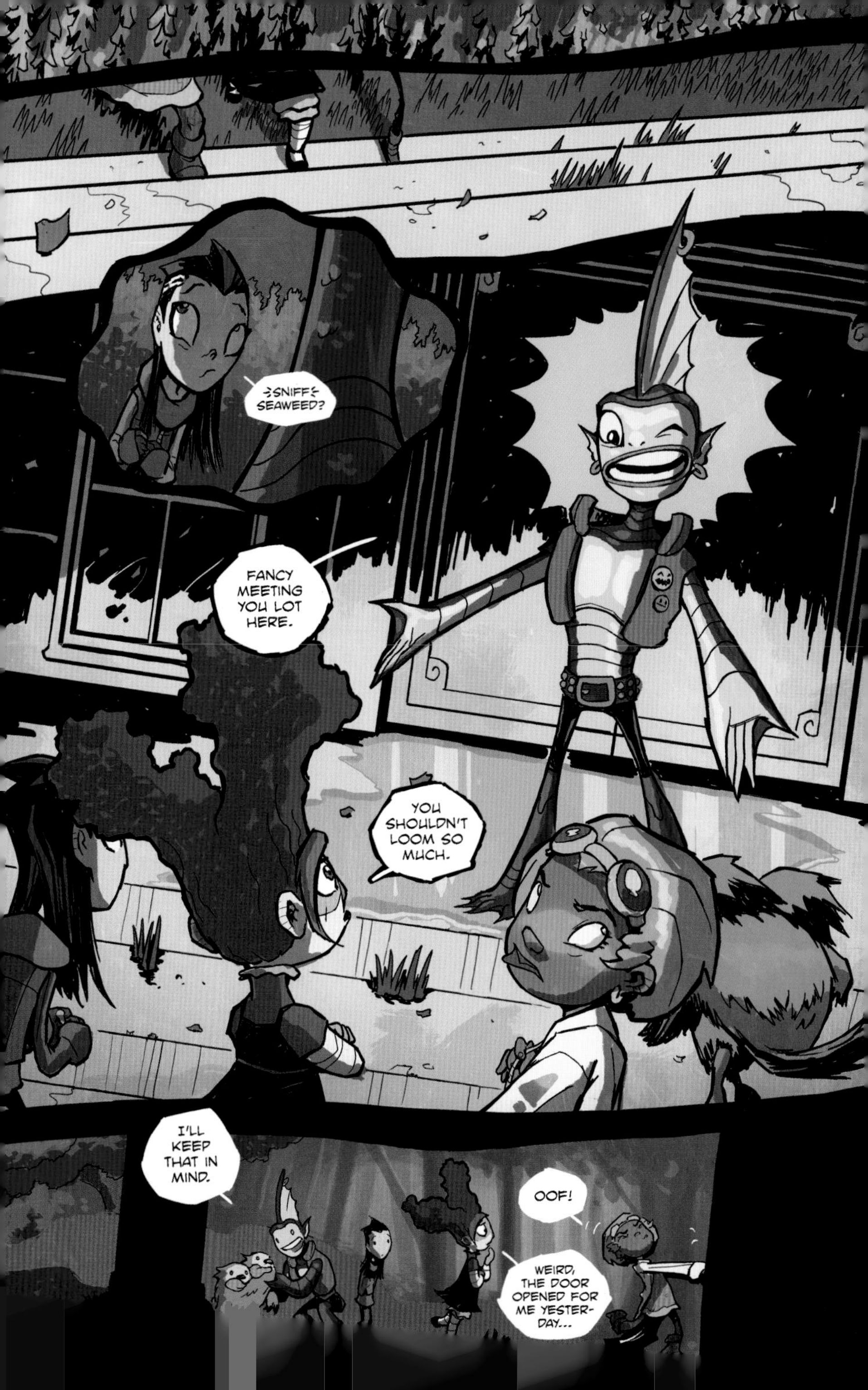

≶SNIFF≶ SEAWEED?
FANCY MEETING YOU LOT HERE.
YOU SHOULDN'T LOOM SO MUCH.
I'LL KEEP THAT IN MIND.
OOF!
WEIRD, THE DOOR OPENED FOR ME YESTER-DAY...

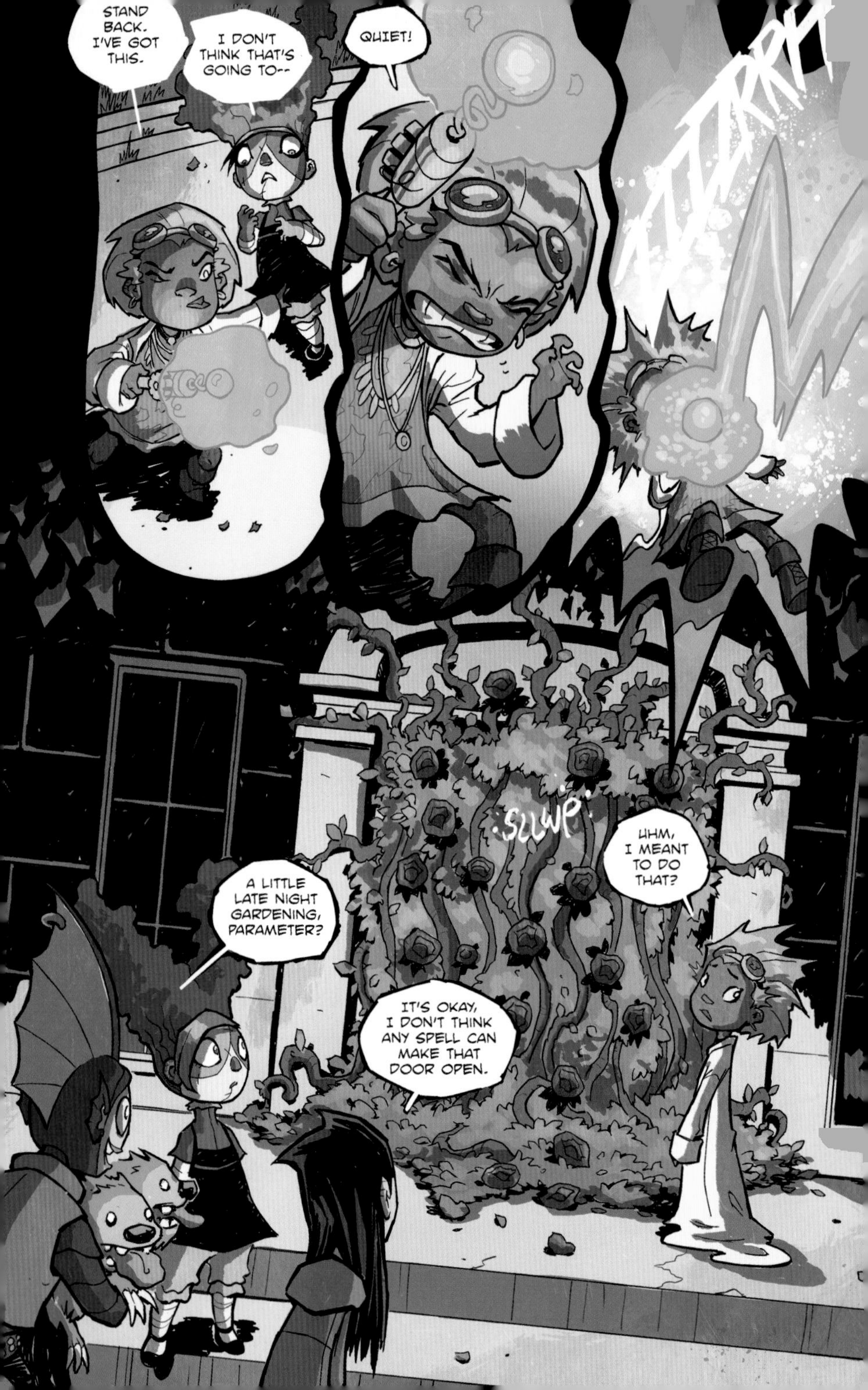
STAND BACK. I'VE GOT THIS.
I DON'T THINK THAT'S GOING TO--
QUIET!
SLLWP
A LITTLE LATE NIGHT GARDENING, PARAMETER?
UHM, I MEANT TO DO THAT?
IT'S OKAY, I DON'T THINK ANY SPELL CAN MAKE THAT DOOR OPEN.

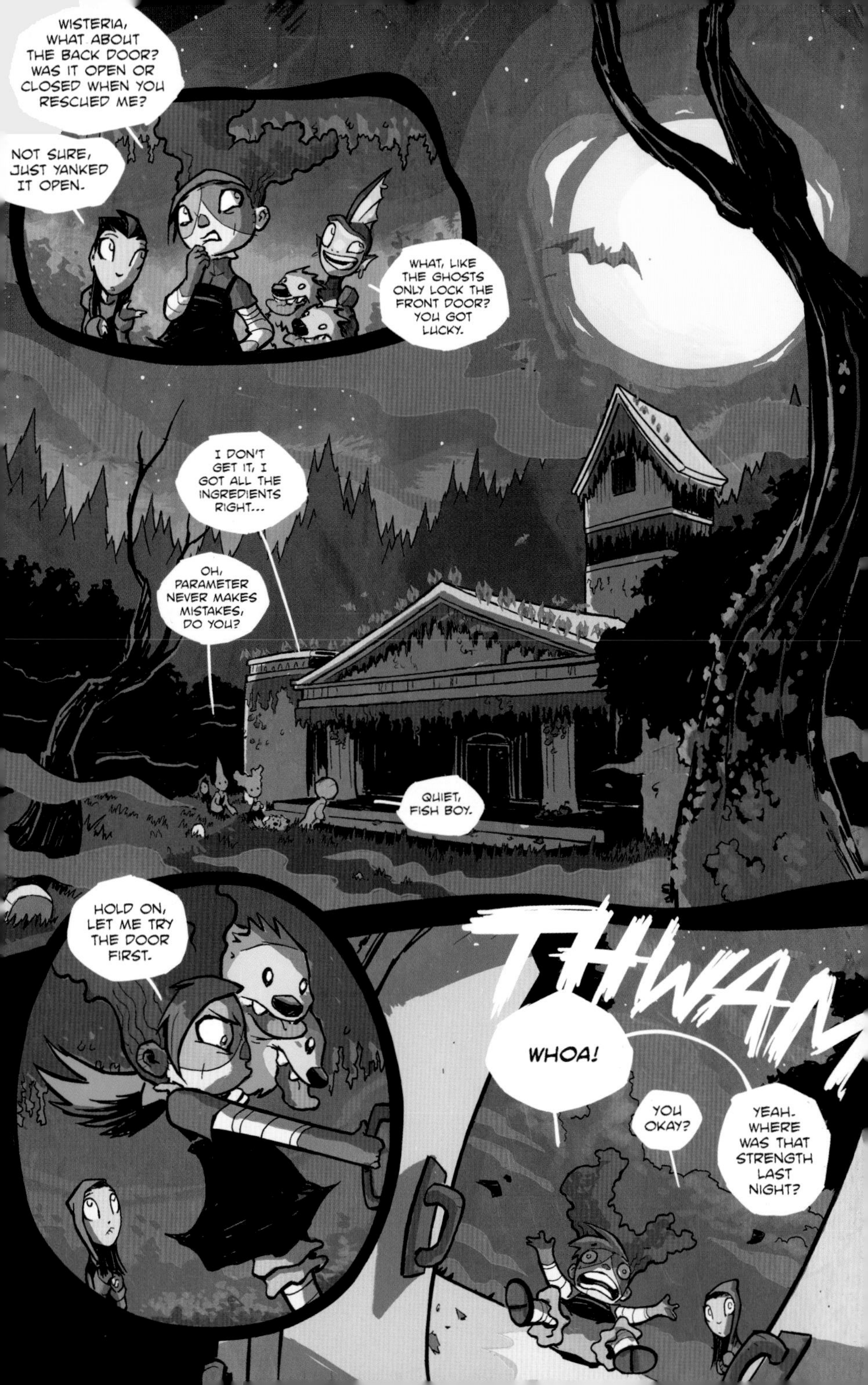
WISTERIA, WHAT ABOUT THE BACK DOOR? WAS IT OPEN OR CLOSED WHEN YOU RESCUED ME?
NOT SURE, JUST YANKED IT OPEN.
WHAT, LIKE THE GHOSTS ONLY LOCK THE FRONT DOOR? YOU GOT LUCKY.
I DON'T GET IT, I GOT ALL THE INGREDIENTS RIGHT...
OH, PARAMETER NEVER MAKES MISTAKES, DO YOU?
QUIET, FISH BOY.
HOLD ON, LET ME TRY THE DOOR FIRST.
THWAM
WHOA!
YOU OKAY?
YEAH. WHERE WAS THAT STRENGTH LAST NIGHT?

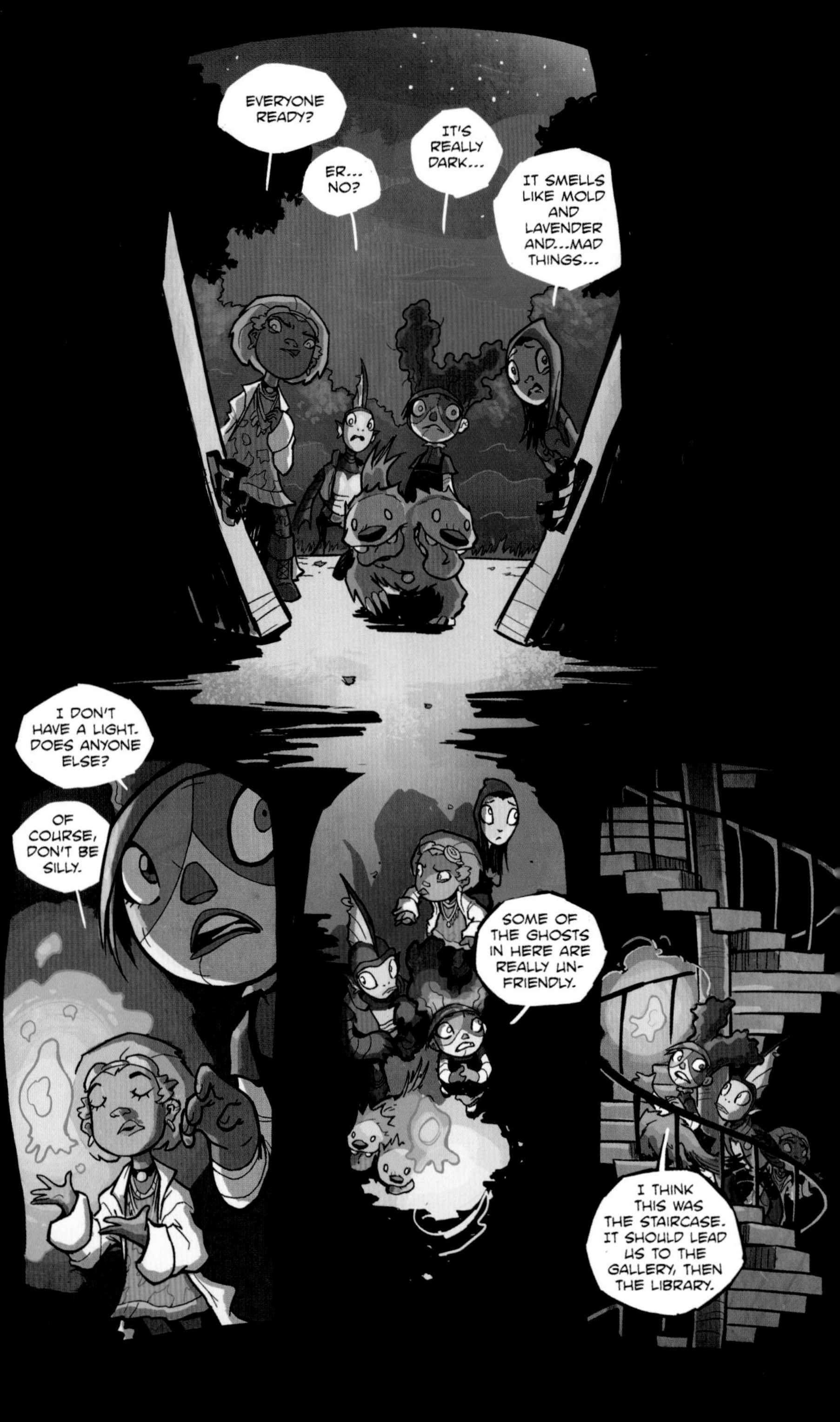

EVERYONE READY?
ER... NO?
IT'S REALLY DARK...
IT SMELLS LIKE MOLD AND LAVENDER AND...MAD THINGS...
I DON'T HAVE A LIGHT. DOES ANYONE ELSE?
OF COURSE, DON'T BE SILLY.
SOME OF THE GHOSTS IN HERE ARE REALLY UN-FRIENDLY.
I THINK THIS WAS THE STAIRCASE. IT SHOULD LEAD US TO THE GALLERY, THEN THE LIBRARY.

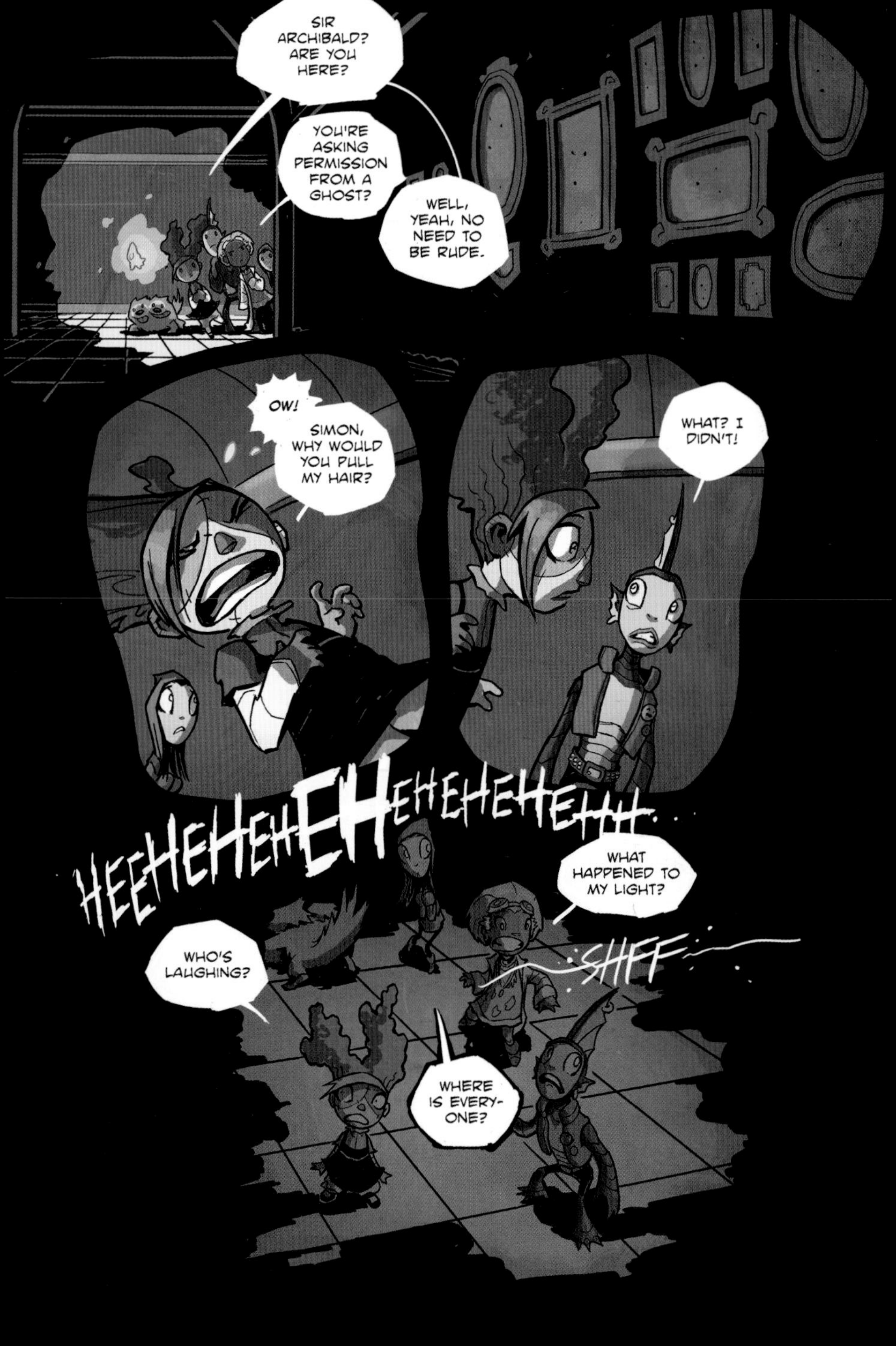
SIR ARCHIBALD? ARE YOU HERE?
YOU'RE ASKING PERMISSION FROM A GHOST?
WELL, YEAH, NO NEED TO BE RUDE.
OW!
SIMON, WHY WOULD YOU PULL MY HAIR?
WHAT? I DIDN'T!
HEEHEHEHEHEHEHEHEHEHEHHH
WHAT HAPPENED TO MY LIGHT?
SHFF
WHO'S LAUGHING?
WHERE IS EVERY-ONE?

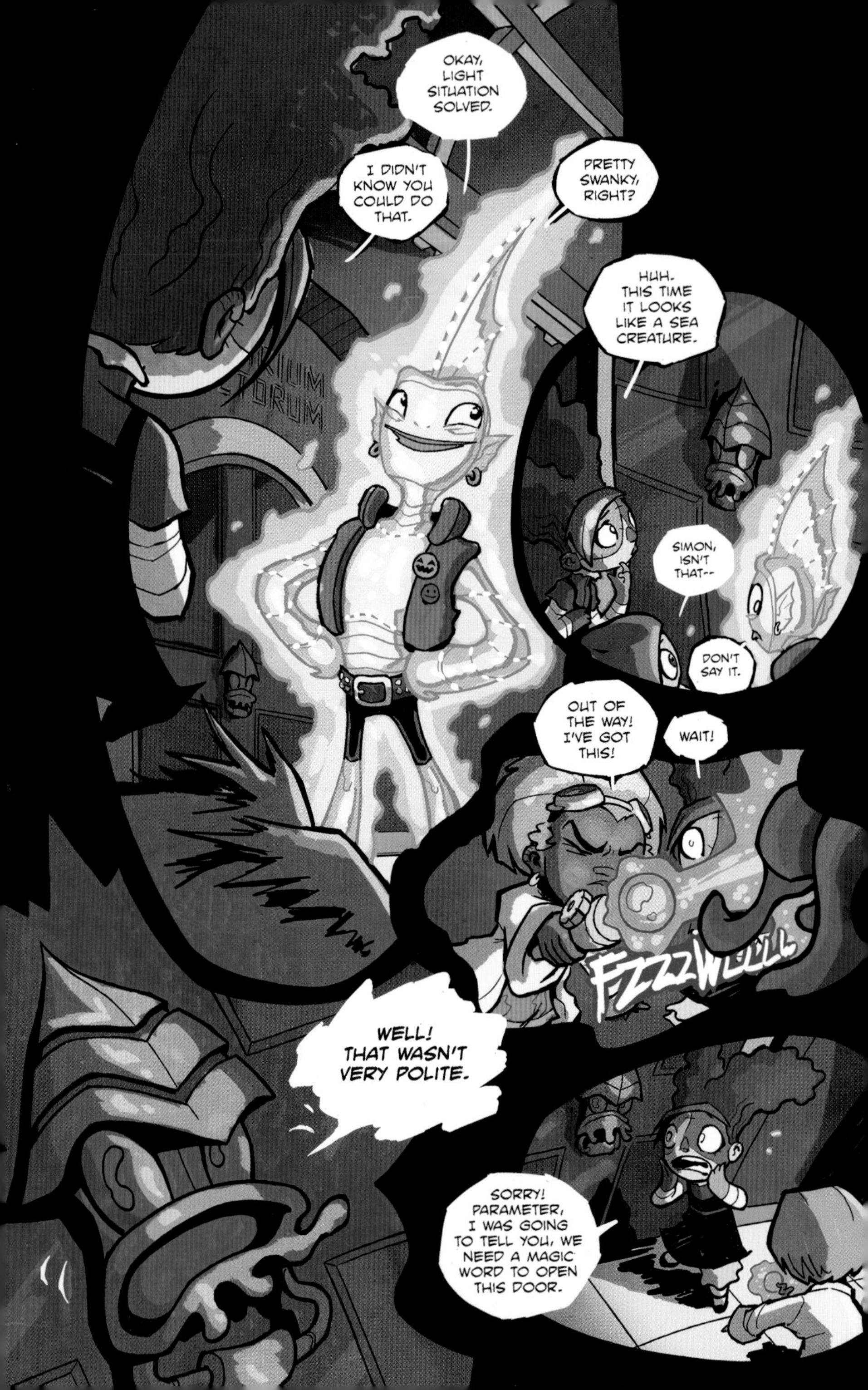
OKAY, LIGHT SITUATION SOLVED.
I DIDN'T KNOW YOU COULD DO THAT.
PRETTY SWANKY, RIGHT?
HUH. THIS TIME IT LOOKS LIKE A SEA CREATURE.
SIMON, ISN'T THAT--
DON'T SAY IT.
OUT OF THE WAY! I'VE GOT THIS!
WAIT!
FZZZWULL
WELL! THAT WASN'T VERY POLITE.
SORRY! PARAMETER, I WAS GOING TO TELL YOU, WE NEED A MAGIC WORD TO OPEN THIS DOOR.

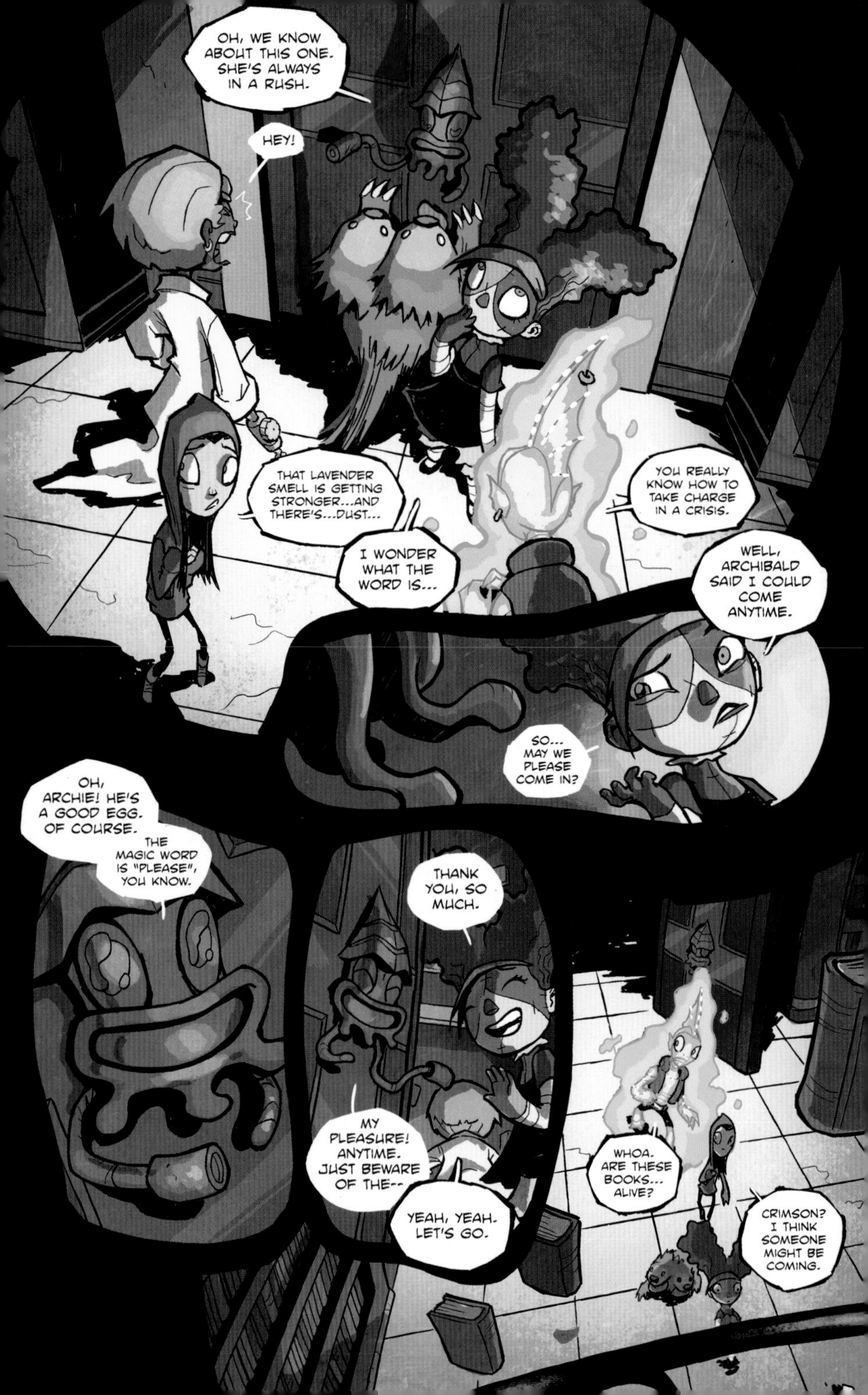
OH, WE KNOW ABOUT THIS ONE. SHE'S ALWAYS IN A RUSH.
HEY!
THAT LAVENDER SMELL IS GETTING STRONGER...AND THERE'S...DUST...
I WONDER WHAT THE WORD IS...
YOU REALLY KNOW HOW TO TAKE CHARGE IN A CRISIS.
WELL, ARCHIBALD SAID I COULD COME ANYTIME.
SO... MAY WE PLEASE COME IN?
OH, ARCHIE! HE'S A GOOD EGG. OF COURSE.
THE MAGIC WORD IS "PLEASE", YOU KNOW.
THANK YOU, SO MUCH.
MY PLEASURE! ANYTIME. JUST BEWARE OF THE--
YEAH, YEAH. LET'S GO.
WHOA. ARE THESE BOOKS... ALIVE?
CRIMSON? I THINK SOMEONE MIGHT BE COMING.

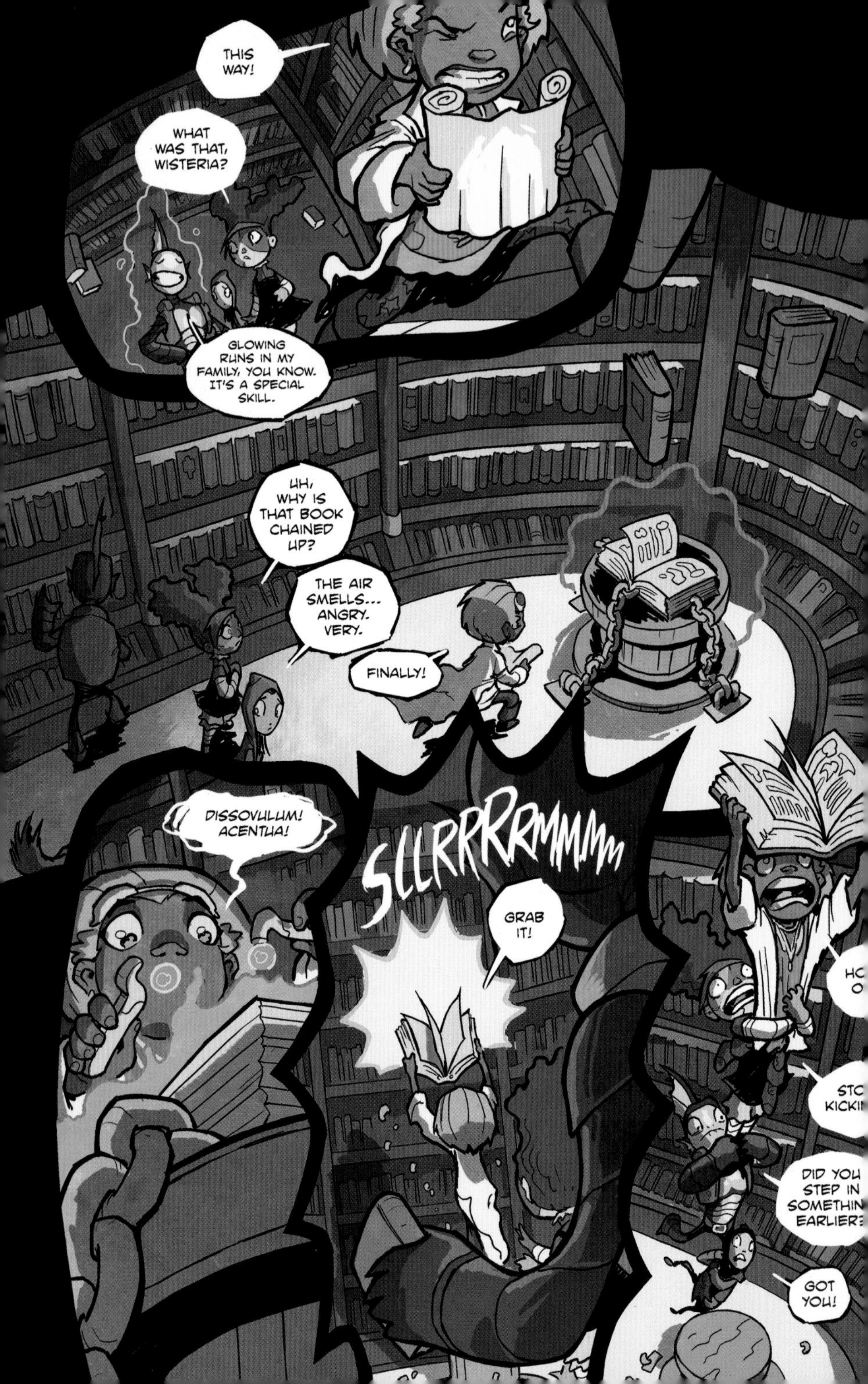
THIS WAY!
WHAT WAS THAT, WISTERIA?
GLOWING RUNS IN MY FAMILY, YOU KNOW. IT'S A SPECIAL SKILL.
UH, WHY IS THAT BOOK CHAINED UP?
THE AIR SMELLS... ANGRY. VERY.
FINALLY!
DISSOVULUM! ACENTUA!
SCLRRRRMMMM
GRAB IT!
DID YOU STEP IN SOMETHIN EARLIER?
GOT YOU!

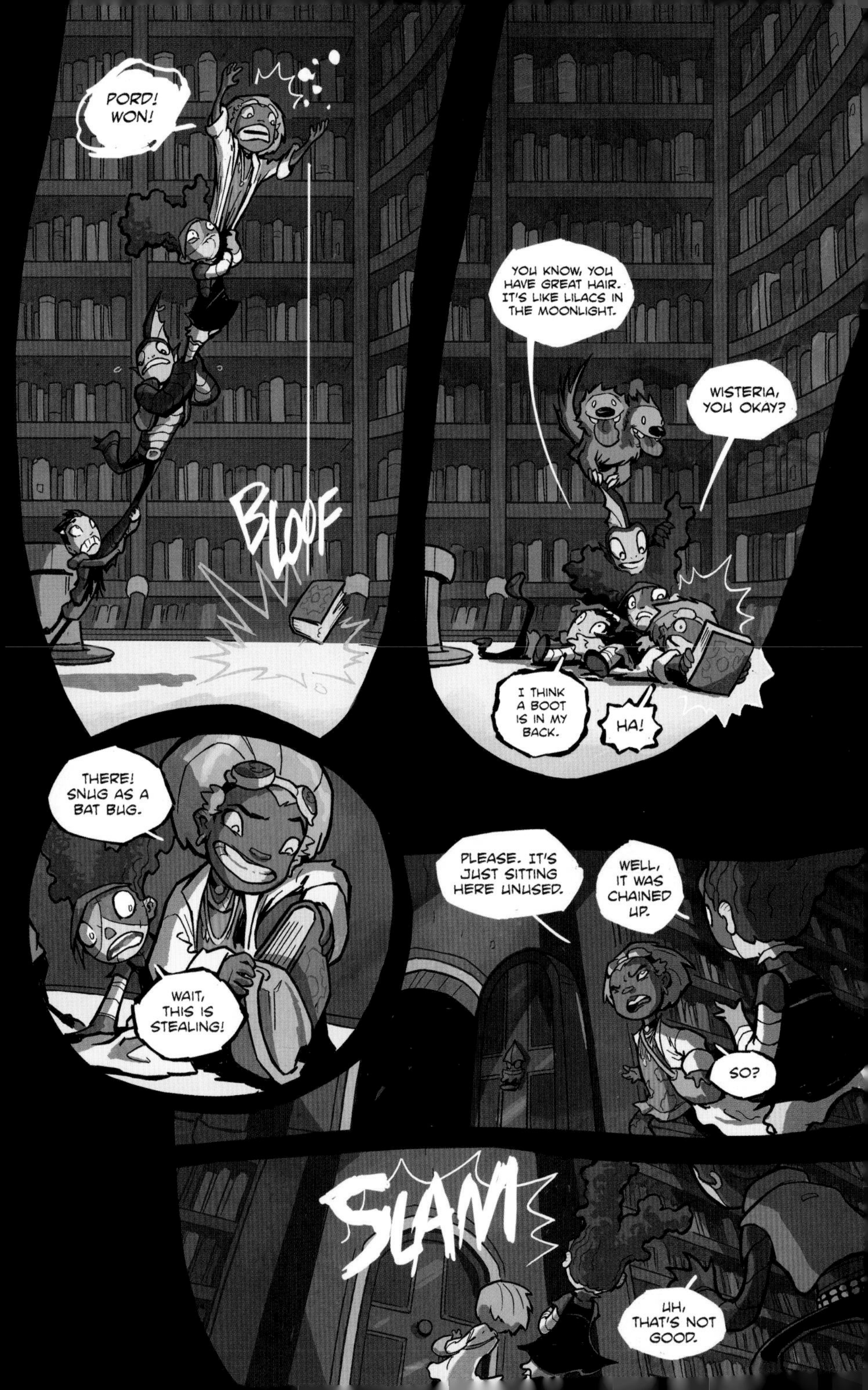
PORD! WON!
BLOOF
YOU KNOW, YOU HAVE GREAT HAIR. IT'S LIKE LILACS IN THE MOONLIGHT.
WISTERIA, YOU OKAY?
I THINK A BOOT IS IN MY BACK.
HA!
THERE! SNUG AS A BAT BUG.
WAIT, THIS IS STEALING!
PLEASE. IT'S JUST SITTING HERE UNUSED.
WELL, IT WAS CHAINED UP.
SO?
SLAM
UH, THAT'S NOT GOOD.

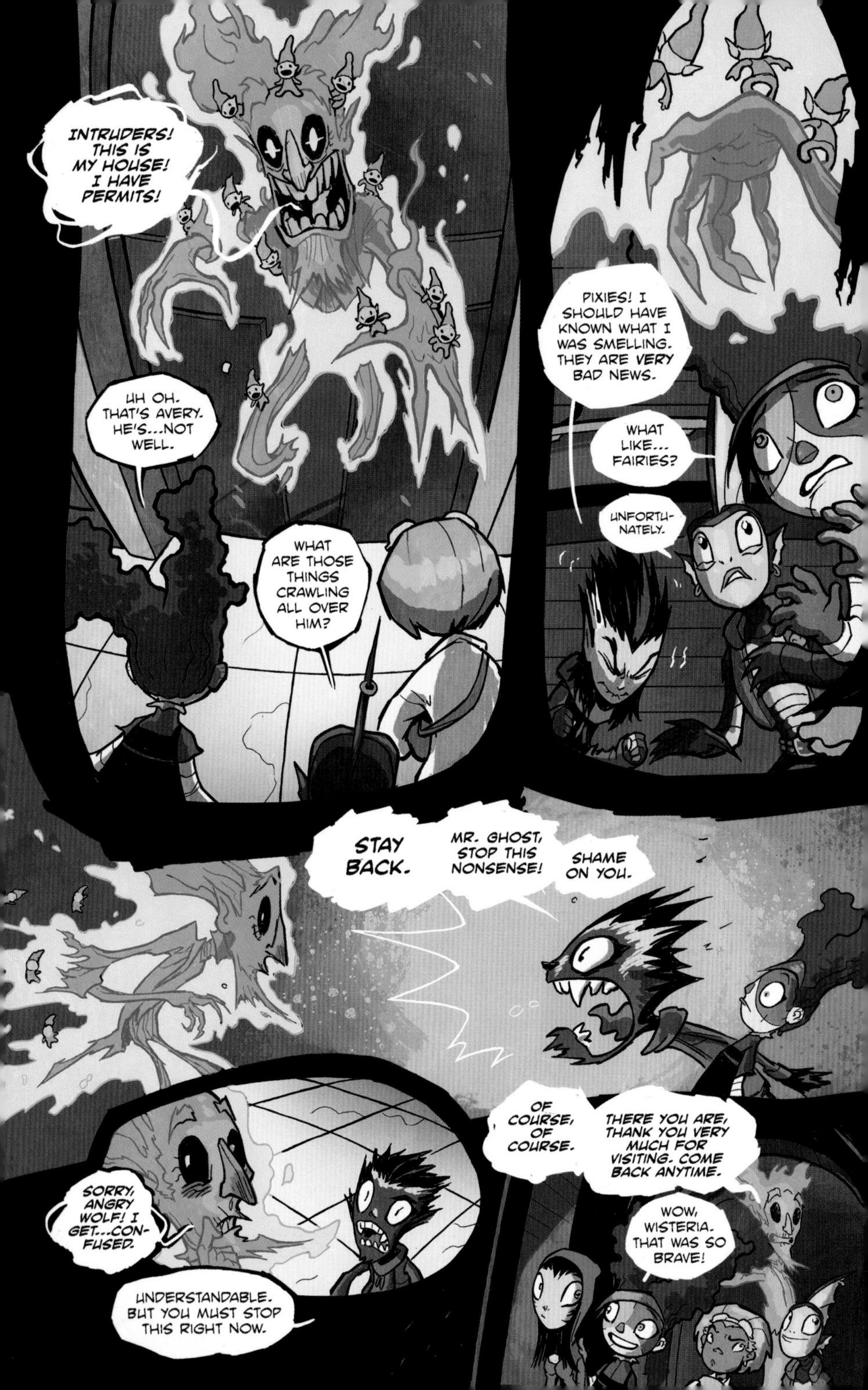
INTRUDERS! THIS IS MY HOUSE! I HAVE PERMITS!
UH OH. THAT'S AVERY. HE'S...NOT WELL.
WHAT ARE THOSE THINGS CRAWLING ALL OVER HIM?
PIXIES! I SHOULD HAVE KNOWN WHAT I WAS SMELLING. THEY ARE VERY BAD NEWS.
WHAT LIKE... FAIRIES?
UNFORTU-NATELY.
STAY BACK.
MR. GHOST, STOP THIS NONSENSE!
SHAME ON YOU.
SORRY, ANGRY WOLF! I GET...CON-FUSED.
UNDERSTANDABLE. BUT YOU MUST STOP THIS RIGHT NOW.
OF COURSE, OF COURSE.
THERE YOU ARE, THANK YOU VERY MUCH FOR VISITING. COME BACK ANYTIME.
WOW, WISTERIA. THAT WAS SO BRAVE!

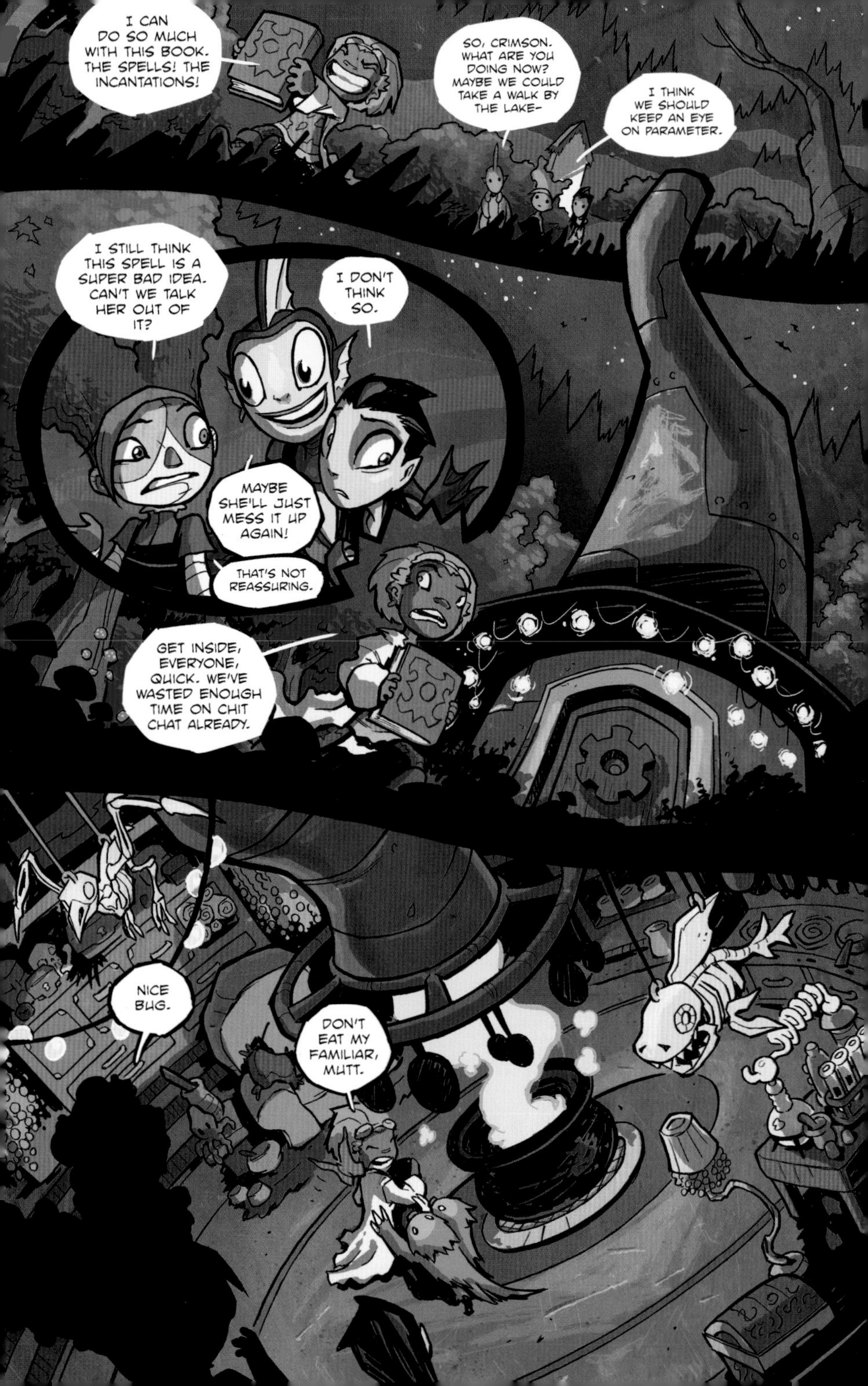
I CAN DO SO MUCH WITH THIS BOOK. THE SPELLS! THE INCANTATIONS!
SO, CRIMSON. WHAT ARE YOU DOING NOW? MAYBE WE COULD TAKE A WALK BY THE LAKE-
I THINK WE SHOULD KEEP AN EYE ON PARAMETER.
I STILL THINK THIS SPELL IS A SUPER BAD IDEA. CAN'T WE TALK HER OUT OF IT?
I DON'T THINK SO.
MAYBE SHE'LL JUST MESS IT UP AGAIN!
THAT'S NOT REASSURING.
GET INSIDE, EVERYONE, QUICK. WE'VE WASTED ENOUGH TIME ON CHIT CHAT ALREADY.
NICE BUG.
DON'T EAT MY FAMILIAR, MUTT.

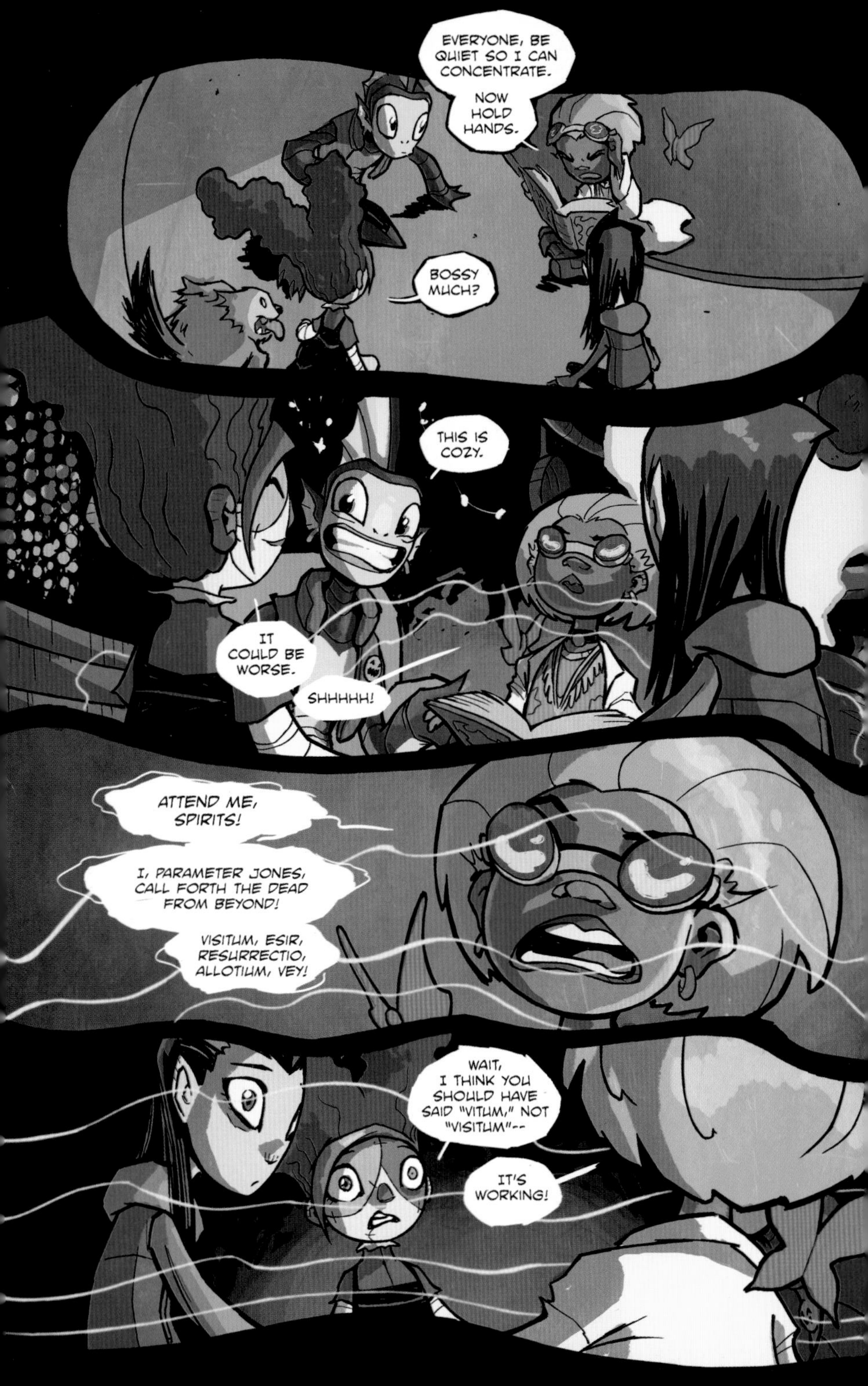
EVERYONE, BE QUIET SO I CAN CONCENTRATE.
NOW HOLD HANDS.
BOSSY MUCH?
THIS IS COZY.
IT COULD BE WORSE.
SHHHHH!
ATTEND ME, SPIRITS!
I, PARAMETER JONES, CALL FORTH THE DEAD FROM BEYOND!
VISITUM, ESIR, RESURRECTIO, ALLOTIUM, VEY!
WAIT, I THINK YOU SHOULD HAVE SAID "VITUM," NOT "VISITUM"--
IT'S WORKING!

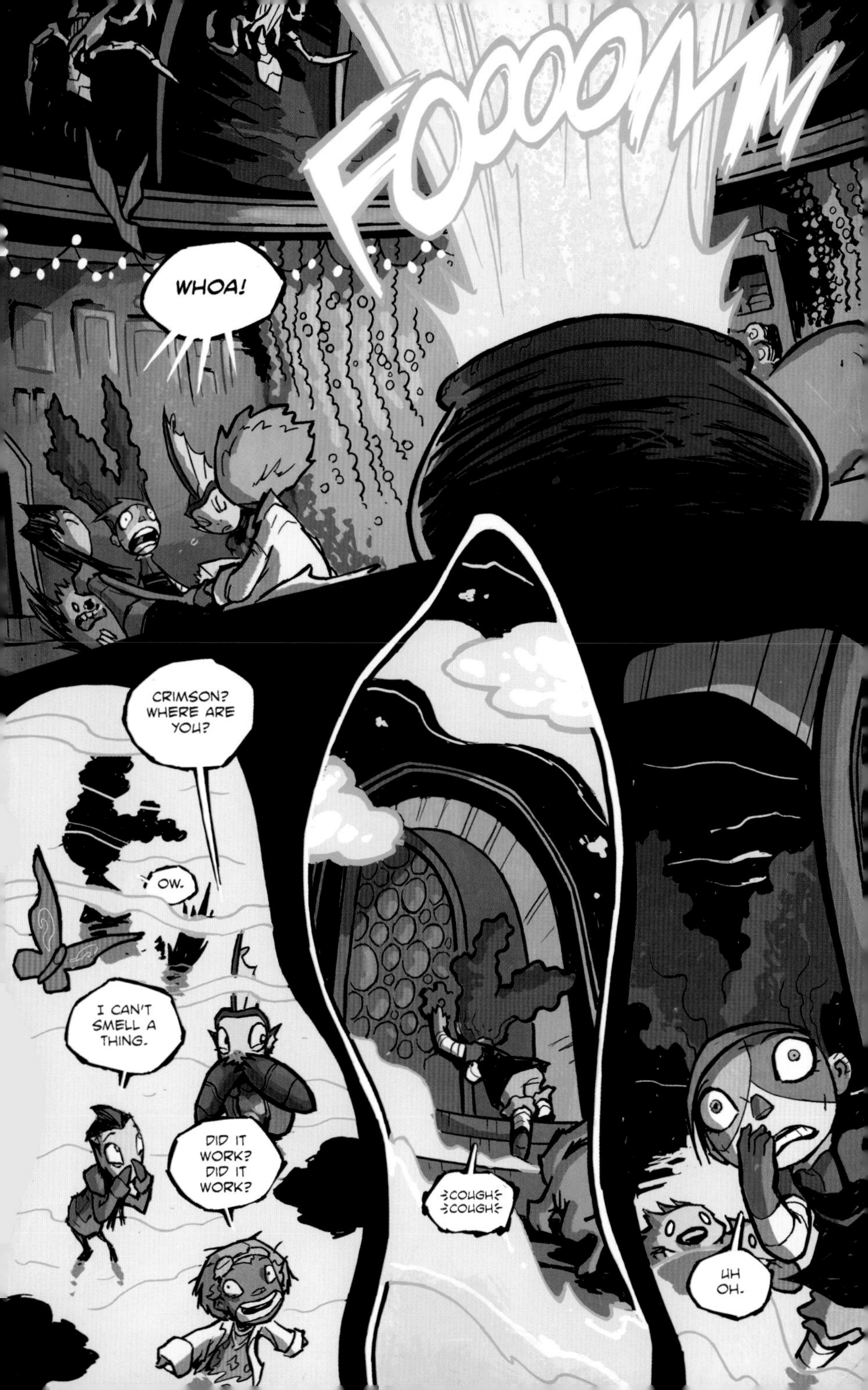
FOOOOM
WHOA!
CRIMSON? WHERE ARE YOU?
OW.
I CAN'T SMELL A THING.
DID IT WORK? DID IT WORK?
COUGH COUGH
UH OH.

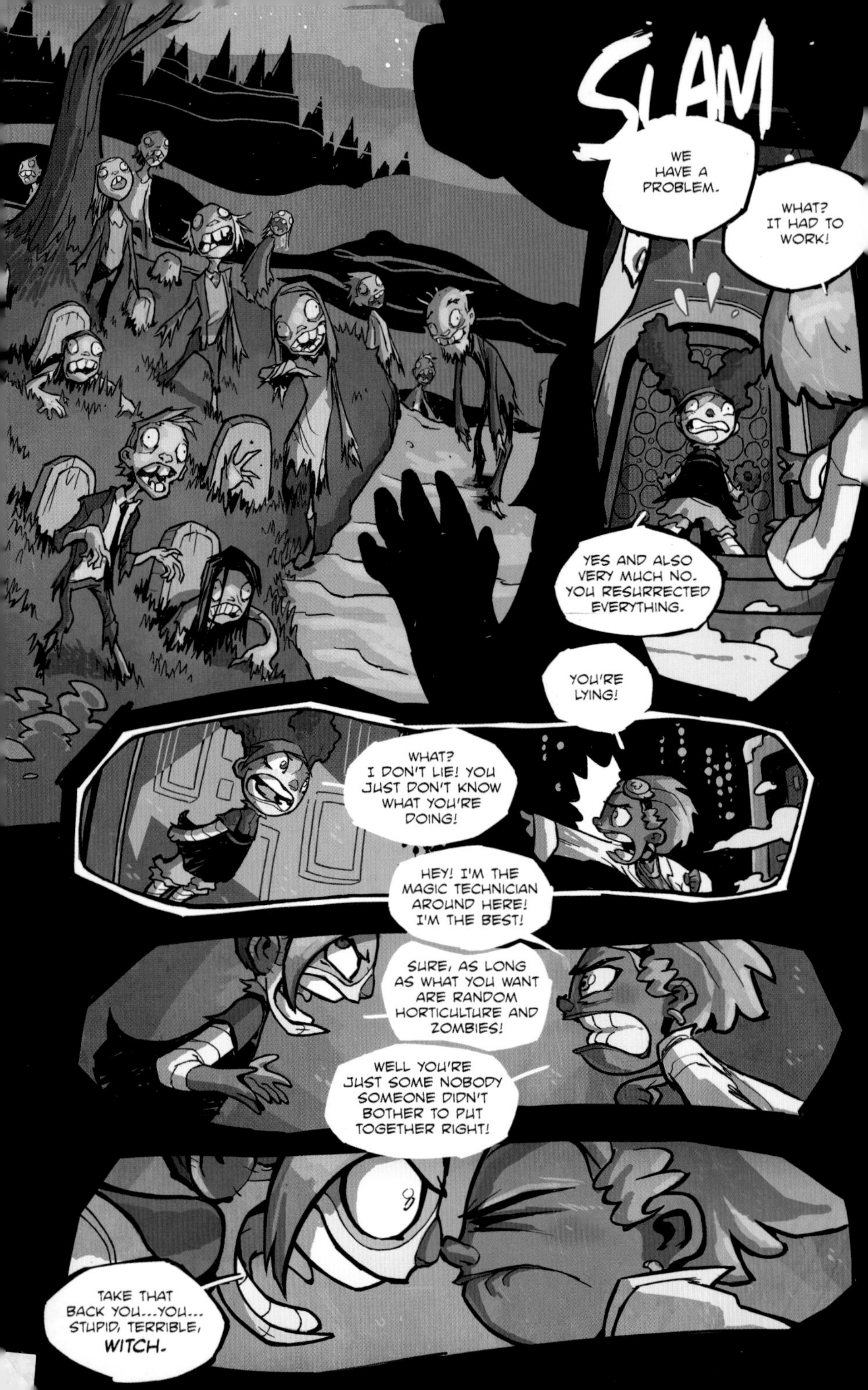
SLAM
WE HAVE A PROBLEM.
WHAT? IT HAD TO WORK!
YES AND ALSO VERY MUCH NO. YOU RESURRECTED EVERYTHING.
YOU'RE LYING!
WHAT? I DON'T LIE! YOU JUST DON'T KNOW WHAT YOU'RE DOING!
HEY! I'M THE MAGIC TECHNICIAN AROUND HERE! I'M THE BEST!
SURE, AS LONG AS WHAT YOU WANT ARE RANDOM HORTICULTURE AND ZOMBIES!
WELL YOU'RE JUST SOME NOBODY SOMEONE DIDN'T BOTHER TO PUT TOGETHER RIGHT!
TAKE THAT BACK YOU...YOU... STUPID, TERRIBLE, WITCH.

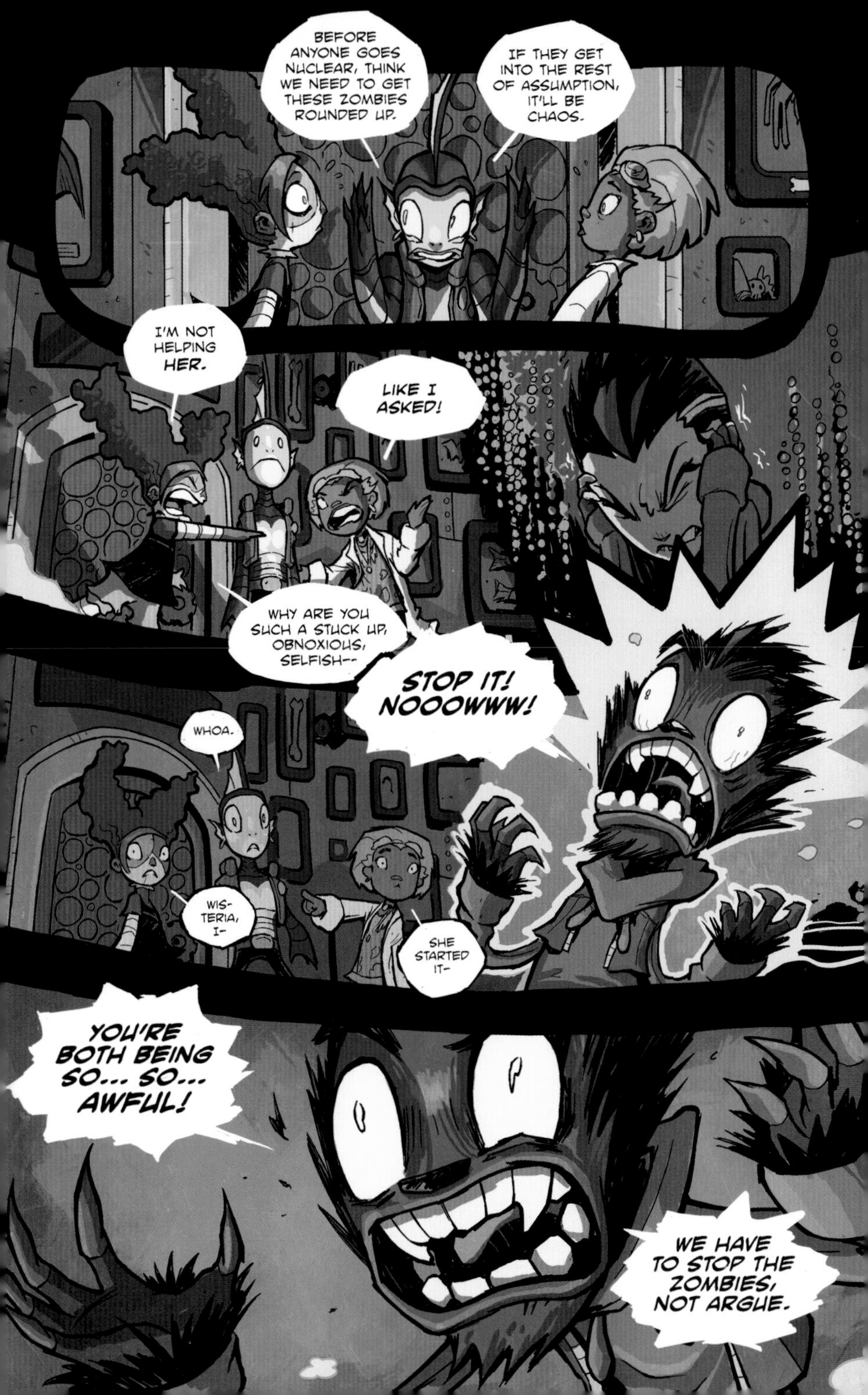
BEFORE ANYONE GOES NUCLEAR, THINK WE NEED TO GET THESE ZOMBIES ROUNDED UP.
IF THEY GET INTO THE REST OF ASSUMPTION, IT'LL BE CHAOS.
I'M NOT HELPING HER.
LIKE I ASKED!
WHY ARE YOU SUCH A STUCK UP, OBNOXIOUS, SELFISH--
STOP IT! NOOOWWW!
WHOA.
WIS-TERIA, I-
SHE STARTED IT-
YOU'RE BOTH BEING SO... SO... AWFUL!
WE HAVE TO STOP THE ZOMBIES, NOT ARGUE.

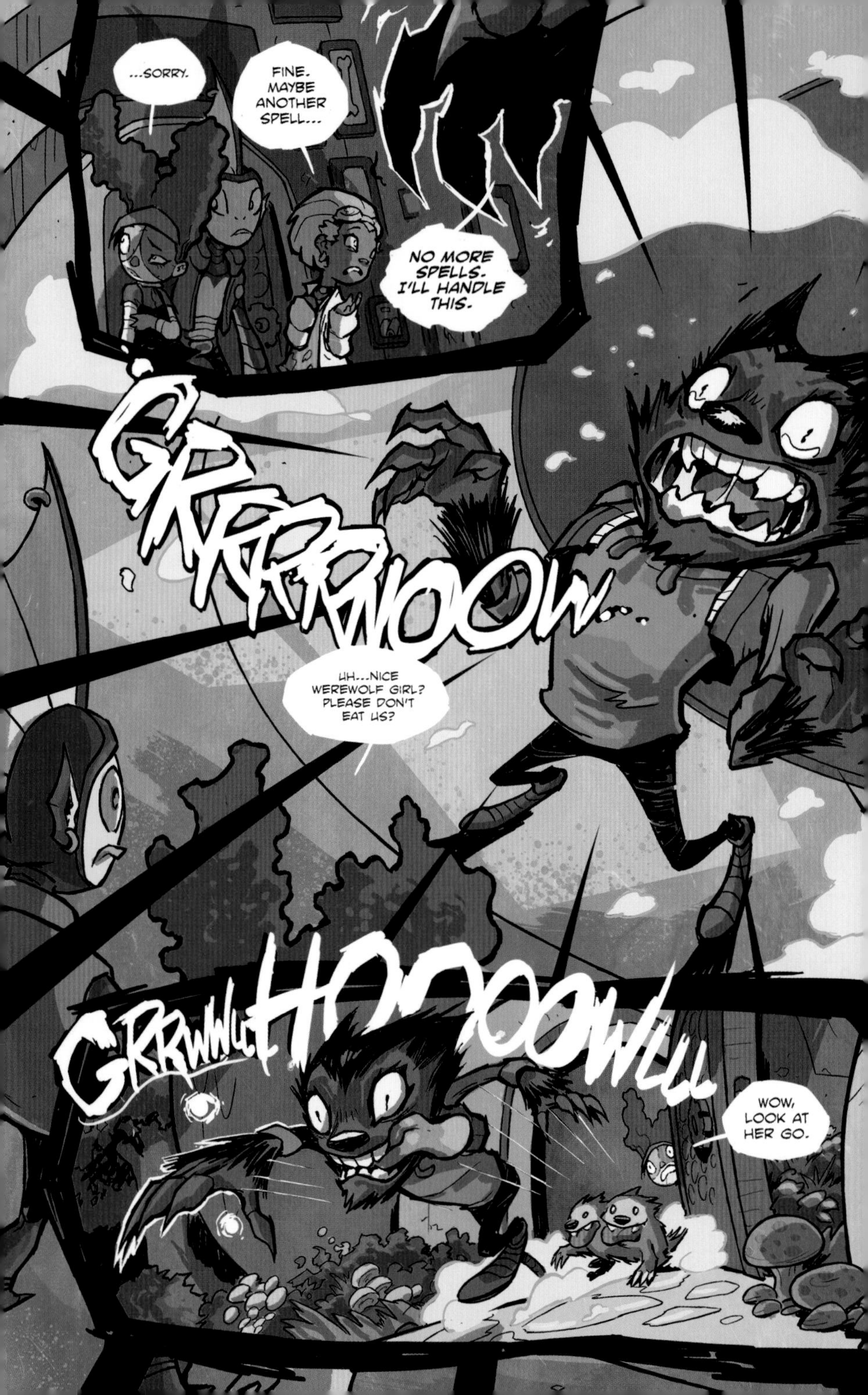
...SORRY.
FINE. MAYBE ANOTHER SPELL...
NO MORE SPELLS. I'LL HANDLE THIS.
GRRRROOOW
UH...NICE WEREWOLF GIRL? PLEASE DON'T EAT US?
GRRWLLHOOOOWLLL
WOW, LOOK AT HER GO.

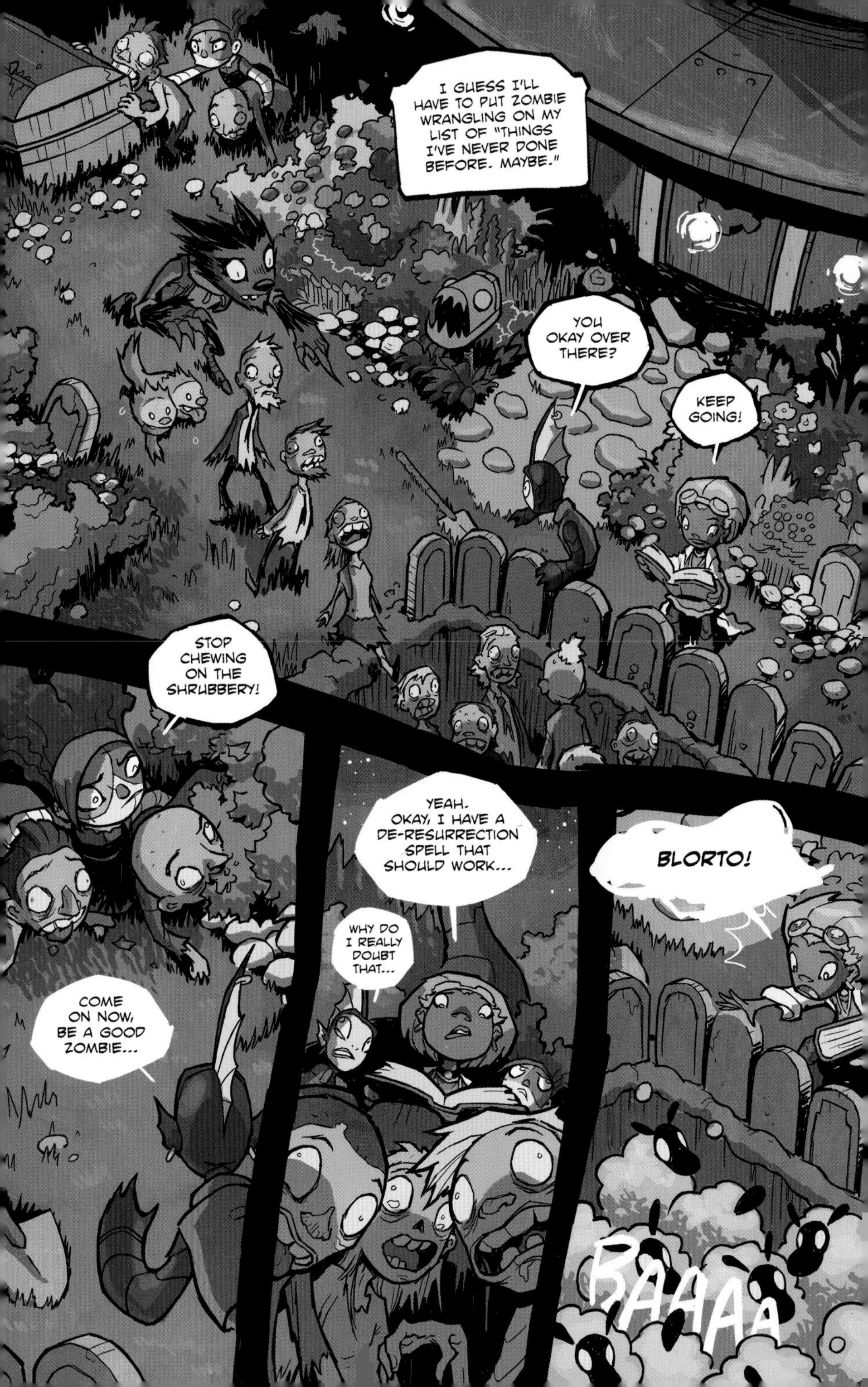
I GUESS I'LL HAVE TO PUT ZOMBIE WRANGLING ON MY LIST OF "THINGS I'VE NEVER DONE BEFORE. MAYBE."
YOU OKAY OVER THERE?
KEEP GOING!
STOP CHEWING ON THE SHRUBBERY!
COME ON NOW, BE A GOOD ZOMBIE...
YEAH. OKAY, I HAVE A DE-RESURRECTION SPELL THAT SHOULD WORK...
WHY DO I REALLY DOUBT THAT...
BLORTO!
BAAAAA

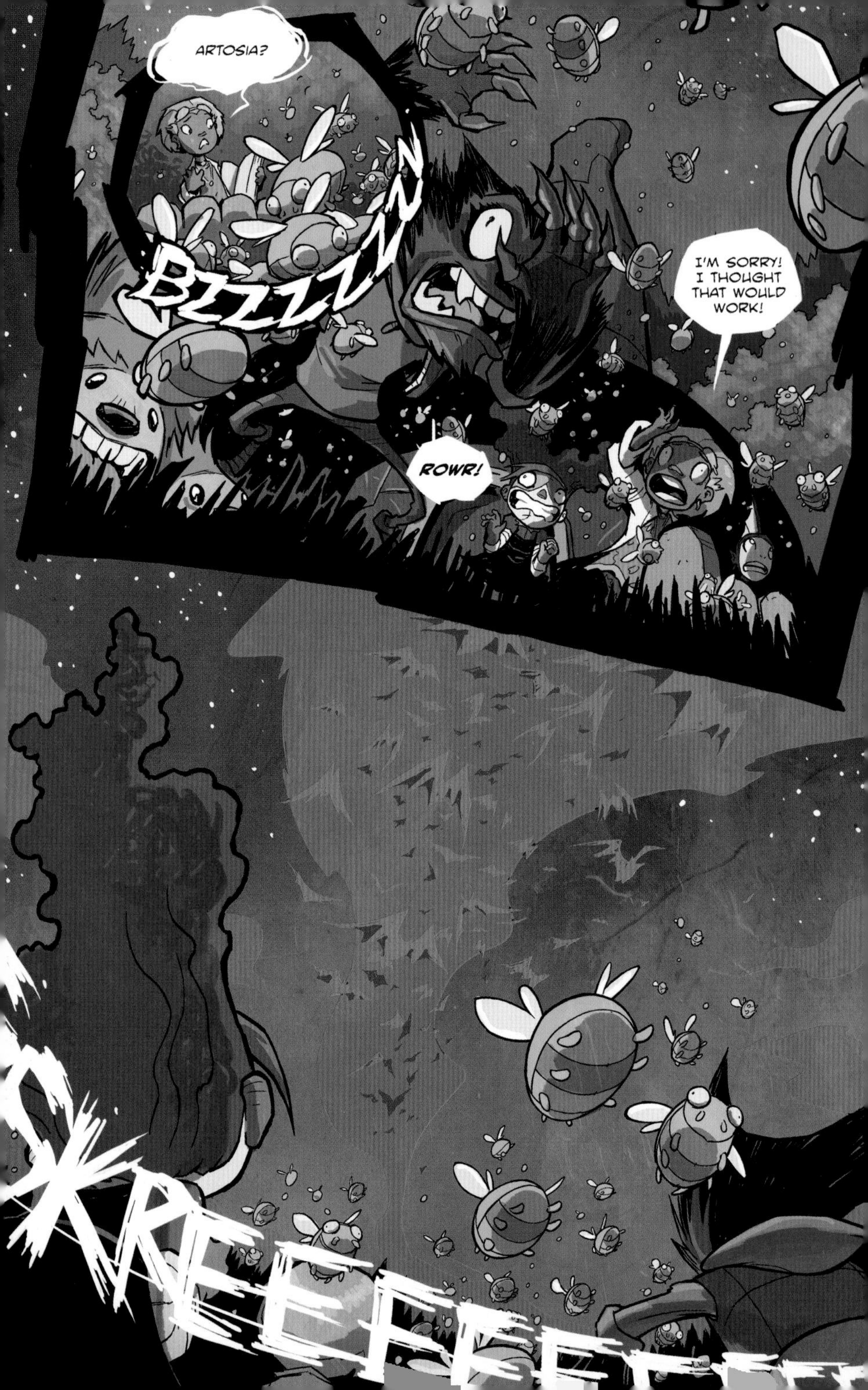
ARTOSIA?
BZZZZZZZ
I'M SORRY! I THOUGHT THAT WOULD WORK!
ROWR!

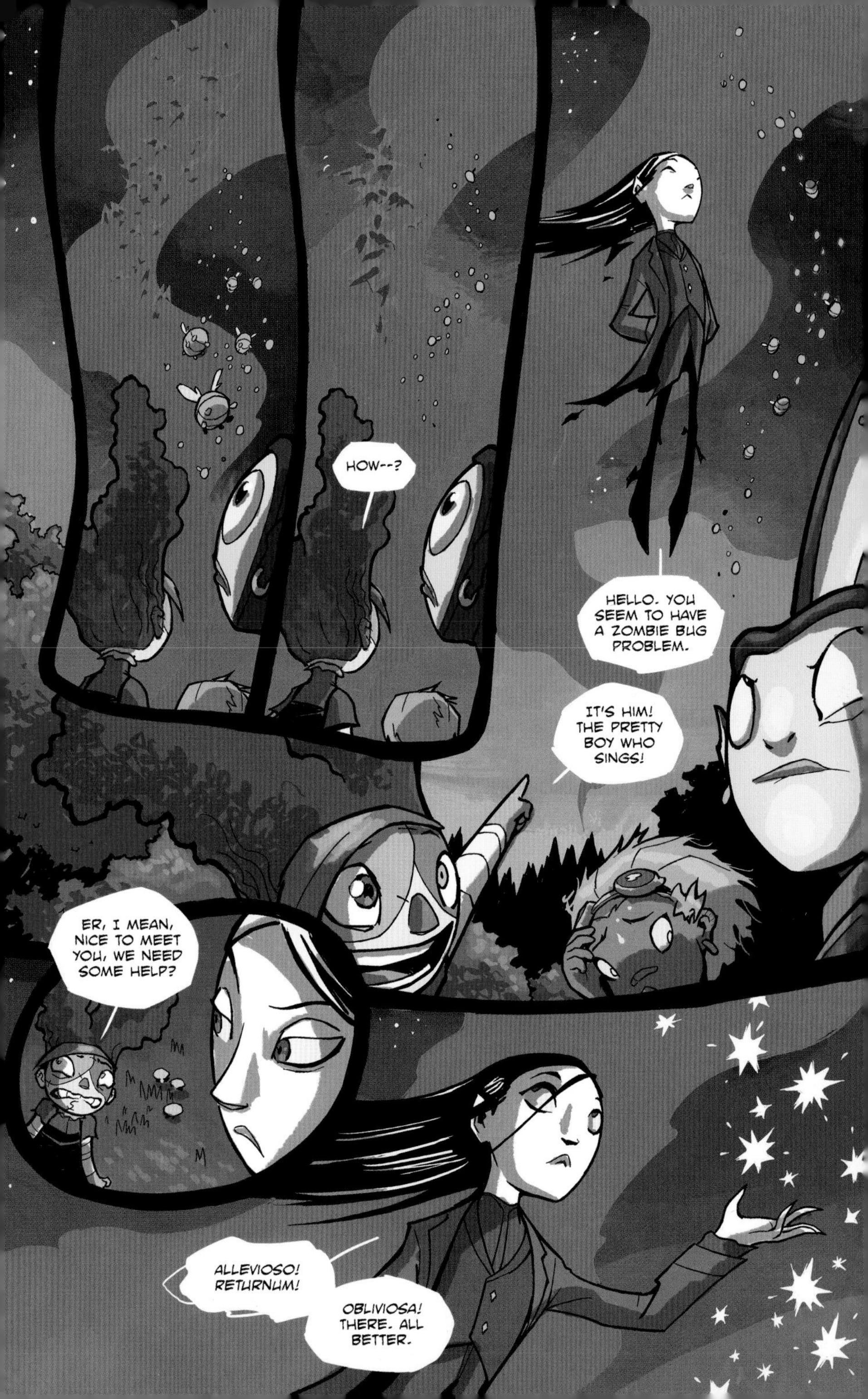
HOW--?
HELLO. YOU SEEM TO HAVE A ZOMBIE BUG PROBLEM.
IT'S HIM! THE PRETTY BOY WHO SINGS!
ER, I MEAN, NICE TO MEET YOU, WE NEED SOME HELP?
ALLEVIOSO! RETURNUM!
OBLIVIOSA! THERE. ALL BETTER.

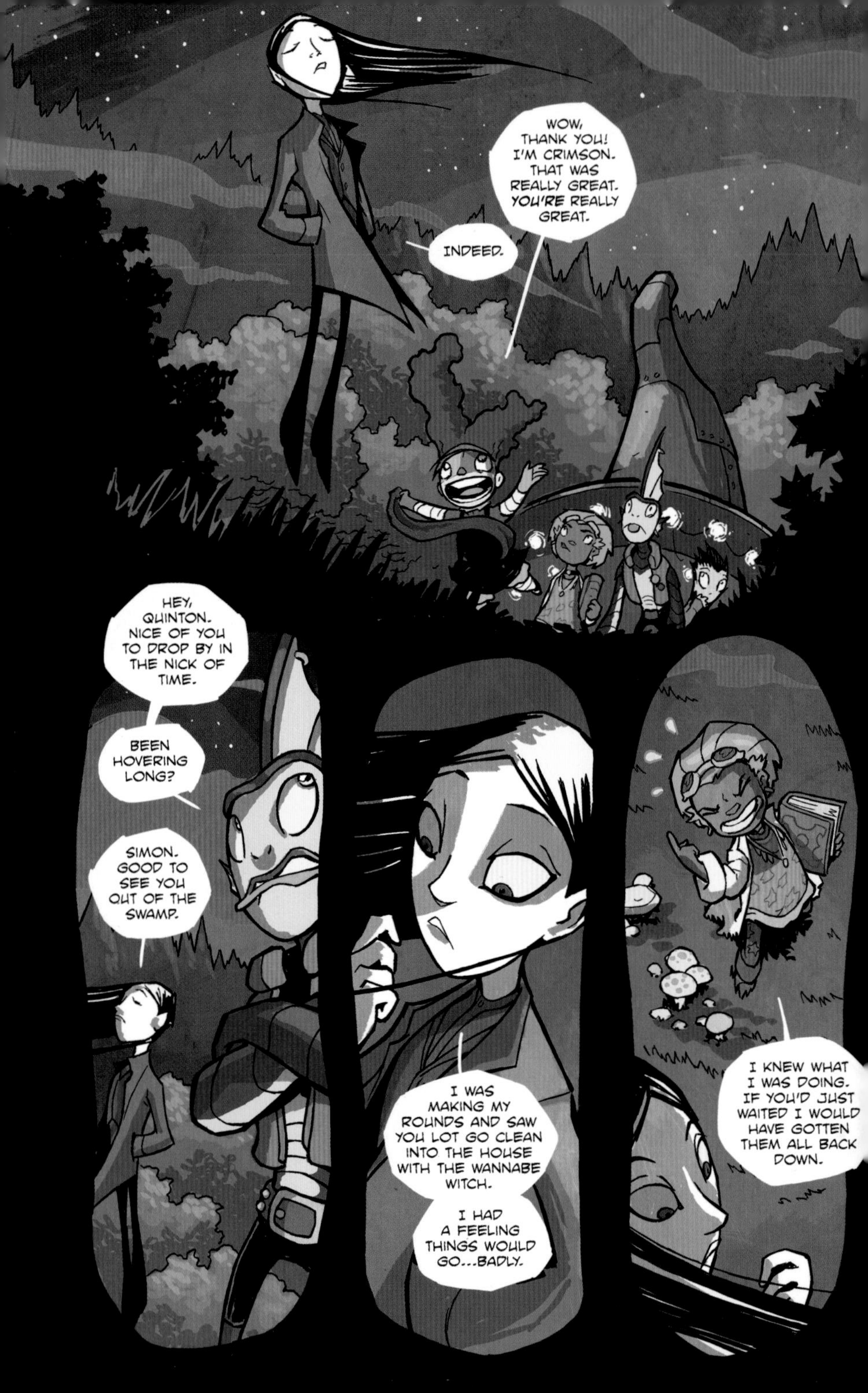
WOW, THANK YOU! I'M CRIMSON. THAT WAS REALLY GREAT. YOU'RE REALLY GREAT.
INDEED.
HEY, QUINTON. NICE OF YOU TO DROP BY IN THE NICK OF TIME.
BEEN HOVERING LONG?
SIMON. GOOD TO SEE YOU OUT OF THE SWAMP.
I WAS MAKING MY ROUNDS AND SAW YOU LOT GO CLEAN INTO THE HOUSE WITH THE WANNABE WITCH.
I HAD A FEELING THINGS WOULD GO...BADLY.
I KNEW WHAT I WAS DOING. IF YOU'D JUST WAITED I WOULD HAVE GOTTEN THEM ALL BACK DOWN.

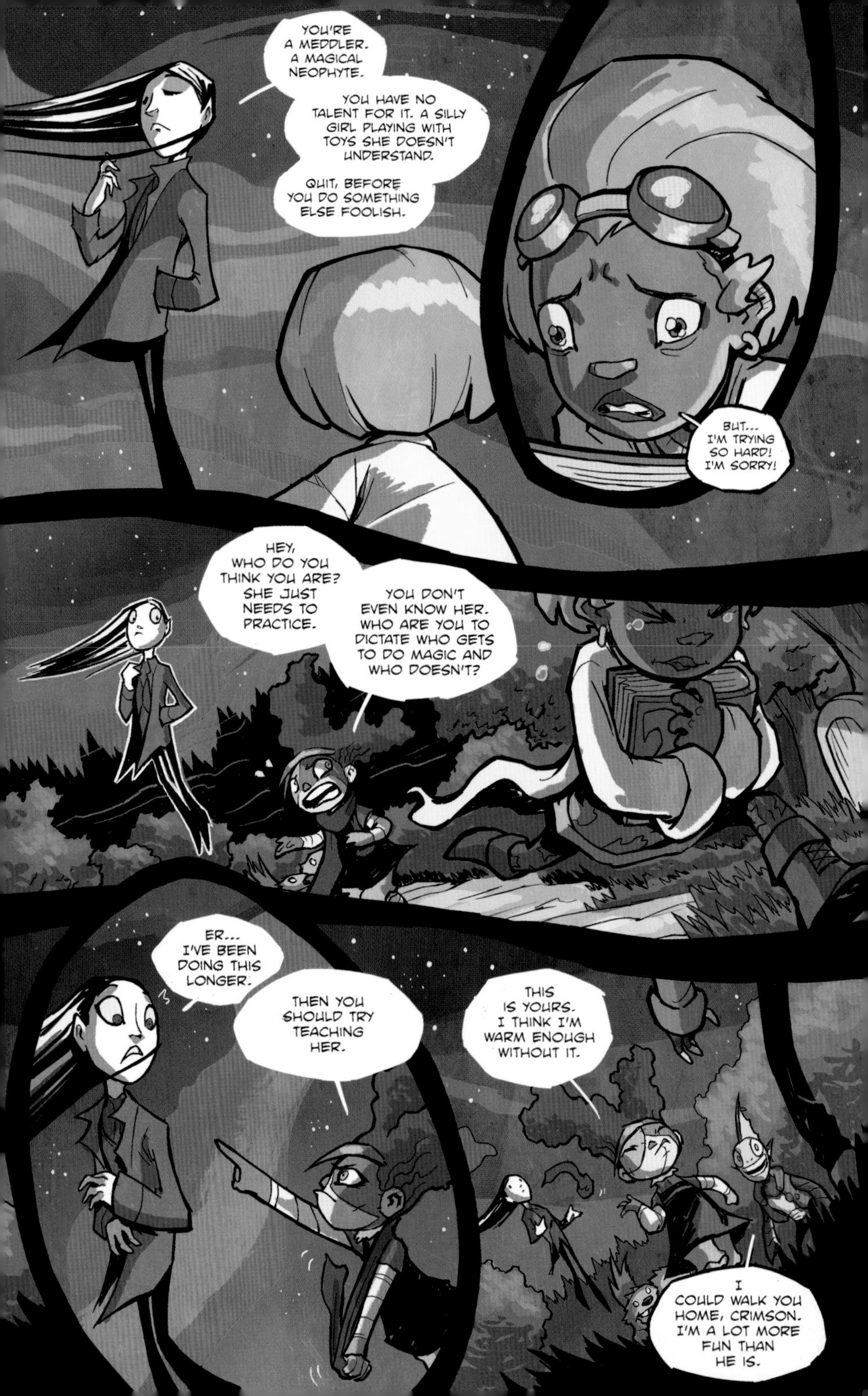
YOU'RE A MEDDLER. A MAGICAL NEOPHYTE.
YOU HAVE NO TALENT FOR IT. A SILLY GIRL PLAYING WITH TOYS SHE DOESN'T UNDERSTAND.
QUIT, BEFORE YOU DO SOMETHING ELSE FOOLISH.
BUT... I'M TRYING SO HARD! I'M SORRY!
HEY, WHO DO YOU THINK YOU ARE? SHE JUST NEEDS TO PRACTICE.
YOU DON'T EVEN KNOW HER. WHO ARE YOU TO DICTATE WHO GETS TO DO MAGIC AND WHO DOESN'T?
ER... I'VE BEEN DOING THIS LONGER.
THEN YOU SHOULD TRY TEACHING HER.
THIS IS YOURS. I THINK I'M WARM ENOUGH WITHOUT IT.
I COULD WALK YOU HOME, CRIMSON. I'M A LOT MORE FUN THAN HE IS.

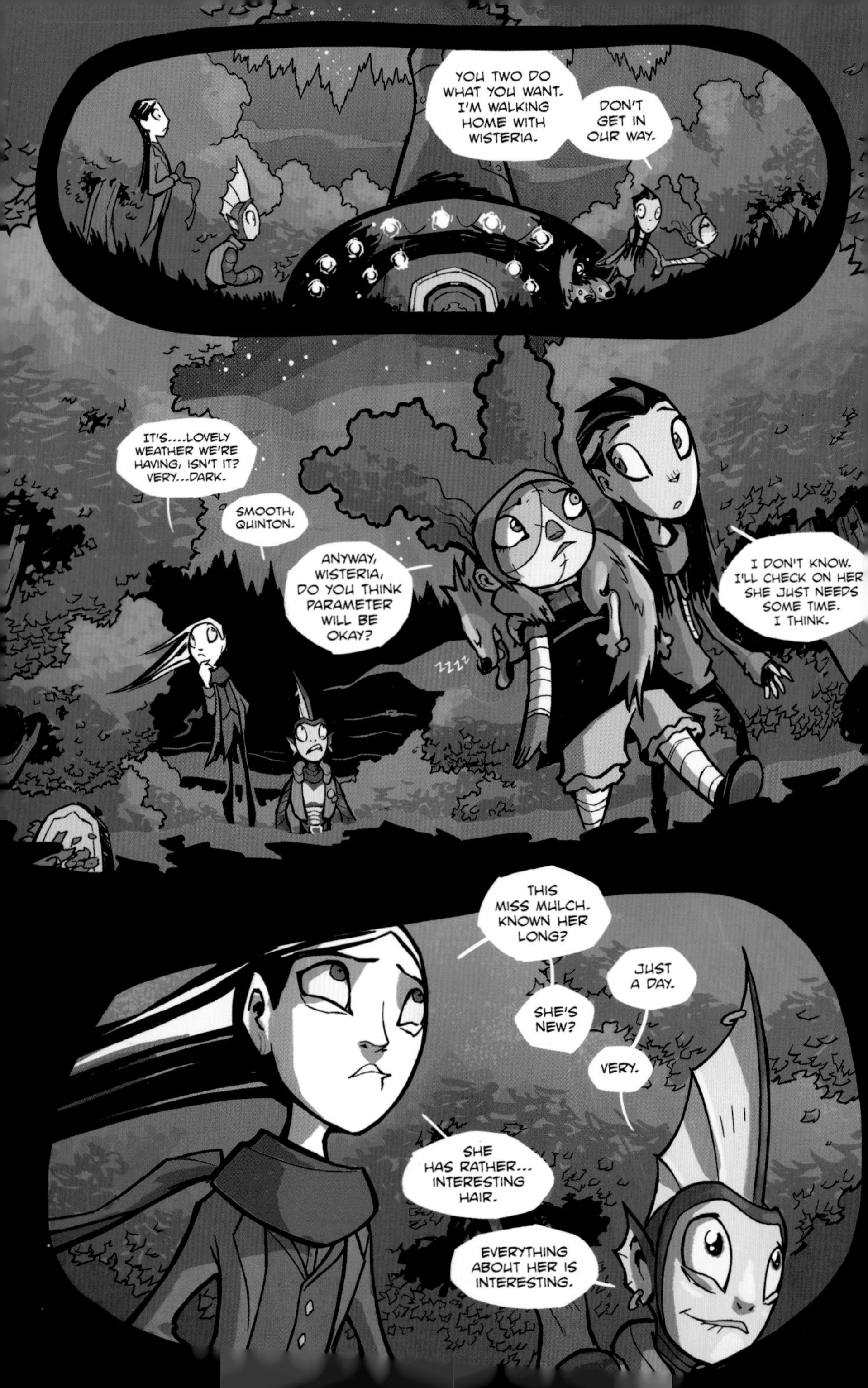
YOU TWO DO WHAT YOU WANT. I'M WALKING HOME WITH WISTERIA.
DON'T GET IN OUR WAY.
IT'S....LOVELY WEATHER WE'RE HAVING, ISN'T IT? VERY...DARK.
SMOOTH, QUINTON.
ANYWAY, WISTERIA, DO YOU THINK PARAMETER WILL BE OKAY?
I DON'T KNOW. I'LL CHECK ON HER SHE JUST NEEDS SOME TIME. I THINK.
ZZZZ
THIS MISS MULCH. KNOWN HER LONG?
JUST A DAY.
SHE'S NEW?
VERY.
SHE HAS RATHER... INTERESTING HAIR.
EVERYTHING ABOUT HER IS INTERESTING.

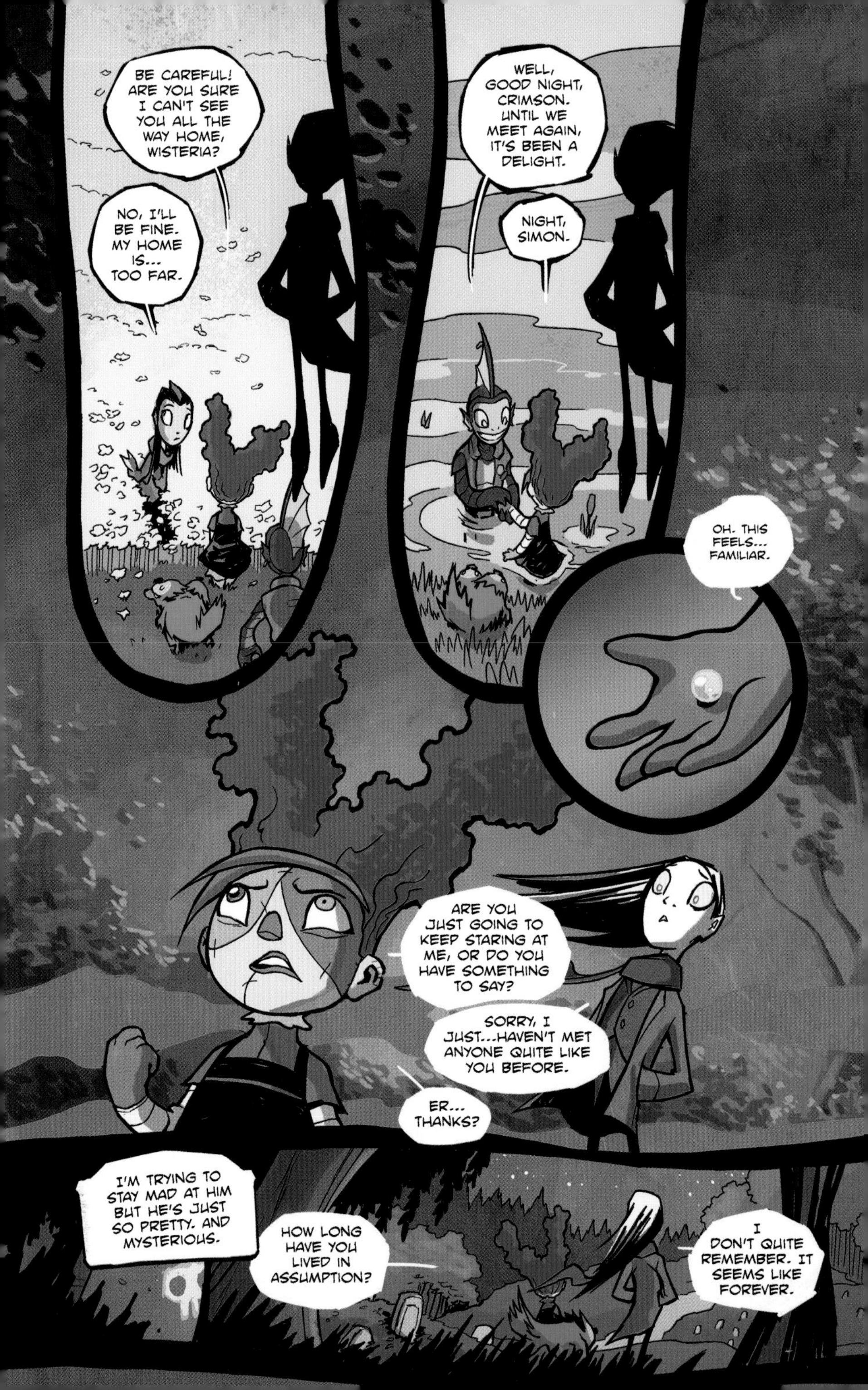
BE CAREFUL! ARE YOU SURE I CAN'T SEE YOU ALL THE WAY HOME, WISTERIA?
NO, I'LL BE FINE. MY HOME IS... TOO FAR.
WELL, GOOD NIGHT, CRIMSON. UNTIL WE MEET AGAIN, IT'S BEEN A DELIGHT.
NIGHT, SIMON.
OH. THIS FEELS... FAMILIAR.
ARE YOU JUST GOING TO KEEP STARING AT ME, OR DO YOU HAVE SOMETHING TO SAY?
SORRY, I JUST...HAVEN'T MET ANYONE QUITE LIKE YOU BEFORE.
ER... THANKS?
I'M TRYING TO STAY MAD AT HIM BUT HE'S JUST SO PRETTY. AND MYSTERIOUS.
HOW LONG HAVE YOU LIVED IN ASSUMPTION?
I DON'T QUITE REMEMBER. IT SEEMS LIKE FOREVER.

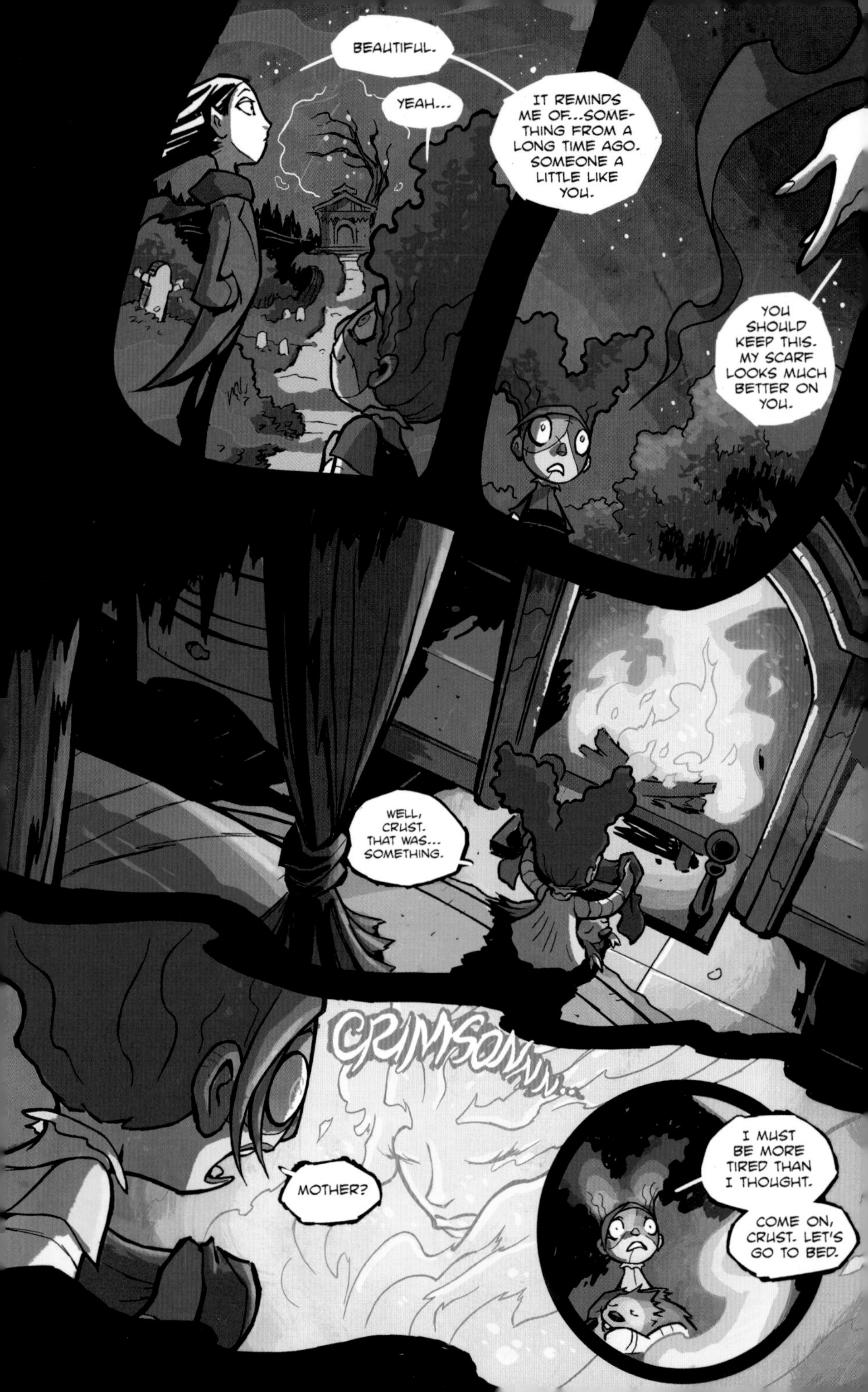
BEAUTIFUL.
YEAH...
IT REMINDS ME OF...SOMETHING FROM A LONG TIME AGO. SOMEONE A LITTLE LIKE YOU.
YOU SHOULD KEEP THIS. MY SCARF LOOKS MUCH BETTER ON YOU.
WELL, CRUST. THAT WAS... SOMETHING.
CRIMSONNN...
MOTHER?
I MUST BE MORE TIRED THAN I THOUGHT.
COME ON, CRUST. LET'S GO TO BED.

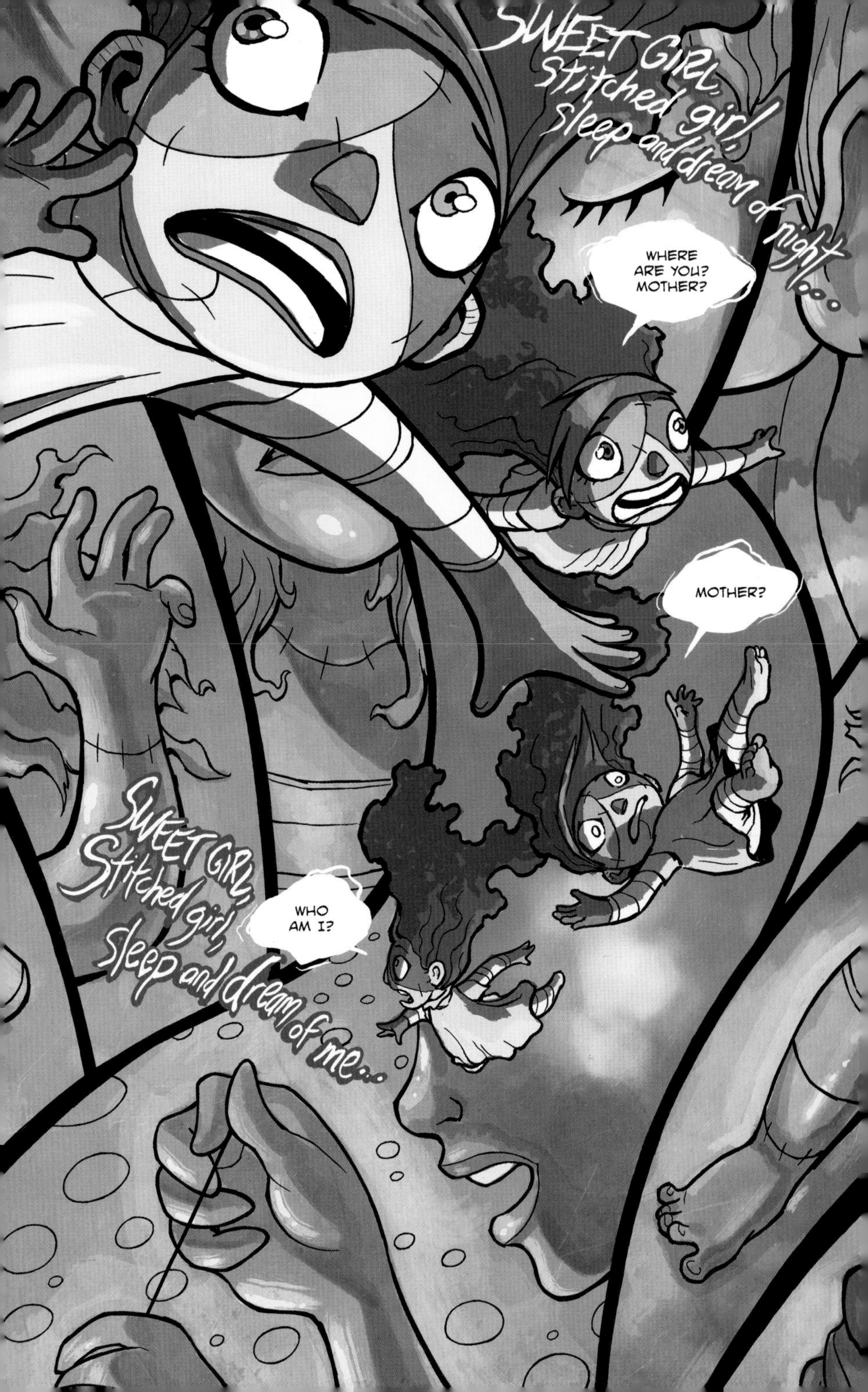
SWEET GIRL, Stitched girl, sleep and dream of night...
WHERE ARE YOU? MOTHER?
MOTHER?
SWEET GIRL, Stitched girl, sleep and dream of me...
WHO AM I?

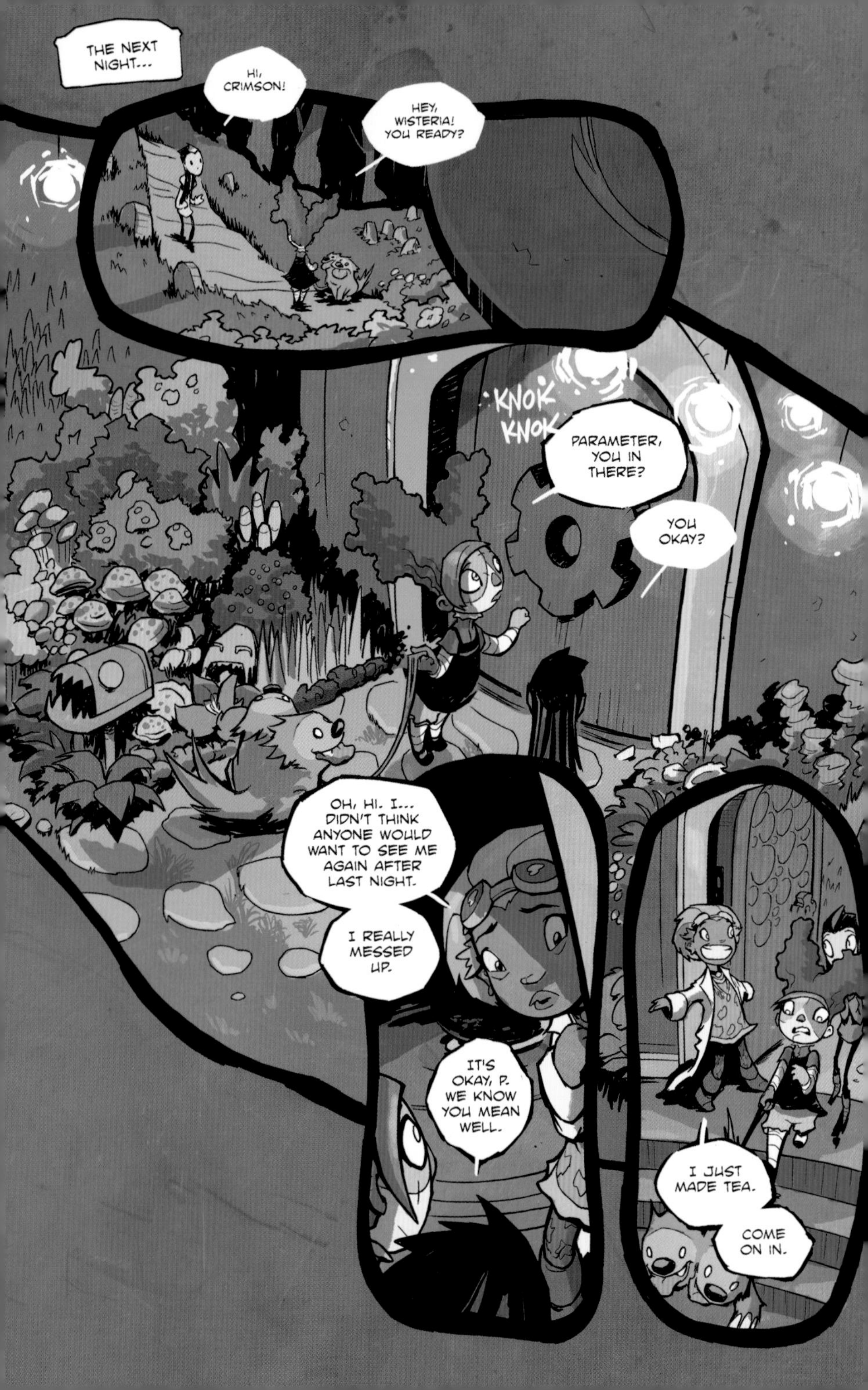
THE NEXT NIGHT...
HI, CRIMSON!
HEY, WISTERIA! YOU READY?
KNOK KNOK
PARAMETER, YOU IN THERE?
YOU OKAY?
OH, HI. I... DIDN'T THINK ANYONE WOULD WANT TO SEE ME AGAIN AFTER LAST NIGHT.
I REALLY MESSED UP.
IT'S OKAY, P. WE KNOW YOU MEAN WELL.
I JUST MADE TEA.
COME ON IN.

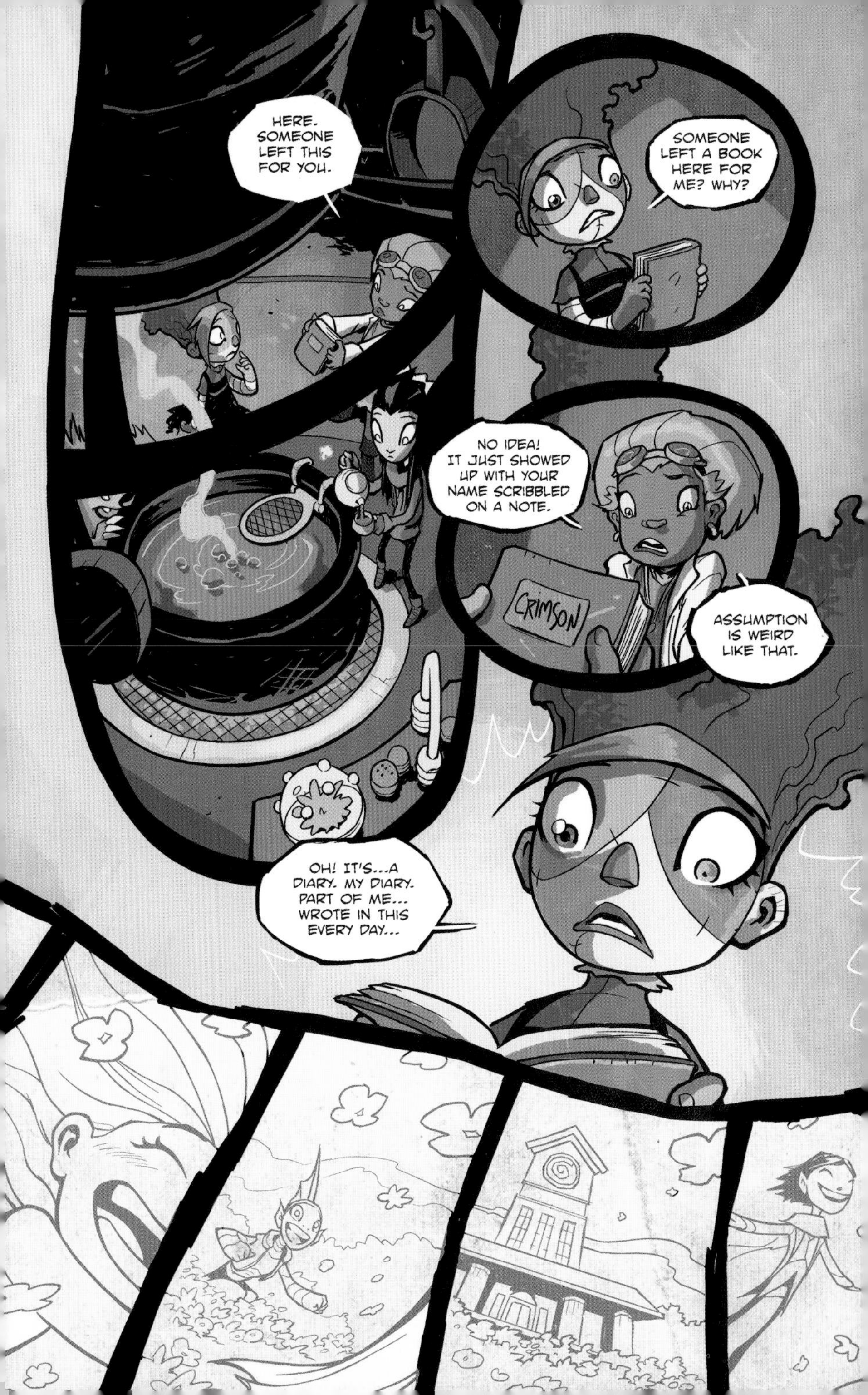
HERE. SOMEONE LEFT THIS FOR YOU.
SOMEONE LEFT A BOOK HERE FOR ME? WHY?
NO IDEA! IT JUST SHOWED UP WITH YOUR NAME SCRIBBLED ON A NOTE.
CRIMSON
ASSUMPTION IS WEIRD LIKE THAT.
OH! IT'S...A DIARY. MY DIARY. PART OF ME... WROTE IN THIS EVERY DAY...

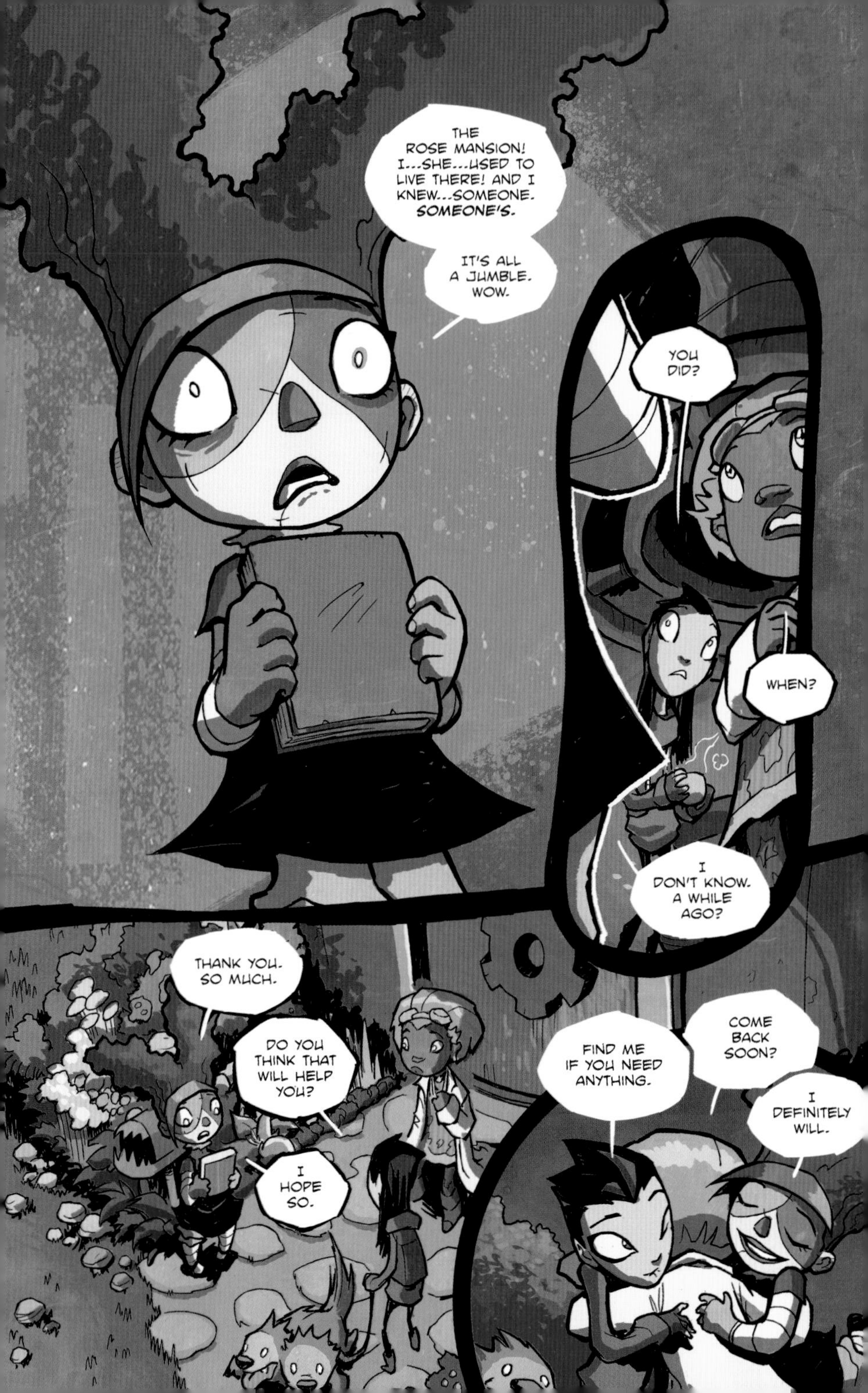
THE ROSE MANSION! I...SHE...USED TO LIVE THERE! AND I KNEW...SOMEONE. SOMEONE'S.
IT'S ALL A JUMBLE. WOW.
YOU DID?
WHEN?
I DON'T KNOW. A WHILE AGO?
THANK YOU. SO MUCH.
DO YOU THINK THAT WILL HELP YOU?
I HOPE SO.
FIND ME IF YOU NEED ANYTHING.
COME BACK SOON?
I DEFINITELY WILL.

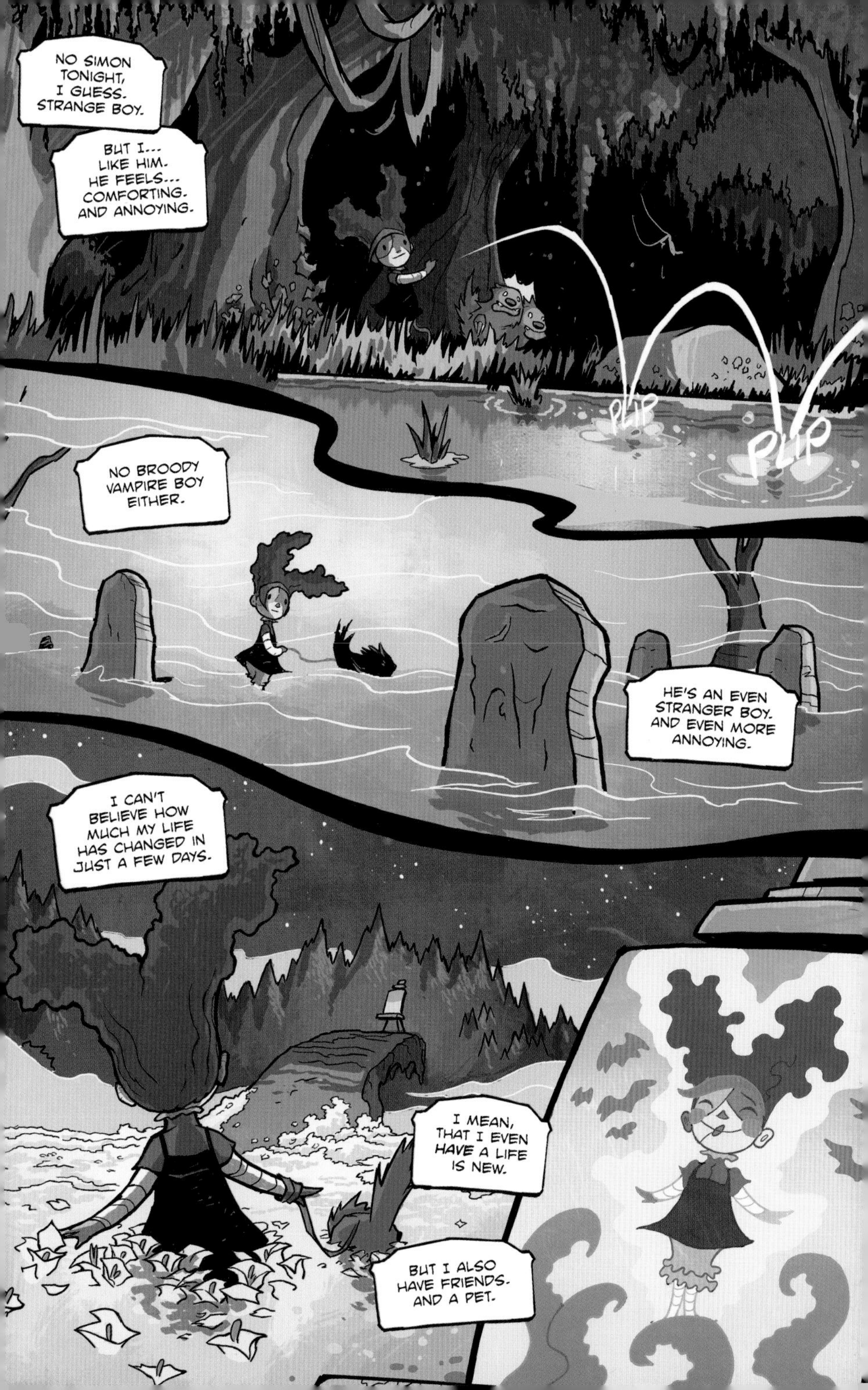
NO SIMON TONIGHT, I GUESS. STRANGE BOY.
BUT I... LIKE HIM. HE FEELS... COMFORTING. AND ANNOYING.
PLIP
PLIP
NO BROODY VAMPIRE BOY EITHER.
HE'S AN EVEN STRANGER BOY. AND EVEN MORE ANNOYING.
I CAN'T BELIEVE HOW MUCH MY LIFE HAS CHANGED IN JUST A FEW DAYS.
I MEAN, THAT I EVEN *HAVE* A LIFE IS NEW.
BUT I ALSO HAVE FRIENDS. AND A PET.

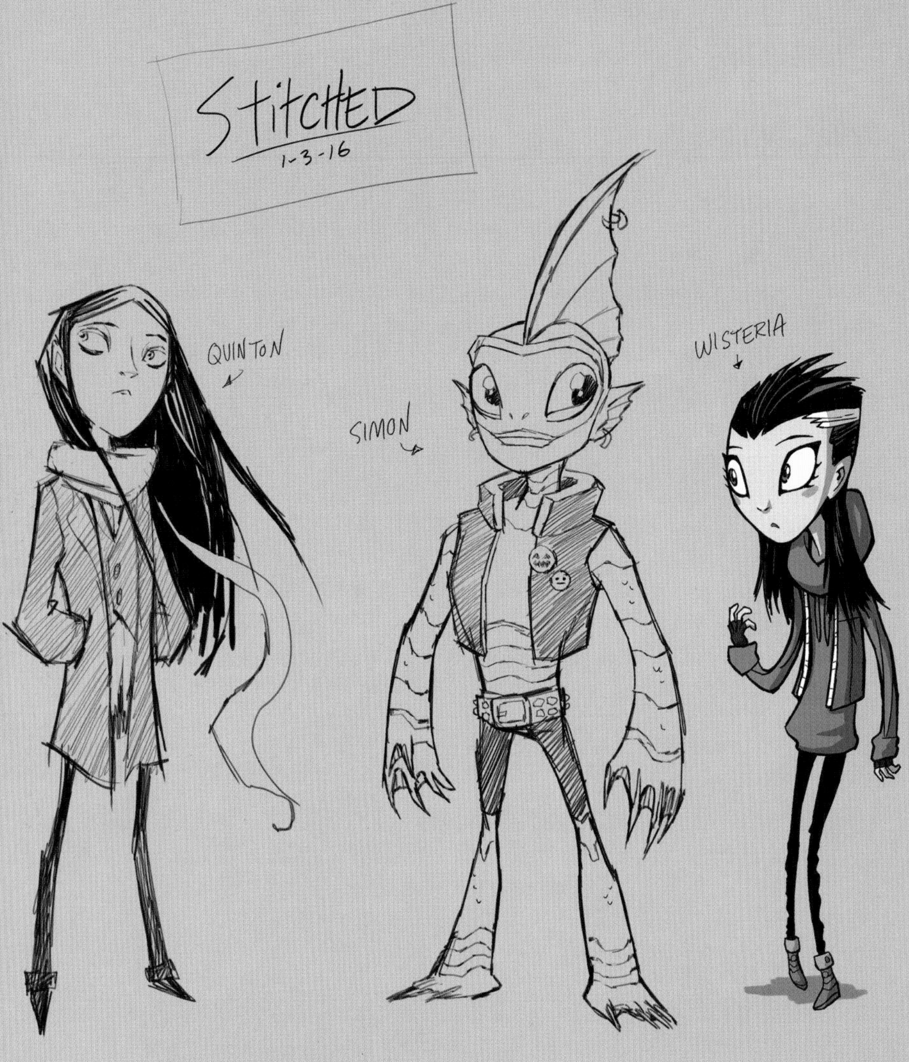
Stitched
1-3-16
QUINTON
SIMON
WISTERIA

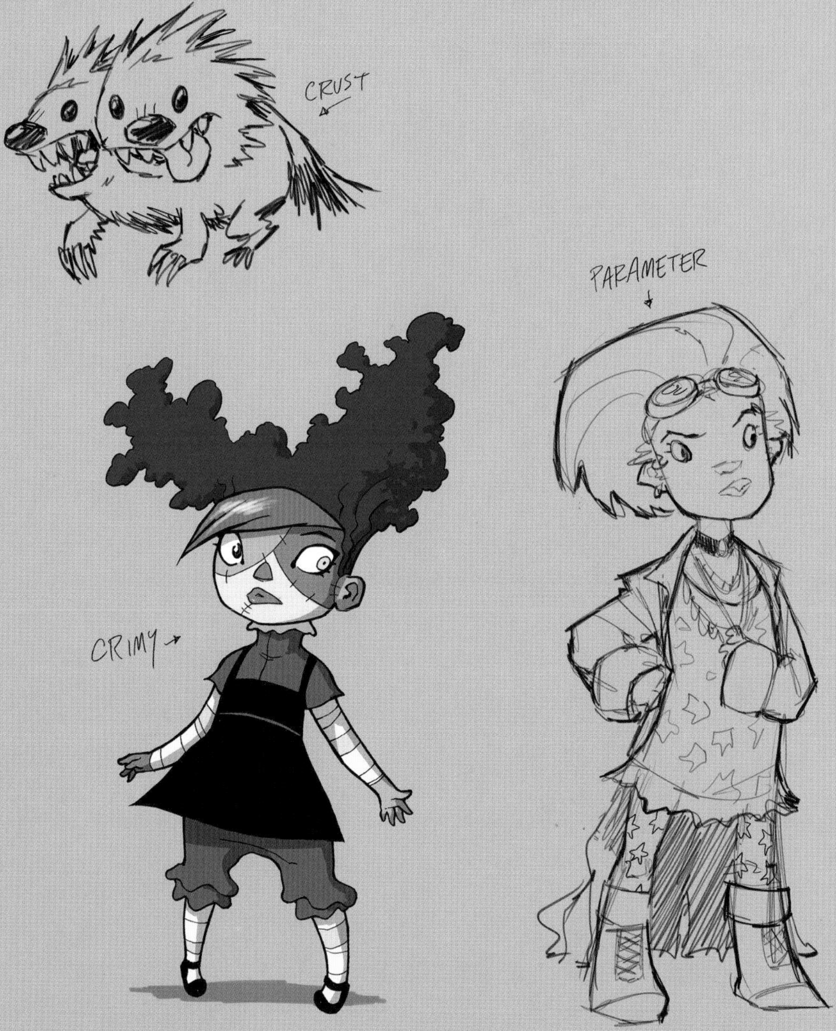
CRUST
PARAMETER
CRIMY

Preview of SWEETIES #1 "Cherry/Skye." A brand new family, a forbidden love, and all the sweets you can handle!

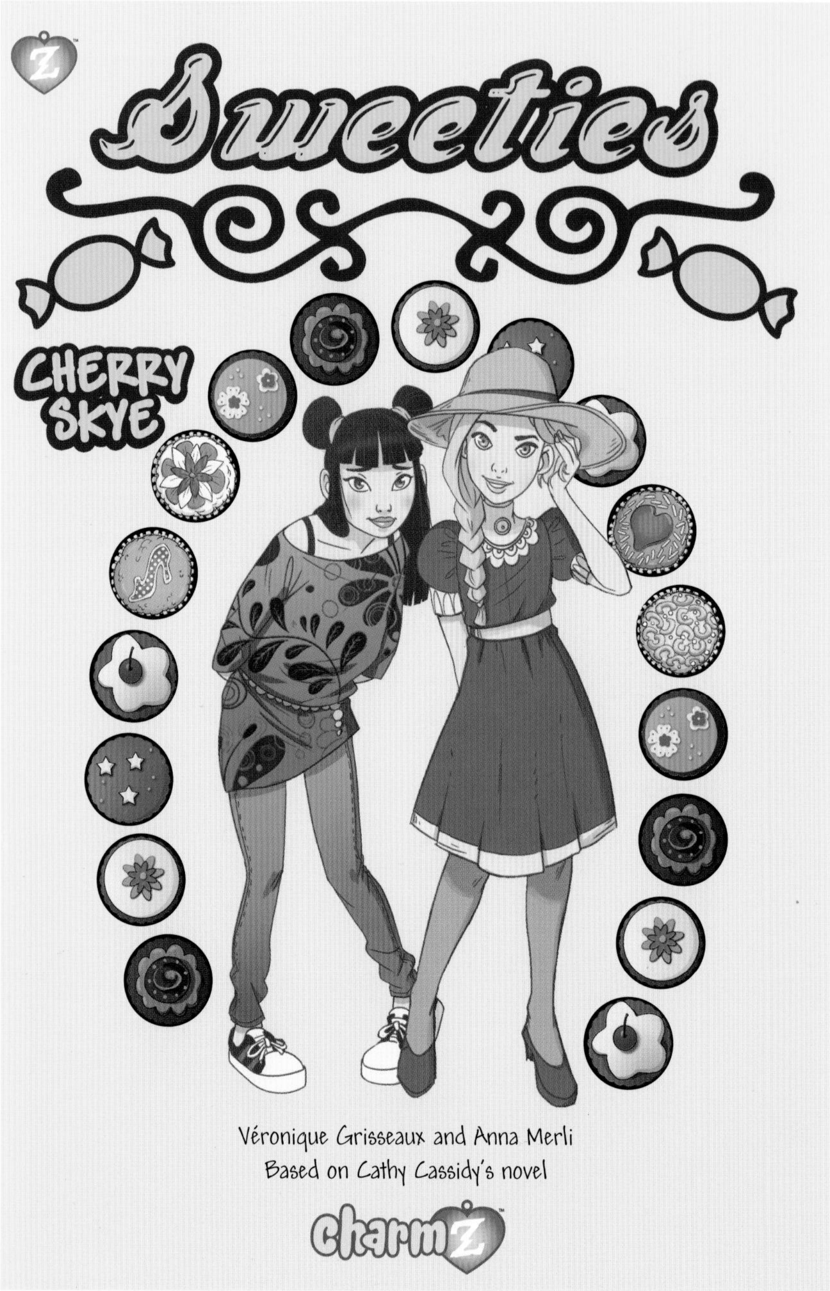
Sweeties
CHERRY
SKYE
Véronique Grisseaux and Anna Merli
Based on Cathy Cassidy's novel
charmz

Sweeties "THE GYPSY GHOST"

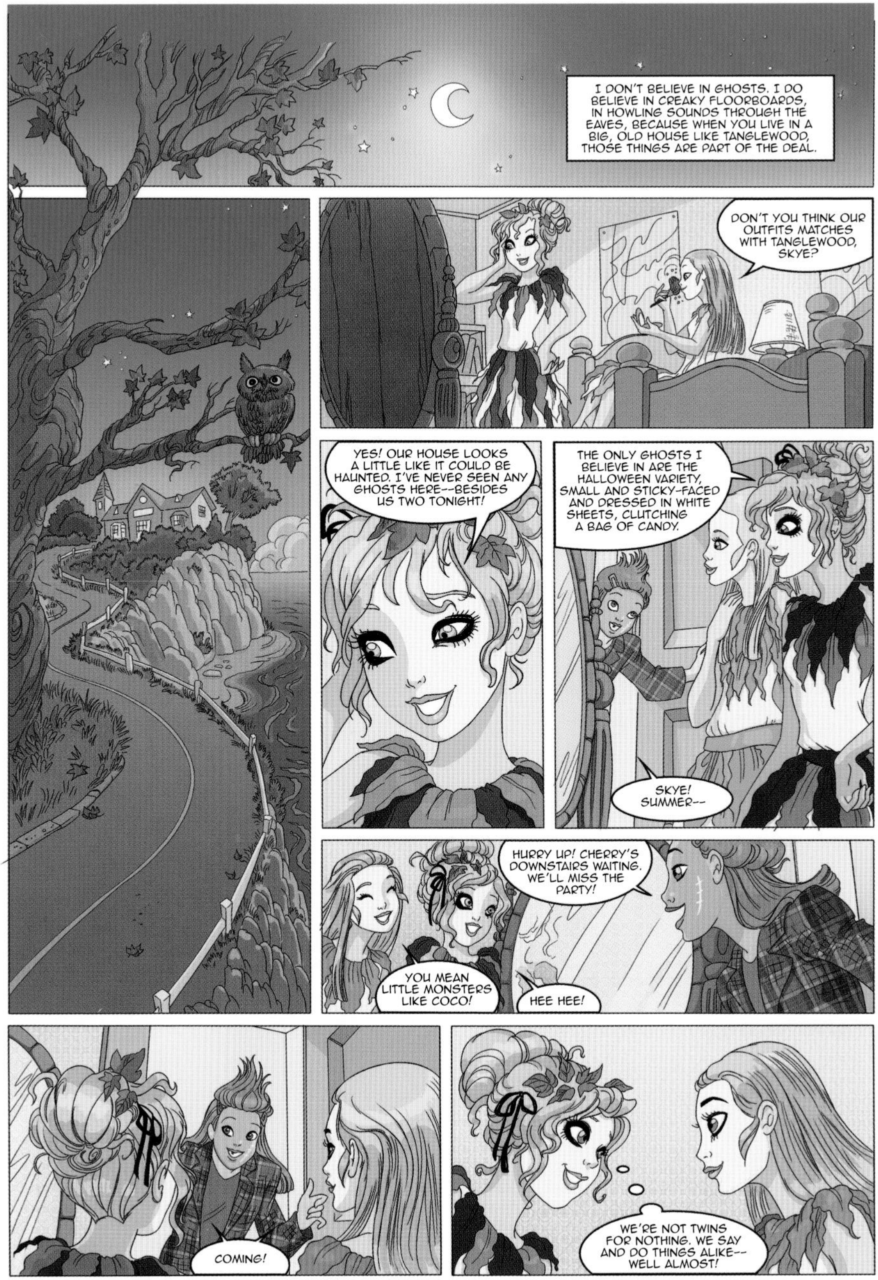
I DON'T BELIEVE IN GHOSTS. I DO BELIEVE IN CREAKY FLOORBOARDS, IN HOWLING SOUNDS THROUGH THE EAVES, BECAUSE WHEN YOU LIVE IN A BIG, OLD HOUSE LIKE TANGLEWOOD, THOSE THINGS ARE PART OF THE DEAL.
DON'T YOU THINK OUR OUTFITS MATCHES WITH TANGLEWOOD, SKYE?
YES! OUR HOUSE LOOKS A LITTLE LIKE IT COULD BE HAUNTED. I'VE NEVER SEEN ANY GHOSTS HERE--BESIDES US TWO TONIGHT!
THE ONLY GHOSTS I BELIEVE IN ARE THE HALLOWEEN VARIETY, SMALL AND STICKY-FACED AND DRESSED IN WHITE SHEETS, CLUTCHING A BAG OF CANDY.
SKYE! SUMMER--
HURRY UP! CHERRY'S DOWNSTAIRS WAITING. WE'LL MISS THE PARTY!
YOU MEAN LITTLE MONSTERS LIKE COCO!
HEE HEE!
COMING!
WE'RE NOT TWINS FOR NOTHING. WE SAY AND DO THINGS ALIKE-- WELL ALMOST!

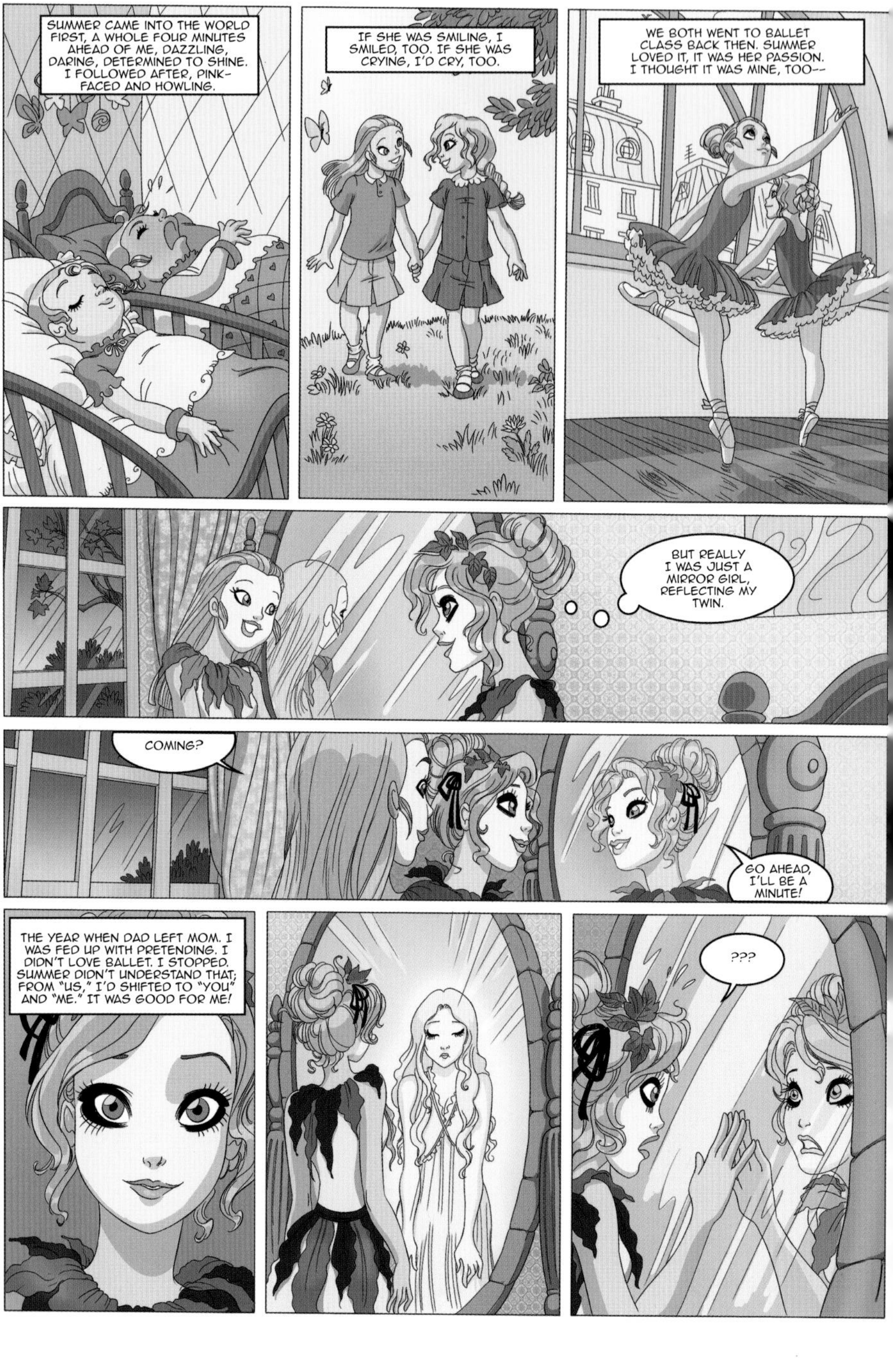
SUMMER CAME INTO THE WORLD FIRST, A WHOLE FOUR MINUTES AHEAD OF ME, DAZZLING, DARING, DETERMINED TO SHINE. I FOLLOWED AFTER, PINK-FACED AND HOWLING.
IF SHE WAS SMILING, I SMILED, TOO. IF SHE WAS CRYING, I'D CRY, TOO.
WE BOTH WENT TO BALLET CLASS BACK THEN. SUMMER LOVED IT, IT WAS HER PASSION. I THOUGHT IT WAS MINE, TOO--
BUT REALLY I WAS JUST A MIRROR GIRL, REFLECTING MY TWIN.
COMING?
GO AHEAD, I'LL BE A MINUTE!
THE YEAR WHEN DAD LEFT MOM. I WAS FED UP WITH PRETENDING. I DIDN'T LOVE BALLET. I STOPPED. SUMMER DIDN'T UNDERSTAND THAT; FROM "US," I'D SHIFTED TO "YOU" AND "ME." IT WAS GOOD FOR ME!
???

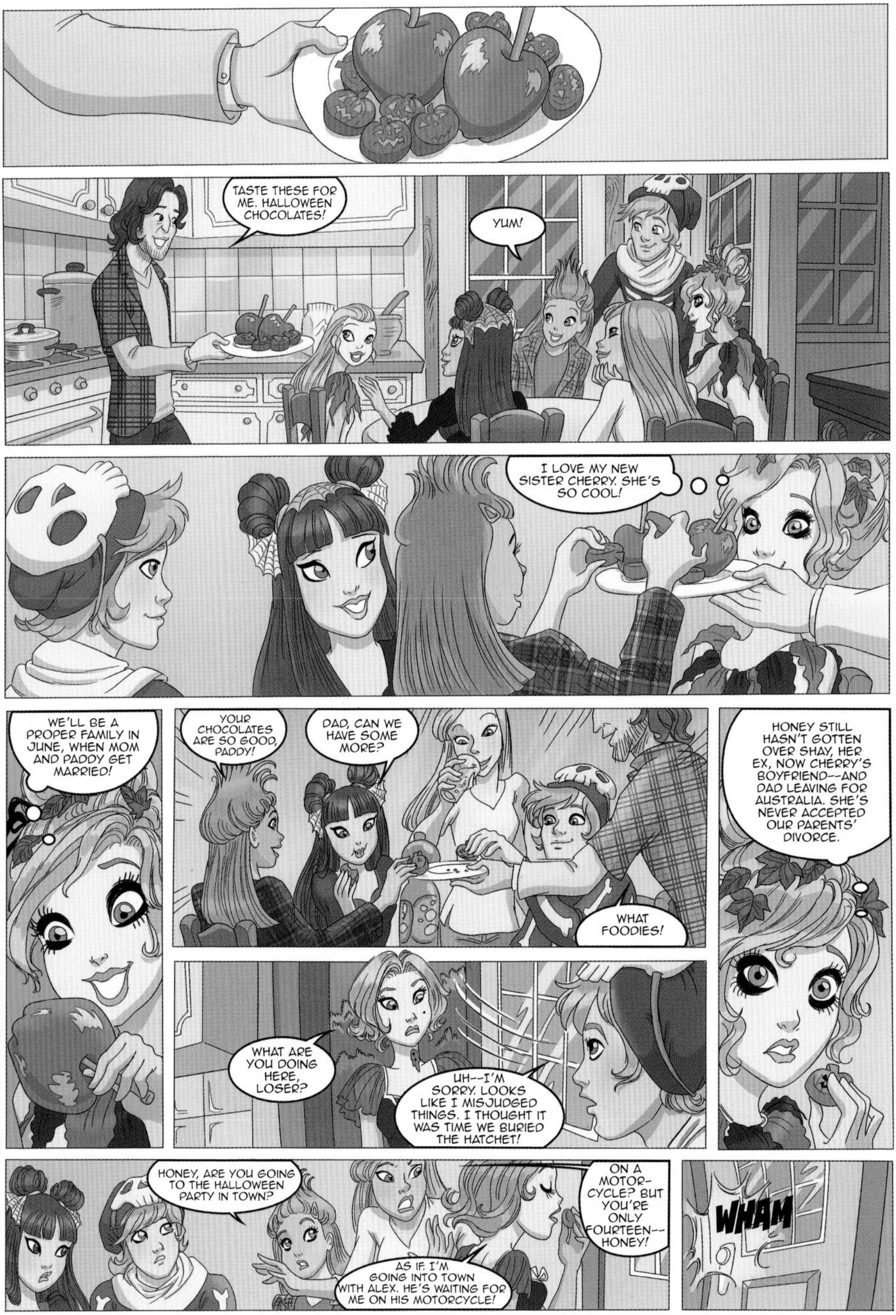
TASTE THESE FOR ME. HALLOWEEN CHOCOLATES!
YUM!
I LOVE MY NEW SISTER CHERRY. SHE'S SO COOL!
WE'LL BE A PROPER FAMILY IN JUNE, WHEN MOM AND PADDY GET MARRIED!
YOUR CHOCOLATES ARE SO GOOD, PADDY!
DAD, CAN WE HAVE SOME MORE?
WHAT FOODIES!
HONEY STILL HASN'T GOTTEN OVER SHAY, HER EX, NOW CHERRY'S BOYFRIEND--AND DAD LEAVING FOR AUSTRALIA. SHE'S NEVER ACCEPTED OUR PARENTS' DIVORCE.
WHAT ARE YOU DOING HERE, LOSER?
UH--I'M SORRY. LOOKS LIKE I MISJUDGED THINGS. I THOUGHT IT WAS TIME WE BURIED THE HATCHET!
HONEY, ARE YOU GOING TO THE HALLOWEEN PARTY IN TOWN?
AS IF. I'M GOING INTO TOWN WITH ALEX. HE'S WAITING FOR ME ON HIS MOTORCYCLE!
ON A MOTOR-CYCLE? BUT YOU'RE ONLY FOURTEEN--HONEY!
WHAM

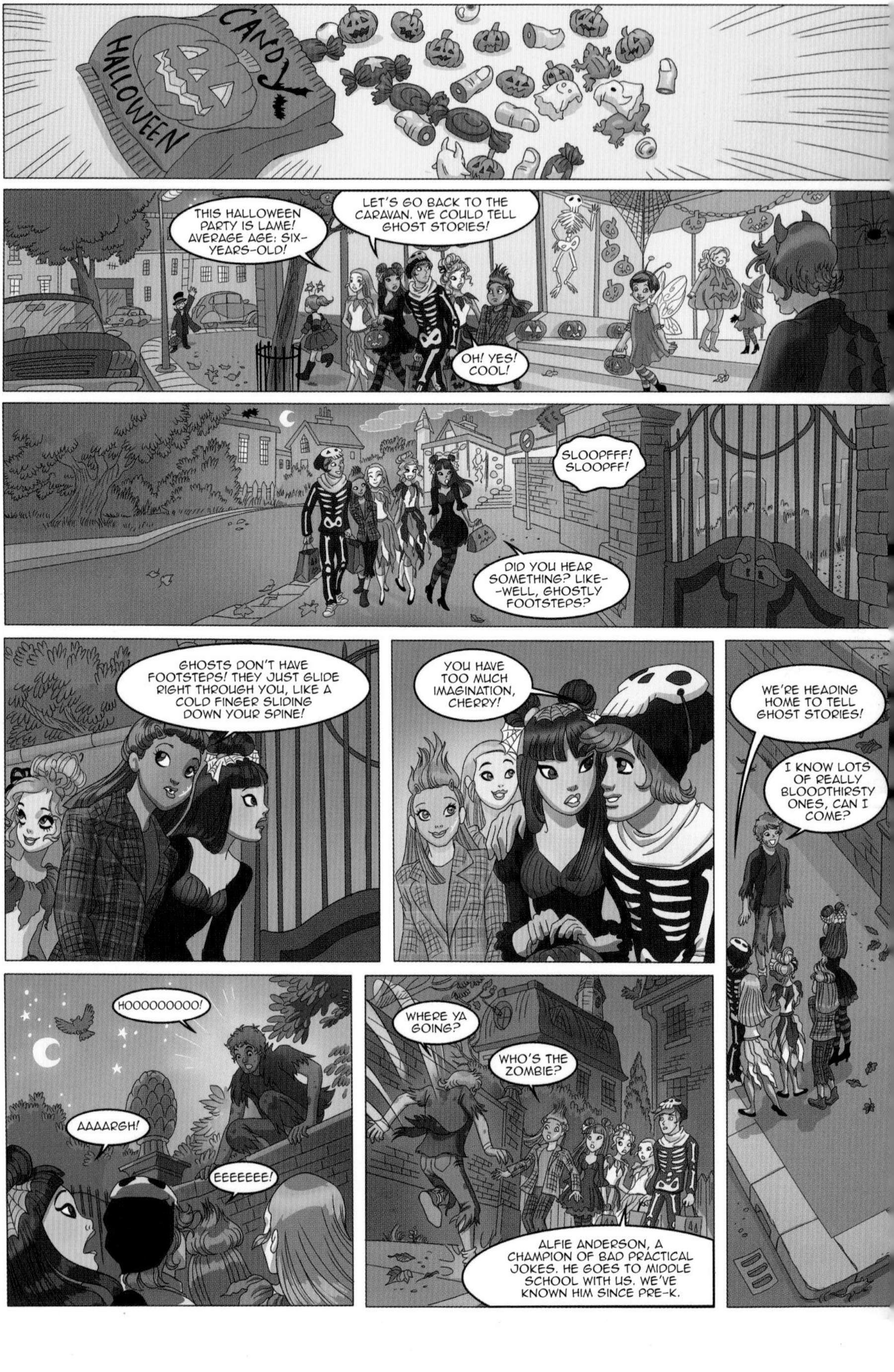
CANDY
HALLOWEEN
THIS HALLOWEEN PARTY IS LAME! AVERAGE AGE: SIX-YEARS-OLD!
LET'S GO BACK TO THE CARAVAN. WE COULD TELL GHOST STORIES!
OH! YES! COOL!
SLOOPFFF! SLOOPFF!
DID YOU HEAR SOMETHING? LIKE--WELL, GHOSTLY FOOTSTEPS?
GHOSTS DON'T HAVE FOOTSTEPS! THEY JUST GLIDE RIGHT THROUGH YOU, LIKE A COLD FINGER SLIDING DOWN YOUR SPINE!
YOU HAVE TOO MUCH IMAGINATION, CHERRY!
WE'RE HEADING HOME TO TELL GHOST STORIES!
I KNOW LOTS OF REALLY BLOODTHIRSTY ONES, CAN I COME?
HOOOOOOOOO!
AAAARGH!
EEEEEEE!
WHERE YA GOING?
WHO'S THE ZOMBIE?
ALFIE ANDERSON, A CHAMPION OF BAD PRACTICAL JOKES. HE GOES TO MIDDLE SCHOOL WITH US. WE'VE KNOWN HIM SINCE PRE-K.

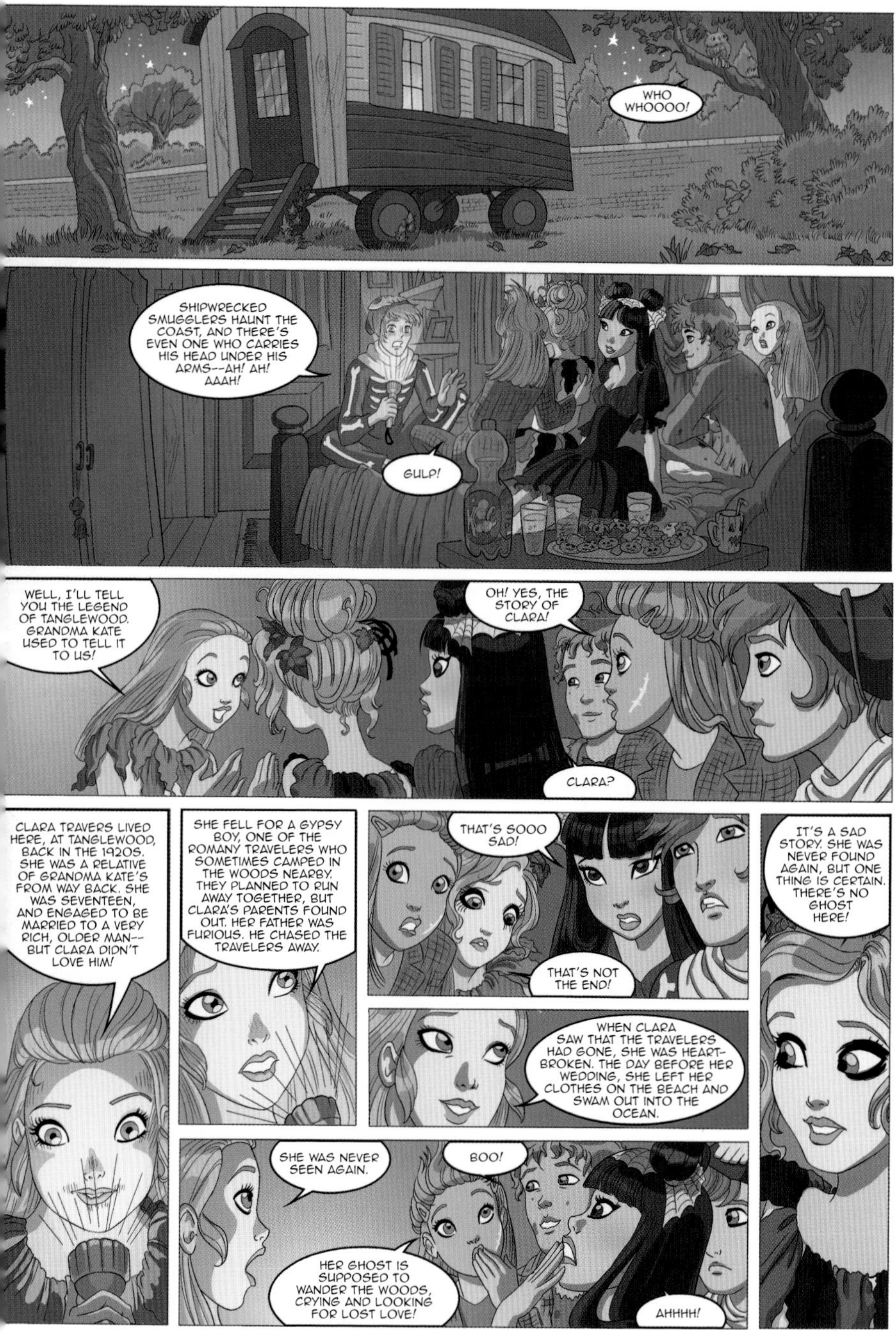
WHO WHOOOO!
SHIPWRECKED SMUGGLERS HAUNT THE COAST, AND THERE'S EVEN ONE WHO CARRIES HIS HEAD UNDER HIS ARMS--AH! AH! AAAH!
GULP!
WELL, I'LL TELL YOU THE LEGEND OF TANGLEWOOD. GRANDMA KATE USED TO TELL IT TO US!
OH! YES, THE STORY OF CLARA!
CLARA?
CLARA TRAVERS LIVED HERE, AT TANGLEWOOD, BACK IN THE 1920S. SHE WAS A RELATIVE OF GRANDMA KATE'S FROM WAY BACK. SHE WAS SEVENTEEN, AND ENGAGED TO BE MARRIED TO A VERY RICH, OLDER MAN--BUT CLARA DIDN'T LOVE HIM!
SHE FELL FOR A GYPSY BOY, ONE OF THE ROMANY TRAVELERS WHO SOMETIMES CAMPED IN THE WOODS NEARBY. THEY PLANNED TO RUN AWAY TOGETHER, BUT CLARA'S PARENTS FOUND OUT. HER FATHER WAS FURIOUS. HE CHASED THE TRAVELERS AWAY.
THAT'S SOOO SAD!
THAT'S NOT THE END!
WHEN CLARA SAW THAT THE TRAVELERS HAD GONE, SHE WAS HEART-BROKEN. THE DAY BEFORE HER WEDDING, SHE LEFT HER CLOTHES ON THE BEACH AND SWAM OUT INTO THE OCEAN.
SHE WAS NEVER SEEN AGAIN.
BOO!
HER GHOST IS SUPPOSED TO WANDER THE WOODS, CRYING AND LOOKING FOR LOST LOVE!
AHHHH!
IT'S A SAD STORY. SHE WAS NEVER FOUND AGAIN, BUT ONE THING IS CERTAIN. THERE'S NO GHOST HERE!

Preview of Chloe #1 "The New Girl." Follow Chloe as she fumbles to find love, popularity, and confidence!

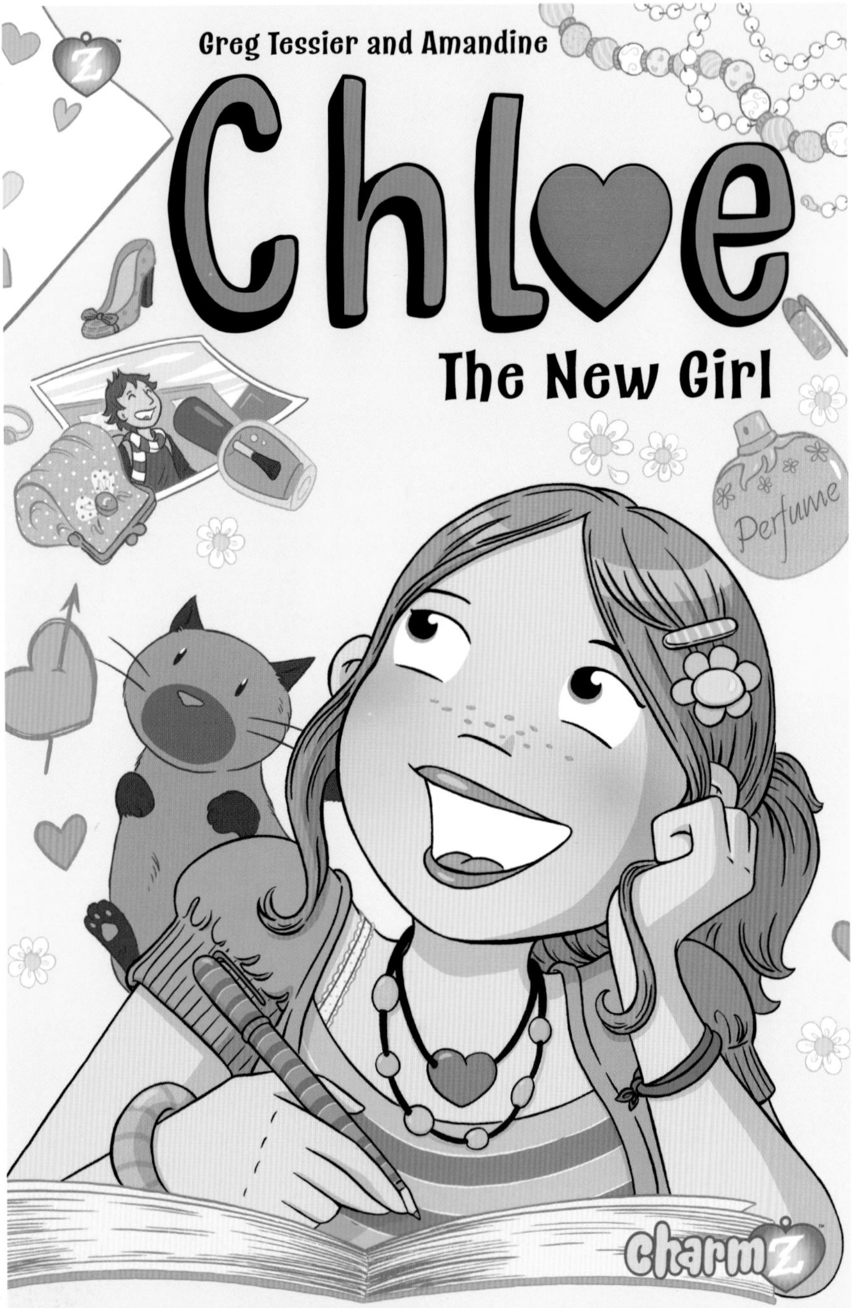

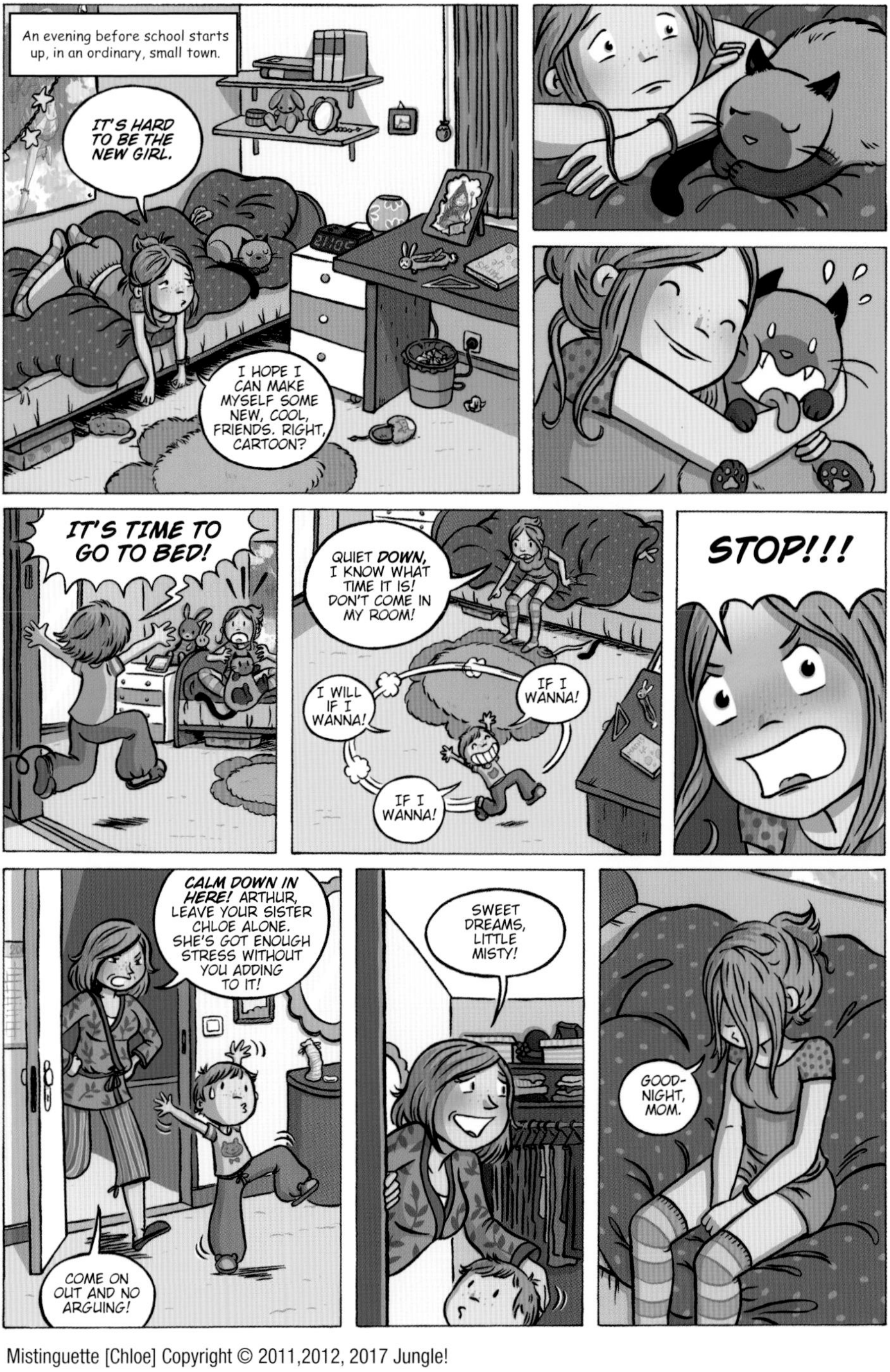
An evening before school starts up, in an ordinary, small town.
IT'S HARD TO BE THE NEW GIRL.
I HOPE I CAN MAKE MYSELF SOME NEW, COOL, FRIENDS. RIGHT, CARTOON?
IT'S TIME TO GO TO BED!
QUIET DOWN, I KNOW WHAT TIME IT IS! DON'T COME IN MY ROOM!
I WILL IF I WANNA!
IF I WANNA!
IF I WANNA!
STOP!!!
CALM DOWN IN HERE! ARTHUR, LEAVE YOUR SISTER CHLOE ALONE. SHE'S GOT ENOUGH STRESS WITHOUT YOU ADDING TO IT!
COME ON OUT AND NO ARGUING!
SWEET DREAMS, LITTLE MISTY!
GOOD-NIGHT, MOM.

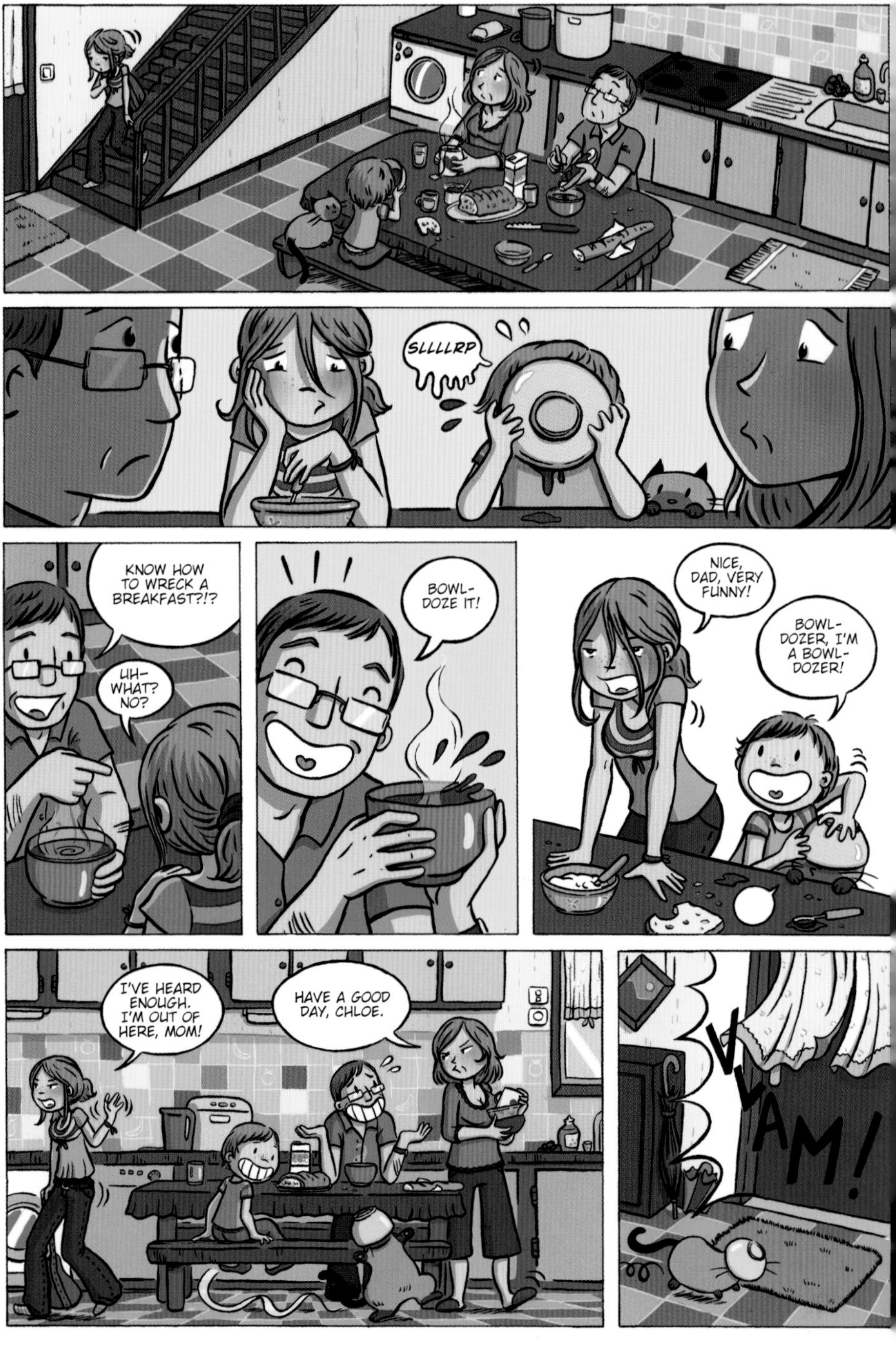
SLLLLRP
KNOW HOW TO WRECK A BREAKFAST?!?
UH-WHAT? NO?
BOWL-DOZE IT!
NICE, DAD, VERY FUNNY!
BOWL-DOZER, I'M A BOWL-DOZER!
I'VE HEARD ENOUGH. I'M OUT OF HERE, MOM!
HAVE A GOOD DAY, CHLOE.
VLAM!

1st Quarter

"Observation Mode "
engaged

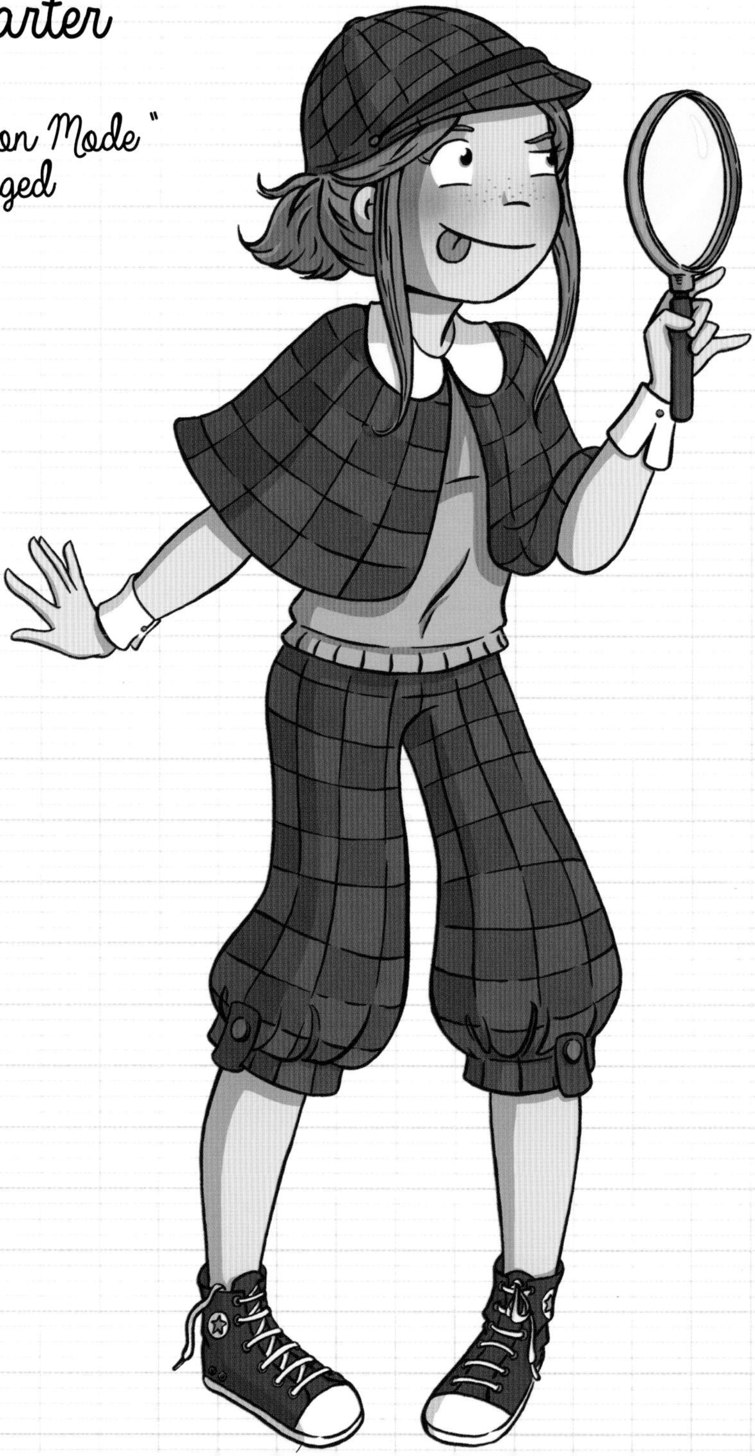

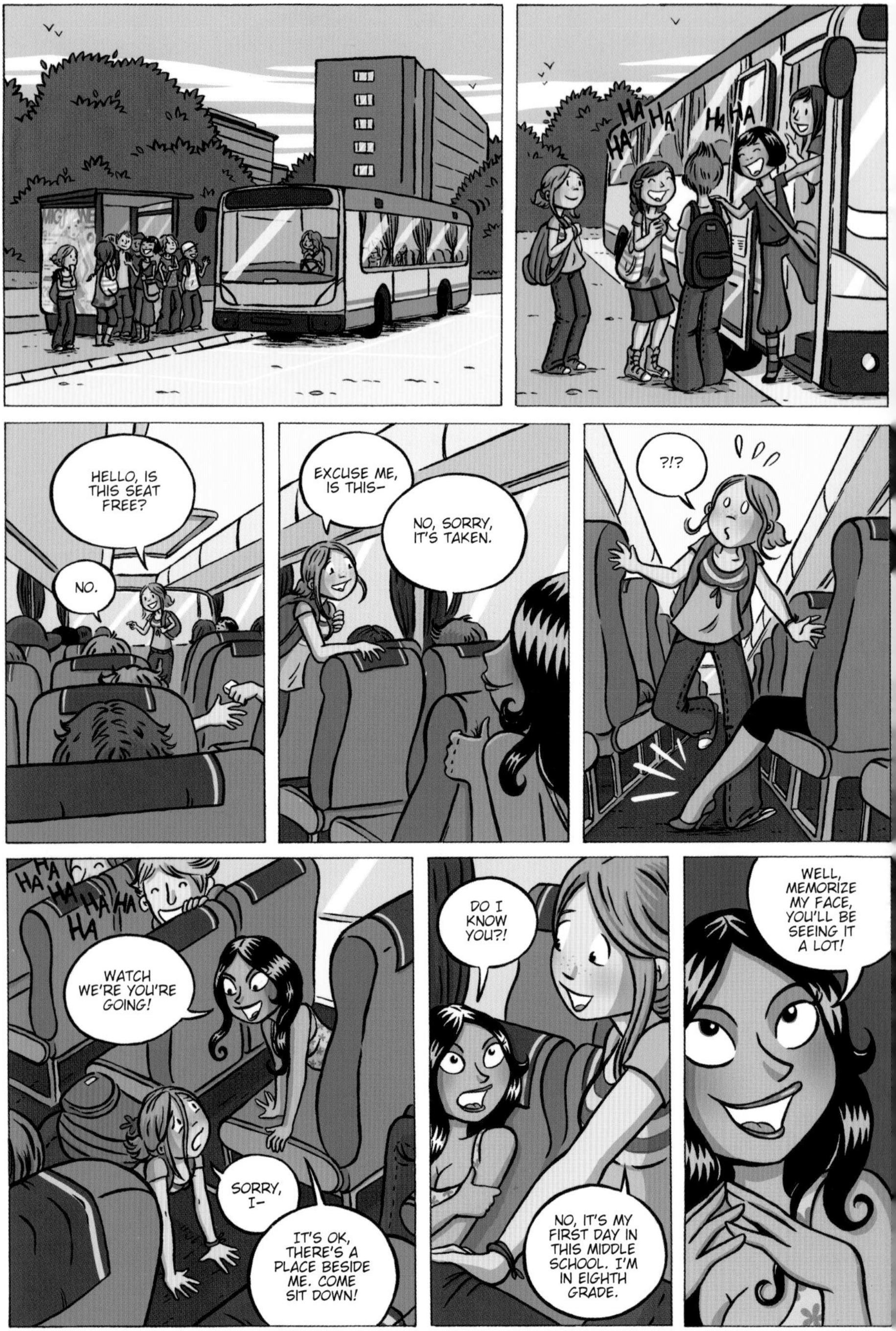
HA HA HA HA HA
HELLO, IS THIS SEAT FREE?
NO.
EXCUSE ME, IS THIS-
NO, SORRY, IT'S TAKEN.
?!?
HA HA HA HA HA HA
WATCH WE'RE YOU'RE GOING!
SORRY, I-
IT'S OK, THERE'S A PLACE BESIDE ME. COME SIT DOWN!
DO I KNOW YOU?!
NO, IT'S MY FIRST DAY IN THIS MIDDLE SCHOOL. I'M IN EIGHTH GRADE.
WELL, MEMORIZE MY FACE, YOU'LL BE SEEING IT A LOT!

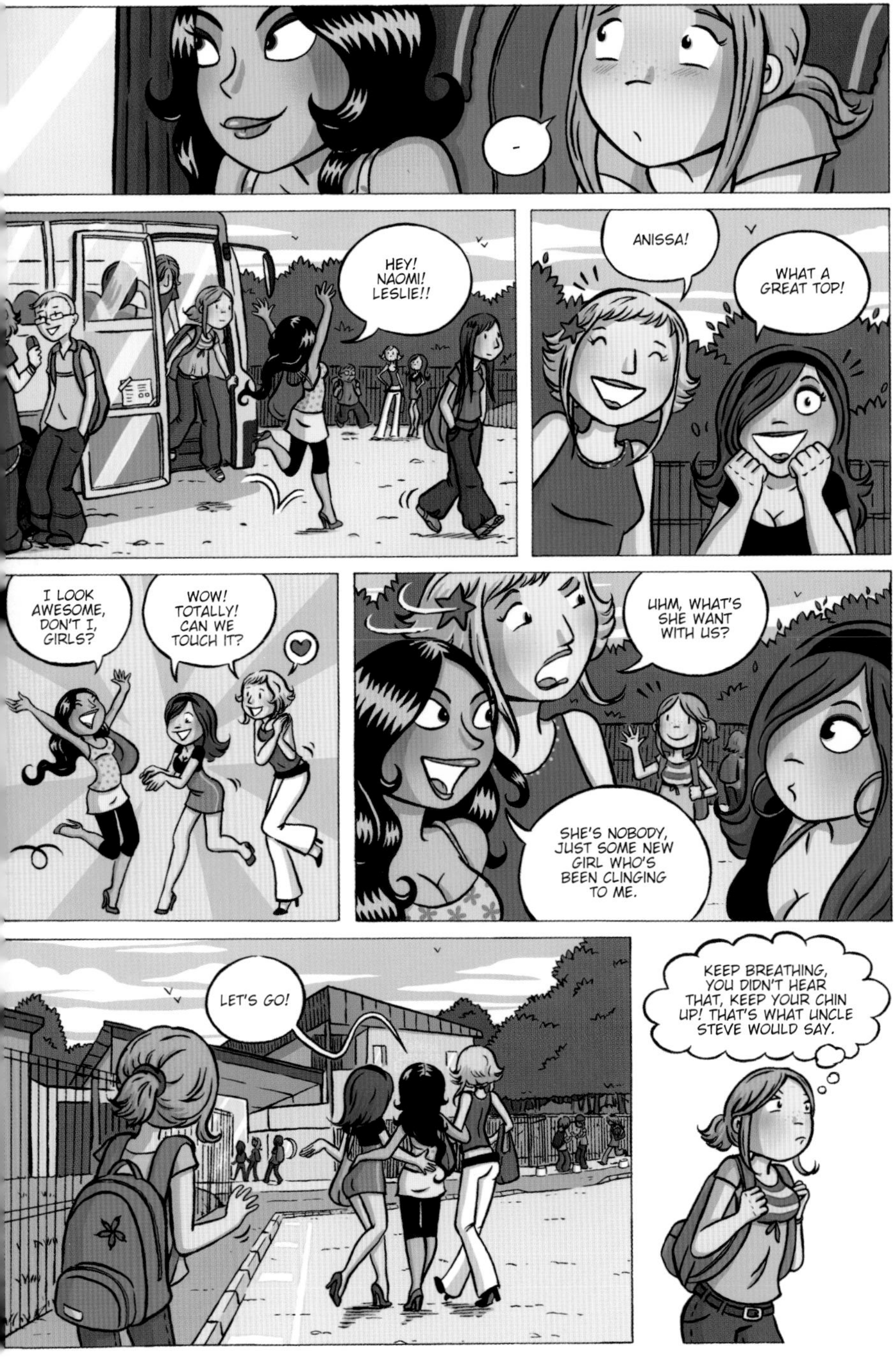
-
HEY! NAOMI! LESLIE!!
ANISSA!
WHAT A GREAT TOP!
I LOOK AWESOME, DON'T I, GIRLS?
WOW! TOTALLY! CAN WE TOUCH IT?
UHM, WHAT'S SHE WANT WITH US?
SHE'S NOBODY, JUST SOME NEW GIRL WHO'S BEEN CLINGING TO ME.
LET'S GO!
KEEP BREATHING, YOU DIDN'T HEAR THAT, KEEP YOUR CHIN UP! THAT'S WHAT UNCLE STEVE WOULD SAY.

Check out more in CHLOE #1 "The New Girl"! Available now!

Here's a preview of another Charmz graphic novel we are working on! ANA AND THE COSMIC RACE #1, on sale June 2017!

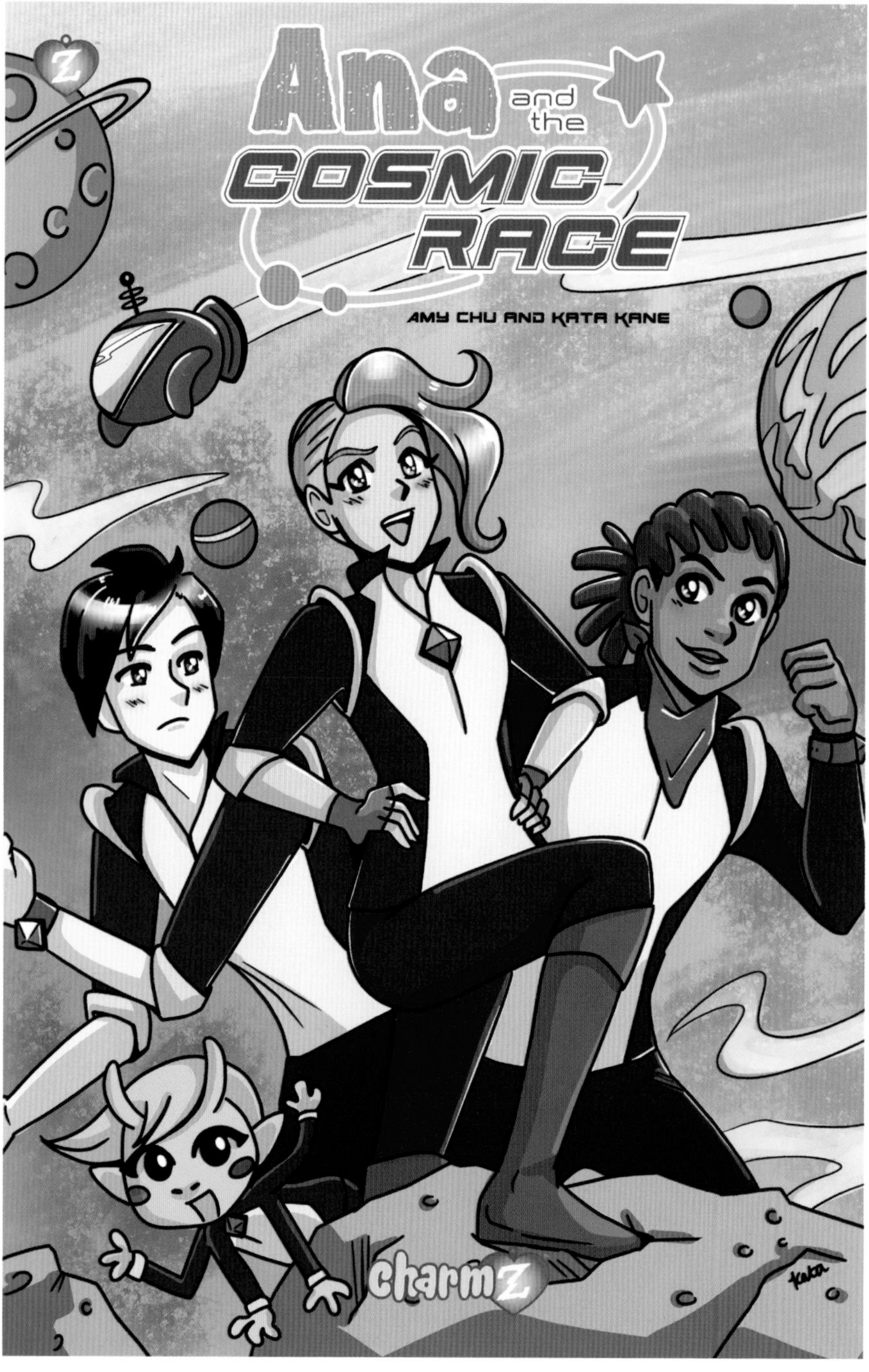
Ana and the COSMIC RACE
AMY CHU AND KATA KANE
charmz

not final art

Layouts for Ana and the Cosmic Race!

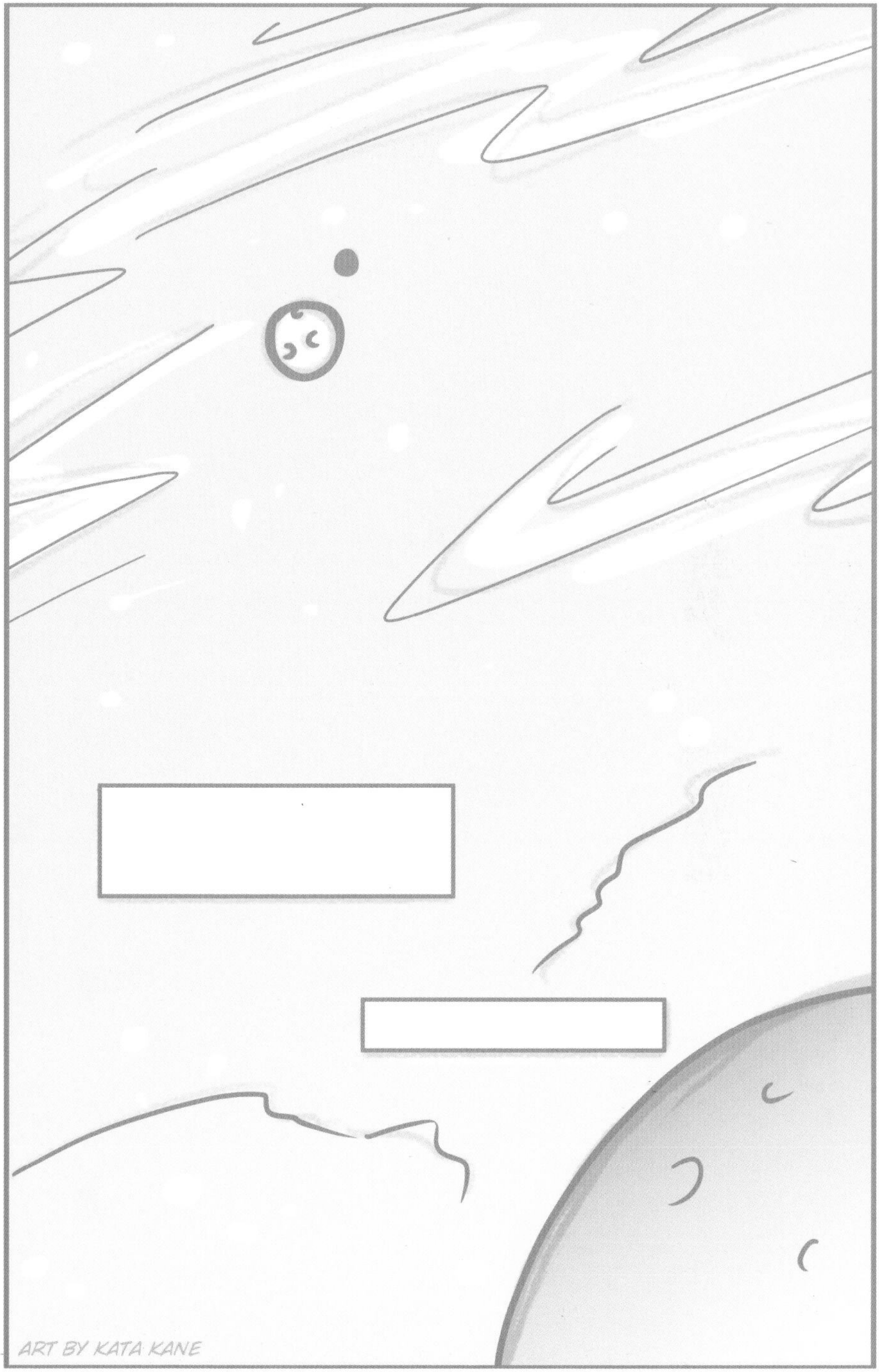
ART BY KATA KANE

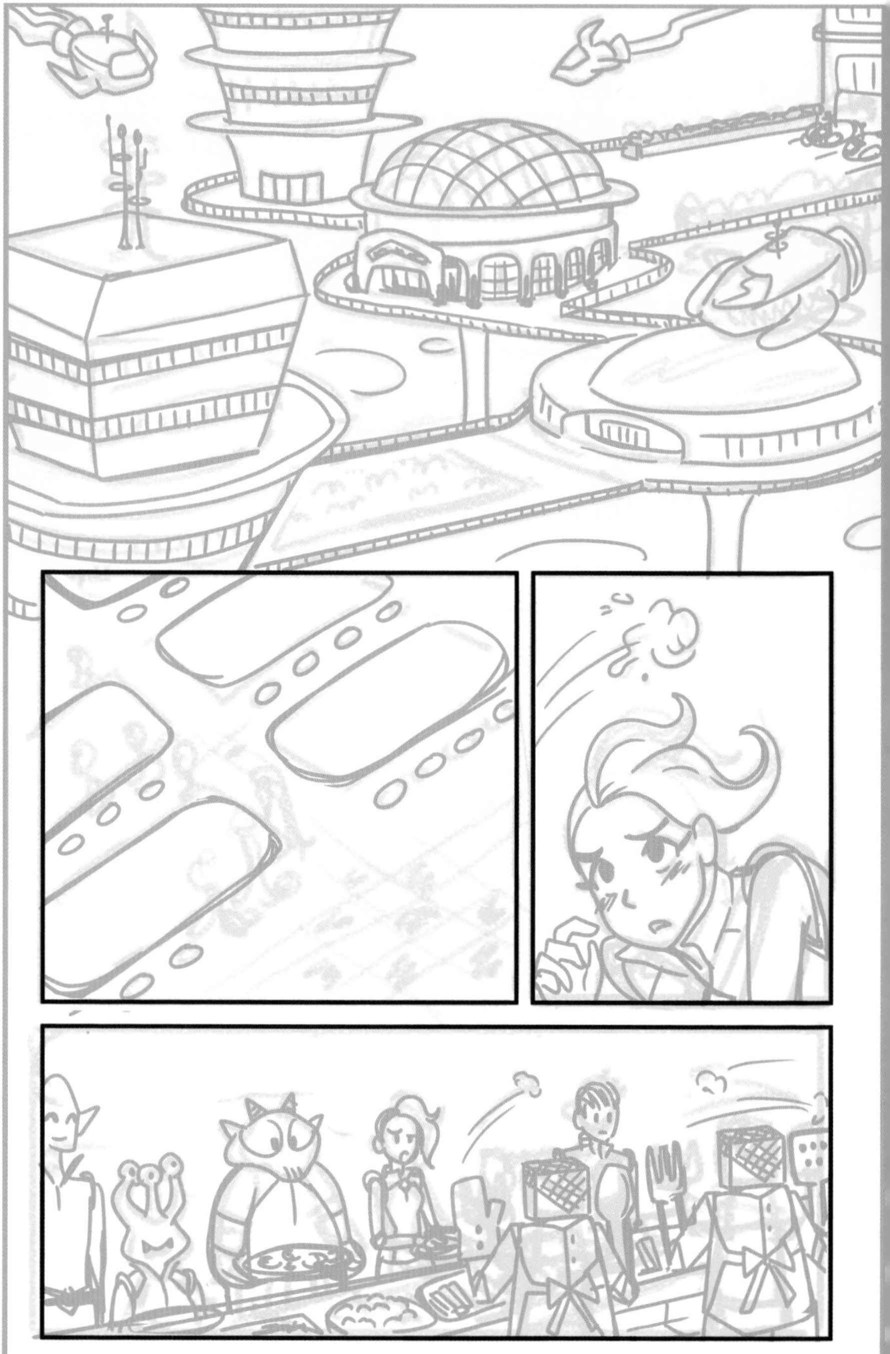

ART BY KATA KANE

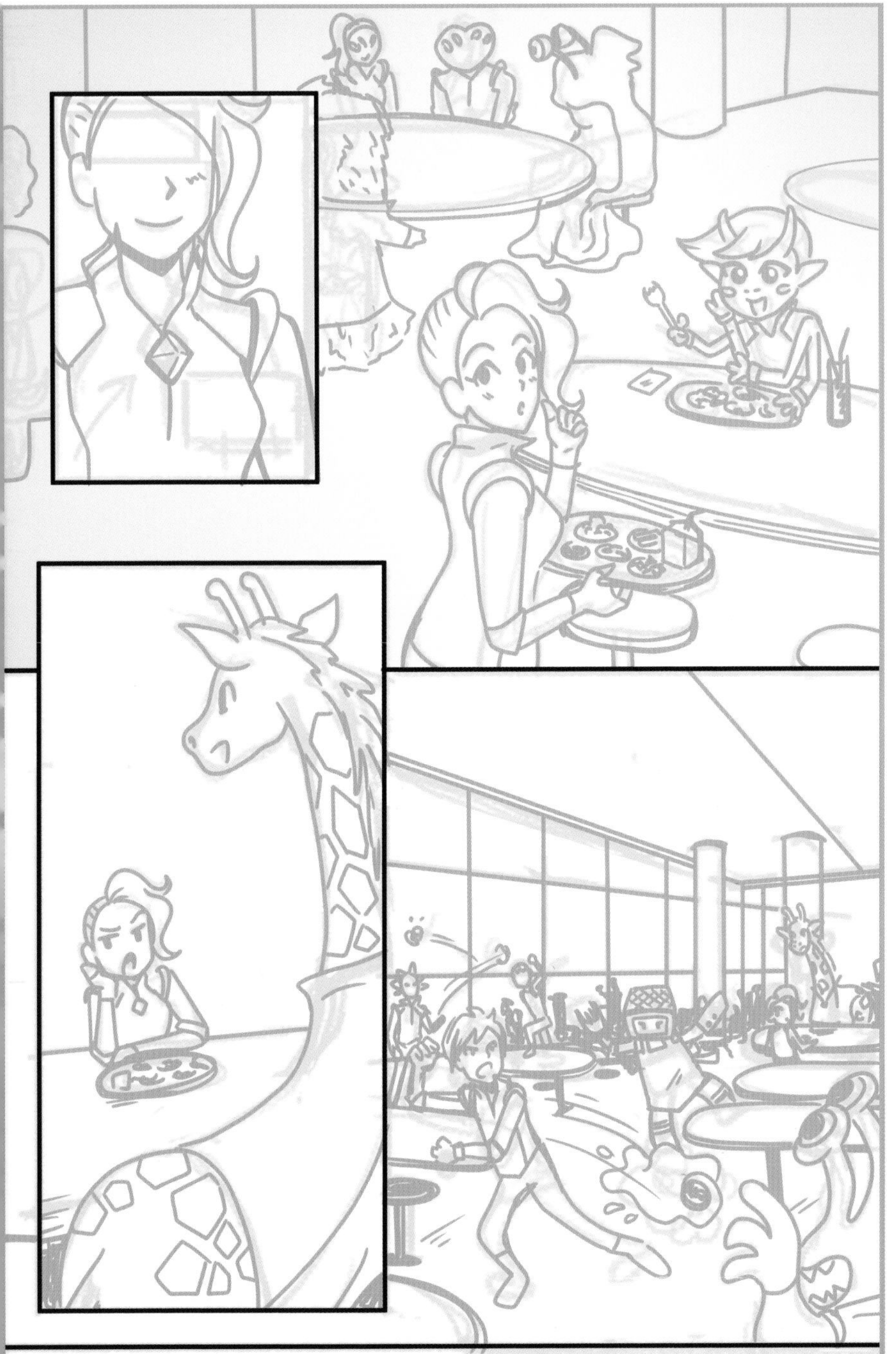

ART BY KATA KANE

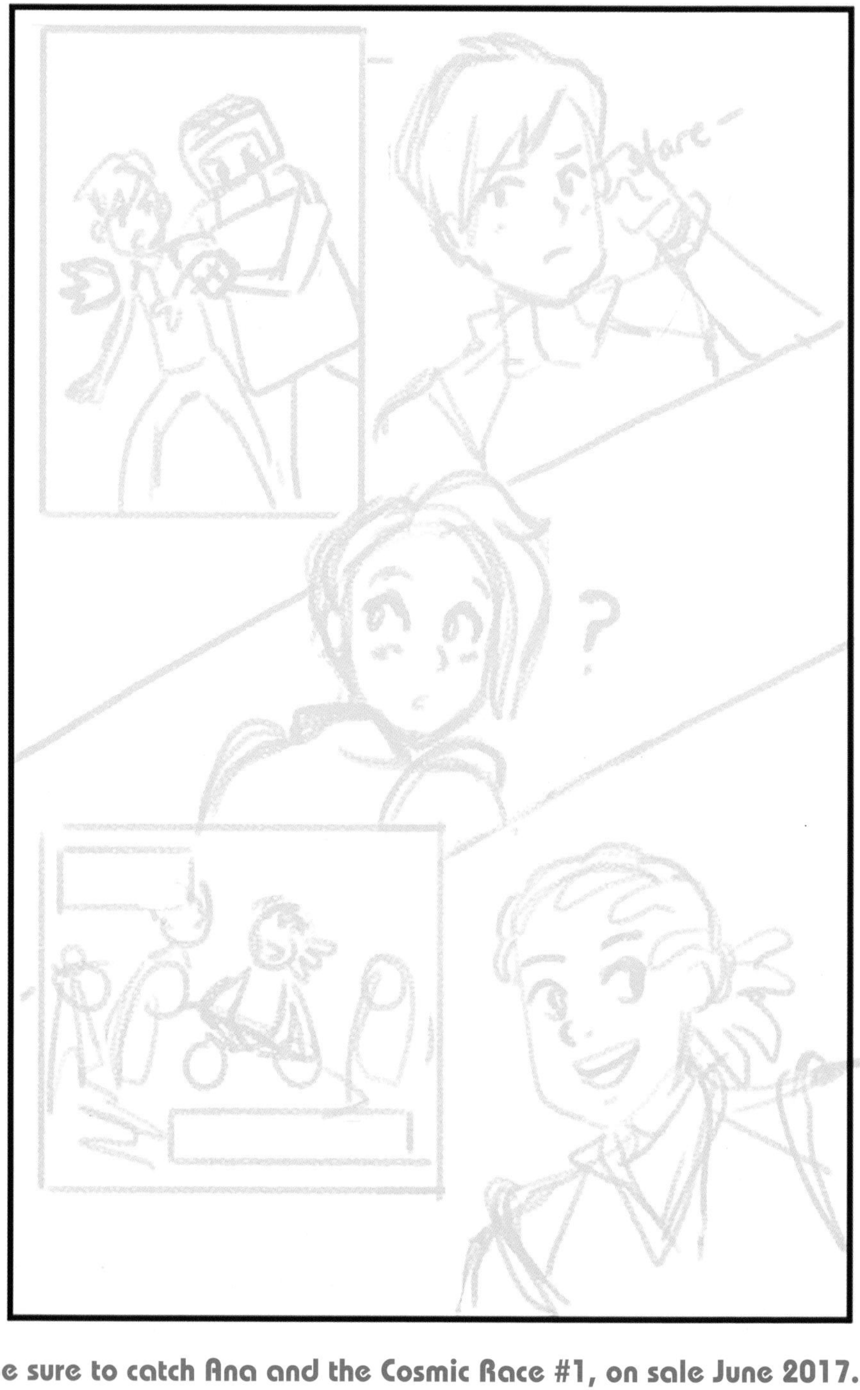
-stare-
?

Be sure to catch Ana and the Cosmic Race #1, on sale June 2017.

Welcome to

I am definitely obsessed with all things romance. It's fun, it's dramatic, and it's all about love. I think love is pretty amazing, don't you? When your heart beats faster at the sound of someone else's voice or the way they smile, you just feel more alive. And terrified! Or how about when just being around that special someone makes you feel like you're flying? Like you could do anything? Falling in love is one of the most incredible feelings, ever.

Of course, love is also complicated and painful sometimes. They don't call them "crushes" for nothing!

Yet, when I'm feeling kind of meh or sad, the first thing I want to do is read a romance. Maybe it's because everyone falls in love, has heartbreak and heartache. Maybe it's because there's really nothing like your first kiss. Whatever the reason, when I want to feel better, I pick up a romance and settle in. Usually with tea and chocolate, if I'm being totally honest.

Which brings us to Charmz, a new line of graphic novels just for you! With stories from all over the world, Charmz wants to celebrate love. Whether we're hanging out in Somerset, UK, the wilds of France, speeding through space, or waking up in a cemetery, love finds our characters and digs right in.

Whether you're in the mood for a (literally!) sweet tale about sisters, chocolate, and forbidden love, or exploring the mysterious darkness of Assumption Cemetery where vampires and swamp boys romance stitched girls, you'll find a lot to relate to.

My favorite kinds of romance are epic, sweeping, and probably just a little bit hilarious. As seriously as I take love, if you don't laugh a little at the things we'll do for it, well, you'll end up actually lovesick. Which is definitely something the girls in our books have to deal with from time to time. Not to mention fashion faux pas, weird chocolate recipes, ghosts, zombie sheep, and puzzles through time and space!

I've read a lot of romances and I definitely have my favorites. I think the one I would take on a desert island would have to be *Pride and Prejudice* by Jane Austen. I know, it's old, but it's so witty, and funny, and real. It's been adapted so many times but it always feels fresh and relevant. Anyone could be those characters. Me. You.

Aside from editing this line of graphic novels, I'm also writing one: STITCHED. This spooky little cemetery book with vampires, werewolves, swamp boys and stitched girls is very dear to me. It's the book I've always wanted to write, with spectacularly weird creatures, spooky adventures, and lots and lots of awkward, splendid, romance. Crimson Volania Mulch is my favorite kind of girl; complicated, smart, curious, kind…but a little bit preoccupied with her own problems. And way too judgmental. No one is perfect! And if I woke up only knowing my name in a strange place, I might be a little self-involved, too. I mean, just who is that pretty boy she meets on her first night "alive," and where is her mother? What does a badger/hedgehog actually eat? Do werewolves like cupcakes?

What I want Charmz to be for you is like the book equivalent of a hot chocolate; sweet, maybe a little dark sometimes, comforting, and made just for you. You can curl up with our tales, settle in, and enjoy falling in love with our characters just like they fall in love with each other.

Remember: stories matter, love is powerful, and there's nothing like a love story to make you feel alive.

–Mariah McCourt

Please write to me any time about Charmz! mariah@papercutz.com

I would love hear from you.

STAY IN TOUCH!

EMAIL:	charmz@papercutz
WEB:	www.papercutz.com
TWITTER:	@papercutzgn
FACEBOOK:	PAPERCUTZGRAPHICNOVELS
REGULAR MAIL:	Charmz, 160 Broadway, Suite 700, East Wing, New York, NY 10038

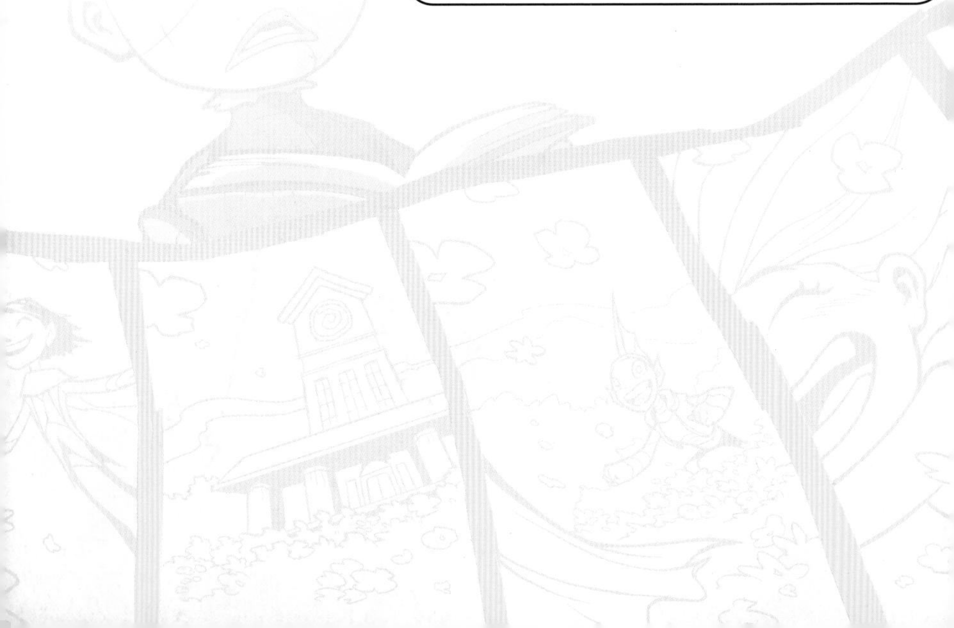